TOO CLOSE FOR COMFORT

A cold wind knifed through my sweatshirt and raised goose bumps on my arms. In October, once the sun went down, it could get cold quick, so, after doing a quick e-mail check on my phone, I decided to take a shortcut home. Granted, it only shortened the walk by a block, but the alleyway I took, which ran between Brown County Custom Furniture and Taylor's Automotive, sheltered me from the wind.

I'd covered about half of the alley's distance when something hit my shoulder. I stopped and looked around, the hair on the back of my neck springing to attention.

"Who's there?" I asked in a shaky voice.

When no response came, I got moving. *Probably some annoying kid.* I laughed out loud to prove to the juvenile delinquent I wasn't afraid.

All of a sudden, I took a sharp blow to the middle of my back, which sent me face-first into the gravel. The moment I landed, someone was on top of me. A knee dug into my spine and hands wrapped around my neck.

"Let it go, Cobb. Let it go."

It was barely a whisper, yet it sent a violent shudder through me...

Books by J.C. Kenney

A Literal Mess

Published by Kensington Publishing Corporation

A Literal Mess

J.C. Kenney

LYRICAL PRESS
Kensington Publishing Corp.
www.kensingtonbooks.com

LYRICAL UNDERGROUND BOOKS are published by
Kensington Publishing Corp.
119 West 40th Street
New York, NY 10018

All Kensington titles, imprints, and distributed lines are available at special quantity discounts for bulk purchases for sales promotion, premiums, fund-raising, educational, or institutional use.

Special book excerpts or customized printings can also be created to fit specific needs. For details, write or phone the office of the Kensington Sales Manager: Kensington Publishing Corp., 119 West 40th Street, New York, NY 10018. Attn. Sales Department. Phone: 1-800-221-2647.

Lyrical Underground and Lyrical Underground logo Reg. US Pat. & TM Off.

First Electronic Edition: January 2019
eISBN-13: 978-1-5161-0856-5
eISBN-10: 1-5161-0856-6

First Print Edition: January 2019
ISBN-13: 978-1-5161-0859-6
ISBN-10: 1-5161-0859-0

Printed in the United States of America

This is dedicated in loving memory to my mom, who once told me it's not about the crime, it's about figuring out the puzzle.

Chapter One

It's a universal truth that a phone call at 2:00 a.m. brings only one kind of news—bad with a capital B. One of two people would be calling, either my brother or sister. Mom would be in no shape to break the news to me. I glanced at the number. It was Luke.

"When did he go?" I had to choke out the last word. My father, my hero and role model, was dead. A plane ticket was on my dining room table, a grim reminder of challenges distance created in life. I was supposed to fly home Friday and spend the weekend with the family and, most importantly, see Dad before he slipped away for good.

Now I'd never be able to speak to my father again.

"He took a sudden turn around eleven and passed about a half hour ago. I'm sorry, Allie." Luke sucked in a long breath. "He asked about you this morning. Wanted to know if you'd sold any books recently."

Even through the tears, I laughed. My father had been a literary agent. Over the course of thirty-five years, he'd represented hundreds of authors and sold thousands of books, a good number of which had become bestsellers.

He'd instilled in me my love of all things bookish and hugged me when I told him I wanted to follow his footsteps into the wild world of book publishing. Since then, we'd joked about who sold more books, got their authors bigger advances, or found the next Stephen King or Janet Evanovich.

I'd spoken with Dad a day and a half ago. He'd promised me he was okay, that he had a book he wanted to finish editing. As recently as twelve hours ago, Mom had texted to let me know he was weak but stable with good vital signs.

And now he was gone.

"Hey, Allie? You still there?"

"Yeah." I wiped the tears from my face. "I'll get a flight this morning. Should be in Rushing Creek by late afternoon. Give Mom and Rachel a hug for me. Love you guys."

"Love you too, Allie. It'll be good to have you home again."

As I set down the phone, I grabbed the tissue box stationed on the nightstand and wiped away more tears. It had been there for weeks, standing at the ready for the moment it was needed. I was nothing, if not prepared.

A sleepy-eyed Ursula got up from her spot at the end of the bed and stretched. After a few licks to make sure her tortoiseshell coat was perfect, she padded up to me and bumped my hand with her head.

I scratched her ears while I used my phone to search for a flight. Sure, I could have fetched my laptop, but my little girl's purring, which rivaled the decibel level of a car without a muffler, was a soothing tonic for my shattered heart.

From the moment of Dad's cancer diagnosis, I accepted he was going to die sooner rather than later. Pancreatic cancer was a devil of a diagnosis, after all. But he sounded fine when we'd Skyped on Sunday and had gotten excited when I told him I'd be home Friday night.

Yet, here I was, in the middle of Tuesday night, or was it Wednesday morning, booking a flight home for his funeral. There were always happy endings in the romance novels I sold, but there sure weren't any in my life.

* * * *

By the time I was in the air, with Ursula snug in her Sherpa kitty carrier underneath the seat in front of me, I'd gotten my emotions under enough control to have a good talk with my boss, Natalie. She and Dad had known each other for years. In a gesture that blew me away, she told me to take the next ten days off.

That was way more than the measly three days the employee handbook said employees could take off for the death of a parent. Though, admittedly, the only reason I knew that was because I'd edited it for grammar in my early days working at her literary agency. Not the most exciting task, but it was another step along the path toward my goal of owning my own literary agency.

Just like Dad had owned his.

You could say I was Daddy's little girl and you'd get no argument from me. I remember one time when I was little, Rachel blew her stack at me over something trivial and called me "Little Walterette." It was meant as an insult, but I responded by saying thanks and running off to tell Dad that Rachel thought I was just like him.

Contrary to popular opinion among the locals, I didn't hate my hometown of Rushing Creek, Indiana, population 3,216. I left my hometown because I wanted to follow in Dad's career footsteps, and it was a lot easier finding a job in the book biz in New York City than it was in Southern Indiana. A lot of folks didn't see it that way, though. They liked to say I turned my back on my dad and my hometown, a sentiment that only grew in intensity after he became ill.

Now it was time to face those people.

So, with mixed emotions, I guided my rental through the twists and turns of the treelined highway that led to Rushing Creek. Sure, it would be good to see Mom and Sloane and my sibs, but I'd never see my father living, breathing again. That hurt worse than when a bookcase fell on me when I was in college.

"There it is, Ursi. Home, sweet home." I scratched Ursula between the ears and gave her a kitty treat as we crested a hill and the Rushing Creek Valley came into view. At a scenic observation area, I wrangled Ursula into her harness and we got out to enjoy the breathtaking view.

The scene was right out of a travel magazine. With the leaves just beginning to turn, we were treated to swaths of green interspersed with touches of glorious yellows, fabulous oranges and heart-stopping reds, my personal favorite. I took in a long breath. The air was clean and sweet, with just a hint of woodsmoke. Not even a trace of exhaust fumes lingered in the air.

I focused on the stream at the south end of town and imagined I could hear the water rushing over limestone rocks as it wound its way through Brown County before eventually emptying into the Wabash River. From my perch, the water appeared high for this time of year. Dad had told me September had been rainier than normal. The creek was the proof.

After snapping a few photos to send to my New York buds, I let Ursi, safely tethered to me by her leash, wander around a bit. The New York cat was used to concrete and fire hydrants, not dirt and plant life, so she had a ball chasing leaves that had already fallen to the ground.

While she played, I went through my e-mails. I was waiting to hear from an editor who was interested in one of my clients' historical romances. Even in challenging times, I owed it to my clients to keep their projects moving forward. It was a lesson Dad taught me, and I intended to make him proud by staying on top of things while I was in Rushing Creek.

"Okay, girl." After fifteen minutes spent on e-mails and text messages, I scooped up Ursi and kissed her on the head. "I know you want to put your inner huntress to work, but we've got things to do and people to see."

It broke my heart there was one less person to see.

My parents' house was on the northern end of town. Since the highway ran through the southern edge, I enjoyed a slow drive through town on Washington Boulevard, the main street and tourist strip. I hadn't been home in six months and was curious to see what was new. While many of the storefronts on the boulevard, like the Brown County Diner and Renee's Gently Used Books, had been there for years, businesses were always coming and going.

One new business that piqued my curiosity was an herbal supplement shop occupying the long-empty space next door to Ye Olde Woodworker. Ozzy Metcalf, the proprietor of the Woodworker, had a reputation as a difficult neighbor. I couldn't wait to meet the person brave enough to open a business next door.

A few blocks after the storefronts came to an end, I turned right onto McMaster Road and came to a stop in front of my parents' home. Despite the late-afternoon sunshine, I broke out in goose bumps as I put the car in park. With the lights in Dad's first-floor office off, the house, a two-story Colonial that had provided so much warmth and happiness over the years, seemed cold, too.

I gathered Ursi in my arms and headed for the house, willing myself not to cry. Rachel opened the front door and greeted me with a sad smile and a hug.

The toll the last few days had taken on my older sister was unmistakable. Her shoulder-length blond hair, which normally looked like spun gold, lacked its usual sheen and had been pulled into a messy top knot. Her eyes were bloodshot, and her blue-green irises were cloudy. She even seemed several inches shorter than her height of five feet, eight inches.

"Thanks for getting here so quickly." She let Ursi sniff her hand. "Who's your friend?"

"Her name's Ursula. I got her from a rescue shelter about six months ago. You know, when Mom suggested I needed a friend close by to help me with," I shook my head, "all of this."

"I don't think a cat was what Mom had in mind." Rachel raised an eyebrow and, after a second, we both laughed. It wasn't a gut-busting laugh, and it didn't cure my somber mood, but it felt good, nonetheless. "Allie, is that you?" Mom came out of the kitchen and stopped a few feet away from me. She looked twenty years older than her age of sixty-one and her eyes were red-rimmed, but every strand of her gray hair was in place. And she was smiling.

"Hi, Mom." I let Ursi down as my mother and I embraced. And the tears fell again.

A little while later, Mom, Rachel and I were in the dining room reminiscing when the doorbell rang. Mom closed her eyes as her chin dropped to her chest. In the two hours since I'd arrived, three casseroles, two lunch meat trays and a case of Rushing Creek wine had been delivered. The town was great at taking care of their own, but Mom needed a break from the well-wishers.

"I'll get it." I nudged Ursi off my lap and, on the short jaunt to the front door, checked my phone. I'd received a handful of text messages and e-mails from coworkers sending their condolences, but nothing from the editor. Nothing from Lance, either. Some boyfriend.

Lance was an attorney specializing in contracts who had come to work at my agency four years ago. A shared passion for Asian cuisine led to a date where we found we enjoyed each other's company. He loved sports, which I did not, and tended to get loud when he was excited, but he made me laugh and was a good listener. After a year of dating, we were happy, and I was beginning to envision a future together.

Then Dad got sick.

Ever since that day I broke down in tears while I gave Lance the awful news, he'd become more and more distant. He'd reassured me more than once he was simply trying to give me space during a tough time. My doubts about his sincerity, and his commitment to us, had grown over time. If he couldn't be there for me when I needed him the most, would he ever be there for me? The answer was becoming more obvious by the day, but it was one I wasn't prepared to face. Not right now.

I opened the door with my eyes still on my phone. Rude, but I was getting tired and was running low on emotional fuel. Before I had a chance to look up, I was wrapped in a hug that forced the air out of me.

"Oh, Allie. I'm so, so sorry. Can I do anything for you? I've missed you so much. Did you bring Ursula? Can I—"

"Hey, Sloane." I put my hands on her shoulders and held her at arm's length. "I'm fine. I mean, given the circumstances. Come on in. Mom and Rachel are in the dining room."

She brushed some strands of her brown hair from her face and pushed the sleeves of her oversized, red Indiana University sweatshirt up to her elbows. Sloane was an elite-class trail runner, so the blousy fit of the sweatshirt emphasized her rail-thin frame. She looked strong, though, not borderline emaciated like so many of her competitors. I had no doubt if I tried to squeeze her biceps or her calves, they would be rock solid. She'd even painted her fingernails a vibrant, sparkly gray that matched her eyes.

Sloane looked good and it lifted my spirits to see her that way.

As I led her down the hallway, my old friend's nervousness radiated off her like a bad sunburn. God love her, she still hadn't overcome her anxiety problems, and situations like this almost incapacitated her. But she came, anyway.

The gesture wasn't lost on Mom, either, as she insisted Sloane join us. We passed the time nibbling on a plate of cheese and crackers the local tourism office had sent. As we chatted, Sloane caught us up on her trail running and Rachel filled us in on the latest exploits of her five-year-old twins, Tristan and Theresa.

After a while, my curiosity got to me and I asked where Luke was.

"He's down at the community center. Said he wanted to clean the place up while he had a chance." Mom sighed. "I think he couldn't stand being here anymore. The last few days have been hard on him."

"They've been hard on all of us, Mom." Rachel tossed her napkin on the table and went to the sink. After a moment of silence, her shoulders began to shake.

"Of course it has, dear. You and your brother have been angels from heaven through all of this." Mom put an arm around her.

I'd always thought of my older sister as prickly as a porcupine and calculating as a criminal. To see her crying left me at a total loss.

And there stood the elephant in the room, too. My sin of leaving Rushing Creek was laid bare. While I was off living the cosmopolitan New York City lifestyle, my siblings had stayed close to home and been there for Mom when she needed them most. Maybe Mom didn't realize how deep her words cut, but they did. All the way to my broken heart.

All of a sudden, the room was too small, too hot and too crowded. I pushed back from the table, escape the only thing on my mind.

"I think I'll go check in on Luke. See if he's okay." I bolted for the door without waiting for a reply.

I was seated on the top step of the front porch, taking long, slow breaths when the door opened with a creak.

Sloane sat beside me and patted my knee. "She didn't mean anything by it, Allie. Your family's hurting right now. Shoot, half the town is. Your dad was a great guy. We all loved him." She nudged my shoulder. "So, do you really want to check in on Luke? If so, I'll drive."

I looked at Sloane, my oldest friend. My best friend, too, even after all the years apart. Her clear, gray eyes were watery.

Sloane and I had been BFFs for as long as I could remember. On the surface, we were as different as night and day. She had long hair. I kept mine short. She ran between five and ten miles almost every day. The only running I did was to catch the subway. She could eat a quart of ice cream in one sitting and there'd be no evidence of it on her rail-thin frame. If I even thought about eating a second scoop of ice cream, I'd have to go get new pants—in a larger size.

Our differences made us such great friends. We took joy in each other's accomplishments. In second grade, I cheered my lungs out watching her beat the boys in our class track meet running events. In middle school, she spent hours drilling me on words for the spelling bee and shed a few tears when I won the district competition in eighth grade.

Even after I moved away from Rushing Creek, we remained as close as peas in a pod. She sent me a bottle of champagne when I signed my first client. I sent her a framed photograph of her atop the podium when she won her first professional trail race. I teased her that the blue nail polish she was wearing in the picture matched the first-place medal's neck ribbon perfectly.

She was the yin to my yang. The peanut butter to my jelly. She made my life better, and I was more thankful than ever to have her in it.

"You'd do that for me?"

She let out a long breath and looked up and down the street. "I don't have anything better to do. And I'll never pass up a chance to ogle your brother while he's working."

"Ewww." I gave her ponytail a playful tug. "That is so gross."

It was no secret Sloane had an incurable crush on Luke, one that she had no interest in getting over. Maybe someday Luke would come to his senses and see Sloane for the woman she was now instead of thinking of her as his little sister's friend. They were both grown-ups, for God's sake.

"Awesome. Let's go." Sloane sprinted for her green SUV. "Last one there's a rotten egg."

Okay, maybe only Luke was a grown-up. I jogged after her, thankful for the moment of youthful silliness. After all, being a grown-up definitely wasn't all it was cracked up to be.

When I visited Rushing Creek, I made a point to support the local businesses, so we took the boulevard through town. I wanted to see if there were any new restaurants I needed to visit. While I was in the mood for a stiff drink, that would have to wait. Seeing my brother to make my mea culpa with alcohol on my breath wouldn't be a good look.

I quizzed Sloane about the new place next to Ye Olde Woodworker.

"You can get aromatherapy stuff there. Beyond that, I don't know much about it. The owner's pretty unique."

"How so?" The shopkeepers in Rushing Creek were always trying to find something new and unusual to draw tourists into their businesses. Over the years, we'd seen folks try everything from housing a reptile zoo to a restaurant that featured raw beef dishes. If Sloan thought the owner of the aromatherapy shop was unique, I wanted to meet the person.

"Remember Professor Trelawney from the Harry Potter movies? This woman looks just like her, except for maybe smaller glasses. People say she's nice."

"I know some people in New York who swear by aromatherapy. I'll have to check it out." To be honest, I had more than a simple passing interest in the new store, though. I'd been having trouble sleeping recently, so maybe the woman would have something to help me sleep. That would definitely be worth a visit.

"Speaking of checking things out..." Sloan pointed down the street.

The diner had a new coat of paint and there was a new chocolate shop next to the general store. Score! It wasn't that I was addicted to dark chocolate. Not at all. It was more that dark chocolate and I had an understanding. It provided moral support when I needed it, and I accepted said support with a smile.

At the south end of town, Sloane took a right onto Madison Street and we oohed and aahed as we passed Rushing Creek Winery. The place had been a godsend for local commerce, thanks to the year-round tourism it attracted. I spent a few summers working there, and they always had a spot for Dad if he wanted to hold some kind of author event.

"What do you say we stop by for a tasting when we're done checking in with Luke?" Forget the stiff drink. A glass of Rushing Creek Traminette was just what I needed at the moment.

Sloane scrunched up her nose. "I dunno. Maybe we can stop by Hoosiers. I'm sure some of the old gang will be there and would love to see you."

Ugh. I was no fan of the bar that was the favored place for locals. Sure, it was friendly and the food was good, if not artery clogging, but I wasn't sure I was ready to see people. At least not today.

"On second thought, how about tomorrow? My pen is running out of ink." Sloane laughed. God love her, she evidently still thought my little literary metaphors were witty. Lance? Not so much. I thought about texting him but shoved my phone in my back pocket as Sloane pulled into the community center's pristine and weed-free parking lot.

The center was a rectangular building that overlooked Rushing Creek. Built to resemble a log cabin, its brown wooden exterior and green tin roof screamed rustic. I found it cliché, but the community loved it. What I loved was the six-foot-wide deck that ran along the side of the center facing the creek. The deck wrapped around the east end of the building to form a fifty-by-fifty-foot deck. The crown jewel of the deck was the fire pit. Maybe it was because Dad donated the money for it, but I'd always loved the fire pit.

We found Luke battling a tangled mess of weeds covering the slope between the deck railing and the creek. Covered in sweat, despite the mild October temperatures, he was hacking away with a garden scythe. I had to shout his name three times to get his attention.

He looked up and smiled, but his forehead was creased.

"Hey, guys. Come to relieve me from my backbreaking labor?" He pulled himself onto the deck.

Sloane let out a sigh as he brushed himself off.

I went to give him a hug, but he put out his hand to stop me.

"You don't want to do that. I'm gross and there's a ton of poison ivy down there."

I sprang back two steps. Poison ivy, and the nightmarish rashes that came with it, was the bane of my existence. One of the things I loved about living in a concrete jungle was the lack of the evil, infectious weed. Shoot, the weed I saw most often in New York was the illegal kind. I avoided that kind like the plague, too.

"How about this?" Sloane tossed him a bottle of water we'd picked up on the drive.

Luke slugged it down in one smooth motion. The old basketball player still had a few graceful moves. Sloane sighed again.

"Thanks, Sloanie." He tossed the bottle back to her with a wink and turned to me. "I take it Mom sent you to check on me? She wasn't happy when I told her I had to go to work."

"No." Okay, maybe she'd suggested her annoyance, but I wasn't going to tell him that. "I wanted to see you." I ran my hand along the deck railing. The smooth, cool surface made me smile. "And to say thanks for calling me. I feel horrible I wasn't here. This looks great, by the way." Sloane and Luke joined me as I gazed at the creek. Despite my grieving soul, I smiled.

"Remember when we were little and Dad dragged us here for Mr. Winchester's book signings? We always ended up out here on the deck."

"Or under it." He chuckled. "One of us always ended up in the creek."

"You guys had it so great," Sloane said. "I was always stuck inside being Daddy's smiling little girl. It was torture, knowing you were out here having a blast, while I had to track the number of books he signed."

"Come on." I gave her a shoulder bump. "At least you never got yelled at for ending up covered in mud."

"I guess so. Still, it wasn't exactly a cakewalk being the daughter of the infamous Thornwell Winchester." She shook her head. "I'm sorry. That was selfish. At least I still have my father."

Sloane put her arm around me as more tears began to fall. No matter what, my father, my hero, was gone. And there wasn't a darn thing I could do to fix that.

Chapter Two

After a night of constant tossing and turning, I woke up the next morning with a ball of orange and black cat fur in my face. After taking a few seconds to get my bearings, I gave Ursi a tummy rub. While that got her to move, all she did was turn around and lick my cheek.

"Ow, girl. Easy with the sandpaper tongue."

In typical Ursi fashion, she yawned and went to the door, where she meowed until I got up. Back home, she had the run of the apartment. Here, even though it was just Mom and me, I wanted some privacy. Okay, given the circumstances, I needed the privacy, as I might have cried half the night.

By the time I made it to the kitchen downstairs, Ursi had her face in her bowl and Mom had laid out breakfast for me. Eggs, sliced fruit and an English muffin. It sure beat my usual breakfast fare of yogurt or a bagel with cream cheese. My stomach growled loud enough to draw a disapproving look from my cat.

I gave Mom a kiss on the cheek. "Thanks. Any coffee, by chance?"

She pointed to a shiny Keurig machine next to the toaster oven. "A gift from your father. He joked that since he wasn't drinking gallons of coffee anymore, it would be more practical." She choked out the last word and eased into a chair.

"Oh, Mom, I'm so sorry. How are you holding up?"

"Like the weather, changes by the minute." She gave me a half-smile.

Mom was a family practice physician. As such, she'd tried to approach Dad's illness with a doctor's clinical detachment. There had been no false hopes. No praying to a higher power. She and Dad faced the facts that pancreatic cancer had a low survival rate with dignified acceptance. It was what it was. In the end, he lasted twenty-two months. It had been a grueling twenty-two months, though. Even from as far away as New York City, I could tell that.

"I'm relieved in a way. Don't get me wrong. I'll miss your father more than anything. But these last few months were so hard on him." She squeezed my hand. "He's at peace now, and for that, I'm happy."

We talked about Dad while I ate breakfast. Mom told me that Tristan and Theresa would spend a few hours with us at the funeral home, but that would be it. They were struggling enough with Rachel's divorce from Matt Roberson, Rushing Creek's chief of police, and Mom was hoping to minimize their time around mourners.

And the awkwardness of having Rachel and Matt in the same room.

* * * *

I wasn't certain what I was expecting from the visitation, but I wasn't ready for a line to have already formed when the funeral director opened the doors. It made me happy I'd finished my work phone calls before we left the house. As we shook hands and shared hugs with tear-filled members of the Rushing Creek community, I marveled at Mom's grace and composure.

And thanked my lucky stars I'd packed a pair of comfortable flats.

In the middle of stifling a yawn, two of Dad's authors, Leslie Fryman and Malcolm Blackstone, greeted me with handshakes and stories about Dad and what a wonderful agent he'd been. When I asked them what their future plans were, they exchanged a look.

Malcolm smoothed his tie. "Leslie's chosen to sign with Suzette Young. I still haven't decided. Your father's sudden turn was…unanticipated."

Suzette was an agent who got her start working with Dad. She'd formed her own agency after working with him for a decade. Because of that, many of his clients moved to Suzette when he got sick, with his blessing. A handful, like Malcolm and Sloane's dad, Thornwell, still hadn't decided on their plans. All I really cared about was that each of them found an agent who was right for them.

"That it was." I gave them each a quick hug. "If there's anything I can do to help, let me know. I'll be in town for another week or so before I have to head back to New York."

Luke cleared his throat to indicate the receiving line needed to get moving, so Malcolm and Leslie hugged me again and moved to Mom.

A little while later, Daniel Godwin, Thornwell's research assistant, came through the line. The man was a little odd but had done wonderful things for his boss over the years and, to his credit, had stuck by Thornwell during the worst of the author's drunken binges.

After exchanging pleasantries, Daniel gave the room a quick scan. "You haven't seen Suzette, by chance, have you? We were chatting the other day and she told me she'd be here. I'd hoped to say hello." He smiled. "Heck of a way to catch up with old friends, I know. If you see her, please let her know I was here."

Figuring he was trying to help nudge Thornwell into signing with Suzette, I promised him I would. Doing business at a funeral home, that was a first.

The visitation started at two and wouldn't end until eight. Talk about a marathon. It wasn't that I didn't appreciate the kind words and stories, but after about four hours of nodding and smiling, all while on my feet, I needed a break. I caught Sloane's eye, and we made a dash for a room in the back, where family members could find refuge for a few minutes.

On the way, I spotted a woman with bottle-blond hair, a skin tone straight out of a tanning booth and stilettos so tall I almost lost my balance looking at them. Sloane must have noticed my gawking, because she gave me a forearm to the back to keep me moving.

"Who was that woman?" I asked once we were alone.

"That's the cling-on, Charissa Mody." Sloane rolled her eyes. When I shrugged, she let out a long sigh. "She works at the winery. Dad met her about a year ago. They've gone out a few times. He's not serious about it, though."

"But she is, I take it? How come you never mentioned her?"

Sloane nibbled on a chocolate chip cookie from a snack tray. "I don't trust her. I think she's just looking for a sugar daddy."

I took a drink from bottled water as I mulled over Sloane's comments. Outside of Dad and Thornwell's accounting firm, nobody in Rushing Creek knew how wealthy the man was. Sure, there was gossip whenever he had a new book published, but he rarely socialized or made public appearances. Most people thought he was either snooty or a weird recluse.

I knew different. The truth was, he was painfully shy. Between my father and Sloane, I'd gotten to know him a little. The man wasn't a warm-and-fuzzy type, but when he was sober, he was pretty decent. Unfortunately, he hadn't been sober very often over the years.

"How are things with your dad?"

Sloane's relationship with her father had been problematic at best and borderline abusive at worst. Her reports about him had changed in recent months, though. For the better.

"He's trying, in a good way, I mean. When your dad got sick, it changed him. He quit drinking and even told me he's working on a secret project."

"That's good, isn't it?"

Thornwell had wounded Sloane in ways that would never heal, but at least she still had a father who could try to repair some of them. That was my hope, at least.

"It is. Like I said, things are better. I just..." She shook her head.

"He turned you down?" Sloane was a blogger and professional trail runner. More accurately, she was trying to be a professional trail runner. Like so many athletes, she needed sponsorship to make a go of it. Despite good results, she'd been trying for years to secure sponsorship with little success. In an act of desperation, she'd talked of turning to Thornwell.

"No. I was ready to ask him, but I couldn't. He was so excited, telling me about his project. It was like he was looking for my approval. I thought if he can change, maybe I can too."

I waited. Whether it was to see if Sloane would tell me more or if it was to avoid returning to the receiving area, I didn't know. And really, I didn't care. I could afford a few minutes to be there for her. God knew she'd been there for me enough, especially in recent months.

"I'm tired of the never-ending money hunt. The income from my blogs pays the rent and day-to-day expenses, but that's about it. If I can't come up with sponsorship by the end of the year, I'm going to give up running." A tear ran down her cheek. She wiped it away with her thumb. "Sorry. You're the one who just lost her dad."

"No. It's okay. Maybe I can talk to him. You know, plant a seed and make it seem like it was his idea."

"You'd do that?"

I nodded.

Sloane hugged me so tight I could barely breathe. "You're the best."

The door opened and Luke came in. "Need you out here, Allie. Oh, and Sloanie? Your dad's here."

I'll freely admit I wasn't on my A-game emotionally, but, at that moment, Sloane could have knocked me over with a poke from a red pen.

"Don't act so surprised, Allie. Your dad was more than just his agent. They were friends. Come on." Sloane offered me her hand as we returned to the fray.

We hadn't gotten very far into the room when Thornwell intercepted us. He was wringing his hands and wiping his brow with a handkerchief every other second, but he was here.

For my dad.

"Alexandra. I'm so sorry for your loss." He was the only person on Earth who called me by my given name, telling me on more than one occasion it was too pretty of a name to ruin it with informality. That was Thornwell Winchester in a nutshell. He'd give you a compliment and insult you at the same time, and you never knew which one to take seriously, if either.

"Thank you. I'm sorry for your loss, as well."

He bit his lower lip. "Your father and I collaborated for so long, I don't know what I'll do without him. We had so many exciting things planned. Well, never mind that."

My heart sank. Here was Thornwell, bestselling author of historical fiction with six books hitting number one, and he looked as if he didn't know whether he should turn left or right. The self-assurance, the swagger he usually exuded when I was in his company was gone. Then again, so was the alcohol.

"Thank you for coming. I appreciate it and I'm sure Mom does, too." I gave him a quick hug.

"Speaking of which, I really should have a few words with her. Sloane, would you do your father a kindness and accompany me? You know how inadequate I am in settings such as this."

"Sure, Dad." She slipped her arm through the one he offered. "Text me if you want to get a drink or just talk, Allie."

Thornwell patted Sloane's hand and led her away as I struggled to reconcile the scene. He'd shown his daughter more respect in our short exchange than I'd seen in years. If I hadn't seen it myself, I wouldn't have believed it, but sobriety seemed to agree with Thornwell.

* * * *

A few hours later, I was seated in a booth at the Rushing Creek Public House, accompanied only by a half-empty glass of Riesling and my gloomy thoughts. At 11:00 p.m. on a weeknight, it was practically deserted, which suited me just fine.

Steve Phillips, a friend from high school, dropped off a basket of tortilla chips with salsa and returned to his post behind the bar. When I lifted my glass to him, he merely nodded and went back to washing glasses. Rachel owned the place, a restaurant and bar adjacent to the Rushing Creek Inn. Located on the boulevard, it catered to the tourist crowd. With a menu full of Indiana staples, like meatloaf and pork tenderloin sandwiches, and a wine and beer list that had been voted best in Southern Indiana, it had become quite the destination point.

It was also a place where a native like me could go to be alone. Steve knew why I was there and was kind enough to leave me in peace as I munched on the salty chips and sipped my white wine. The day had been beyond exhausting. My feet hurt from standing for hours on end, my eyes hurt from crying and my neck hurt from the overarching tension.

I was telling myself to take things one hour at a time to get through the funeral then the wake when the melodic dingdong of the doorbell broke the silence. Steve was halfway to my booth with another glass of wine when the people who had entered came into view.

It was Thornwell and the last woman on Earth I would have expected to see in his company—his ex-wife, Kathryn. They took a seat at a table in the middle of the room. I scooted to the far end of the booth to keep from being seen, while still being able to keep an eye on them. They shared a laugh with Steve when he took their orders. The last time I'd seen them together, and not screaming at each other, was Sloane's college graduation dinner.

Things between them had gone downhill fast after that night, as Thornwell's drinking and abusive behavior worsened. The divorce had been as nasty as the ongoing battle between the husband and wife from *Gone Girl* and had been gossip fodder for months. I'd lost track of the times Sloane called me in tears, needing a sympathetic ear.

Now, here they were, clinking glasses and smiling at each other. Did Sloane know her parents were back on friendly terms after years of treating each other like a real-life version of Cronus versus Zeus? Did Sloane even want to know? My mind reeled as I considered the implications of a reunion.

Taking a drink, I almost choked as another thought came to me. If Thornwell and Kathryn were making googly eyes at each other, where did that leave the woman at the funeral home who Sloane had said was claiming to be Thornwell's girlfriend?

Chapter Three

The next morning, I had time to waste before the funeral, so after leaving a message with the editor about the historical romance, I started in on the one thing Dad asked me to do for him after he was gone, go through his office. Before he got sick, Dad had more than fifty clients. He'd worked with folks who wrote everything from historical fiction, like Thornwell, to cop mysteries, like Malcolm Blackstone, who had his first bestseller earlier in the year. I'd held Malcolm for a good five minutes at the viewing while he cried his eyes out.

Though Dad had notified all of his clients of his diagnosis and pledged to help them find new agents, some chose to stick with him until the literal end. My job was to account for all of his records so I could make sure those authors found new agents and then help Mom close out the agency.

I took a deep breath and pushed open the door. Thanks to the east-facing windows, the room was bathed in a soft, yellow light. The glorious smell of old books welcomed me as I wandered toward the bookcase that housed his authors' published novels. I ran my fingers across the spines of the hardbacks and smiled. I'd read every single one, from the first book Dad sold, Thornwell's *Pottawatomie Bride*, to his most recent published sale, a military thriller entitled *Defcon Two*.

From the bookcase, I went to a table where he kept paper copies of the manuscripts he was editing. I picked up one and laughed at the editorial marks he'd made in red ink. He was no literary dinosaur, though. When finished bleeding all over the story, he'd make the same changes to an electronic version, which he'd send to the author. He told me countless times going old school was the only way to really get to know the story, to get to the heart of the author's message.

I put the manuscript down and settled in front of Dad's laptop. He'd written all of his passcodes on a notecard and taped it to the desktop so I'd have an easy go of it when the time came. Again, his attention to detail. With no goal in mind, I nosed around in the folders on the hard drive to get a sense for how he organized things. My jaw almost hit the desk at how similar my system was to his. Like father, like daughter. Once I was comfortable with the file organization, I opened his e-mail. The inbox was flooded, so it took me an hour to weed through messages I could delete, flag ones that needed a response and ID others I didn't know what to do with.

A knock on the door brought my work to a halt.

"Time to go, hon." Mom was as regal as a queen in a royal blue suit and sapphire stud earrings. Blue was Dad's favorite color, and Mom had made it clear she was going to honor the love of her life by wearing it. The outfit was such a touching tribute to Dad I had to blink away a tear.

"Give me two minutes." I closed e-mail and was about to shut down the system when a folder on the desktop brought me to a stop. It was labeled Locker. Curious about its contents, I clicked to open it but got a message asking for a password. The notecard didn't include information for Locker so, pressed for time, I made a mental note to ask Mom about it later.

I had my father's funeral to attend.

Per Dad's request, the funeral service was short and simple. As the eldest child, Luke gave a eulogy that, God bless him, left everyone in attendance laughing about Dad's lovable foibles. Then Rachel read a selection of passages from Dad's published books. There wasn't a dry eye in the house by the time she finished. I had to hand it to her, she and I had our differences, but nobody had worked harder for Dad during his illness than Rachel.

When the funeral was over, we made our way to the community center for the wake. Pulling into the parking lot, I smiled at the results of Luke's recent efforts. The parking lot and flower beds were Disney-like in their perfection. A blaze was already going in the fire pit, and a sizable stack of wood had been placed next to it.

I wandered around the deck before heading indoors. Luke had cleared almost all the weeds between the deck and the creek. All that remained appeared to be low ground cover. I lingered against the rail, eyes closed, and let the steady rushing of the water calm me. It was a happy sound, and one that brought back great memories of my childhood.

"It's so nice here. I wish we didn't have to go in." Rachel's voice brought me out of my daydream.

"Very true." I turned to look my sister in the eyes. "The passages you read during the service. They were beautiful. Thanks for doing that."

"Yeah, well, you're not the only one of Dad's kids who cares about literature." She let out a sigh that felt as if it carried the weight of the world. "Sorry. That was mean. I like your new haircut, by the way. Ready to head inside?"

It took me a minute to recover from Rachel's apology. She hadn't done that in years. And complimenting me on my pixie cut? Hadn't seen that coming. Well, losing our father was going to affect each of us differently. Maybe some good would come out of this and my sister and I could get past our issues with each other once and for all.

Growing up, Rachel had always been part of the in-crowd. She was gorgeous, dressed impeccably, could have any guy she wanted, and reveled in her lofty status. Since I was only two years younger than Rachel, many people, including Rachel, expected me to be heavily influenced by her and follow her lead in all things.

At first, I tried. Mom and Dad knew how hard I tried to live up to my sister's lofty expectations, but no matter what, all of my efforts to be another Rachel Cobb failed. And with each failure, the resentment between us grew.

By the time I entered middle school, I'd had enough of being Rachel Number Two and focused on being Allie Number One. The acceptance of myself for who I was brought me peace and happiness. Doing my own thing often embarrassed Rachel, though, so among her and her friends, I became little more than the "annoying little sister."

That was a label I carried with pride. I reveled in books and nerd culture and tromping around the woods at Sloane's house. If I found out Rachel thought something was stupid, like role-playing board games, I embraced it.

When I left for college, I hugged Mom, Dad and Luke. Rachel and I just nodded to each other. In the ensuing decade or so, the hostility and silly, teenage game-playing had come to an end. The scars remained, though. Living eight hundred miles apart and only seeing each other a few times a year made it easy to avoid acting like adults and talking out our problems. Perhaps now, it was finally time.

That was me, the eternal optimist.

I hadn't been inside more than a minute when Steve handed me a glass of white wine. "A bunch of us at the pub wanted to do something for you guys, so we asked Rachel if we could cater this. We figured one less thing for your family to have to think about." With a sweep of his arm, he guided me toward the buffet. "Eat, drink and, if you can, be merry." The buffet featured Italian, Dad's favorite, and tasted like the angels in Heaven had prepared it. Drinks flowed freely, and I found myself enjoying the evening until reality reared its ugly head.

Sloane and I were outside chatting by the fire pit when raised voices interrupted our conversation. We went around the corner of the building to find Thornwell and Suzette glaring at each other.

"Stop badgering me. I won't do it." Thornwell took a long drink from a wineglass, spilling some on his jacket lapel in the process. "I don't need you."

"Look at yourself." Suzette ran her fingers across the wine stain. "Not a single agent knows you as well as I do. Without me, you'll be lost."

Sloane froze in place. Unsure of whether to break up the argument or slip away, I was unable to do anything beyond hold my breath. Just as I had built up the courage to confront them, a door opened and Daniel emerged.

"I heard voices. Is there a problem?" He took a spot on the railing next to Thornwell and put a hand on the man's shoulder, the loyal assistant at his boss's side.

Daniel had worked for Thornwell for two decades. Over the years, Dad had often joked Daniel was Robin to Thornwell's Batman. He lived in Indianapolis, but e-mailed the author weekly, daily if they were on a deadline, and visited monthly.

Sloane and I backed away, satisfied that, with a mediator present, cooler heads would prevail.

"I don't need any more drama tonight," I said. "Join me inside for another drink?"

"Good idea. I'll buy."

After we got drinks and some melt-in-your-mouth breadsticks, Luke insisted we join him and some of his buddies. That was one thing about growing up the bookish introvert of the Cobb family. Other than Sloane, I didn't have any friends in Rushing Creek. I was fine with that, but Luke's invitation was welcome. The more friendlier faces I saw this night, the better.

A little while later, Daniel tapped Sloane on the shoulder. "I'm so sorry, but I think it's time for your father to go home and he said you're his ride."

Sloane closed her eyes for a moment before she got to her feet. "And I thought I was going to be your designated driver, Allie. Ah, well, duty calls."

"Don't worry, Sloanie. I'll make sure Allie gets home safe. Text me when you get home." Luke gave her a peck on her cheek. "Thanks for everything." With cheeks the shade of red roses, she gave me a rib-crushing hug. "Love you, Allie. I'll stop by tomorrow, okay?" She had a few words with Rachel and Mom, gathered up her father, who, by now, could barely walk a straight line, and made for the door.

When they were gone, Luke let out a low whistle. "I'd heard he'd cleaned up his act. Guess not."

I stared at him. "Why do you have Sloane's phone number?"

He rolled his eyes. "Relax. Sloanie was part of the phone tree after Dad got sick. She helped with his chemo appointments."

"She never told me."

Luke patted my knee. "She knew there was only so much you could do from New York. My guess is she didn't want you to feel guilty. Like you're trying to feel right now. Am I right?"

"I guess. No need to make a mountain out of a molehill." I got up and yawned. "You know what? I need some fresh air. I think I'm going to walk home." Before Luke could object, I pulled out my phone. "I'll text you when I get there, just like Sloane. Forty-five minutes tops, promise."

After the stuffy air of the community center, the briskness of the early October evening rejuvenated me. As I strolled past the winery, the only sounds to break the silence were the hoots from a nearby barred owl.

I'd forgotten how peaceful my hometown could be. Living in the City That Never Sleeps, I was used to the constant white noise of traffic, music and people living life at breakneck speed.

Here in Rushing Creek, I could take a ten-minute walk and find myself surrounded by the woods, with nothing but squirrels and other wildlife to keep me company. It was calming, peaceful.

Even the boulevard was fairly quiet. A few cars were parked in front of the inn, and Marinara's, the pizza place, still had its lights on. Beyond that, all was quiet.

The peacefulness ended the moment I inserted my key into the front door of the house. Ursi howled a greeting to me and her meow, meow, meow didn't stop until I fed her. Once I was certain she wouldn't curl up and die from malnutrition, I changed into my pj's and returned to Dad's office, compelled by a need to be near him in some way.

I picked up a manuscript that caught my attention and snuggled into a leather recliner in the corner of the room. For years, Dad had sat in the recliner as he read and edited manuscripts. Tonight, I'd pretend to be him with the hope that the worst of my visit home was over.

* * * *

I was startled awake the next morning by an insistent banging on the front door. When I opened it, Sloane grabbed me.

"Ohmigod, Allie. Thank God you're here. I can't believe it. It's so awful. I can't do it alone. Will you come with me?"

The words had spilled out so fast, I barely understood them. I put my hands on her forearms and gave them a gentle squeeze. "Sloane, come inside and tell me what's wrong."

"We need to go. Right now." She started crying. "They're waiting for me."

"Who's waiting for you?" This time I shook her, hoping to get her to stop babbling. "Where do we need to go? Sloane, what is going on?"

Her eyes cleared for a moment and then she wrapped her arms around me, tears falling with such force, my shoulder was soaked in seconds.

"Chief Roberson came by a few minutes ago. He said it was about Dad. They found him under the Rushing Creek Bridge.

"Allie, my dad's dead."

The world swam before me as I held my distraught best friend. Thornwell dead? Couldn't be. I guided Sloane into Dad's office and sat her in the recliner then dashed upstairs to throw on a sweatshirt and pair of jeans. By the time I returned to the office, Ursi had climbed into Sloane's lap.

My friend looked at me with bloodshot eyes. "He can't be dead. Tell me they're wrong."

One of the lessons I'd learned as an agent was to never lie to a client. There were times when tact was needed to ease the blow of bad news, but I always needed to be honest. This was a time for tact.

"I don't know. This must be why they want you to go there. To make sure, one way or the other." I took the hand she wasn't using to pet Ursi. "You can do this. I'll be by your side the whole way."

She smiled. "Just like old times?"

"Yeah, just like old times, bestie."

It was a quiet drive to the hospital. All I managed to get out of Sloane was Matt had given her the news and offered to take her to identify her father. She told him she wanted me to drive her. Evidently she'd been determined enough to convince him to let her have her way. An advantage of small-town life, I guess.

The situation was awful enough, without adding Matt to the mix. He and Rachel had been the perfect small-town couple—high school sweethearts who got married right out of college. When the twins came along, the town saw a family that belonged in a Norman Rockwell painting. What I saw were the first cracks in a marital foundation that turned out to be built of sand. A nasty divorce that included charges of infidelity was finalized just before the twins turned four. Over a year later, hard feelings remained between not just Rachel and Matt, but between the Cobb and Roberson families.

As Sloane and I entered the hospital, I crossed my fingers Matt would be professional and not hold anything against Sloane on account of my presence. He greeted me at the door with a quick nod and nothing more. All things considered, it could have been a lot worse.

I held Sloane's hand as we followed him to a nondescript door on the hospital's lower level. A stone-faced officer with dark hair stationed by the door wrapped his arms around Sloane and shared a few quiet words with her. When she nodded, they stepped inside.

Matt held out his hand when I tried to follow. "Sorry, Allie. Next of kin only." He took out a notepad. "While you're here, I'd like to ask you a couple of questions about last night."

Over the next few minutes, I told him everything I could recall from the wake. I also confirmed Thornwell had been very drunk. Based on Matt's questions, word about his condition had already gotten around town.

When he asked how Thornwell got home, the hair on the back of my neck stood on end.

"Sloane drove him."

He scratched his chin. "And that was the last time you saw or heard from her?"

"Yeah, until she showed up on my doorstep this morning. Wait a minute." My blood went cold. "You can't possibly think Sloane had something to do with Thornwell's death, can you?"

"I don't know. She may have been the last person to see him. They had a rocky relationship." He looked up and down the hall. "I'm only going to tell you this next thing because you're her best friend. We found a credit card statement on him. The account was maxed out and past due. It was Sloane's."

I literally fell against the wall, Matt's words rocked me like a kickboxing shot to the gut. The chief of police was accusing my best friend of murdering her father. What was I going to do?

Chapter Four

After a few deep breaths, I pushed off from the wall as my shock turned to anger. Sloane wasn't a killer. Whatever happened to her father, my best friend wasn't involved. She couldn't be.

"Look, Matt, I'm sorry you and Rachel hate each other's guts, but there's no need to take it out on me." I poked his chest with my finger. "Now stop playing games and tell me what really happened."

He chomped down on the gum he was chewing twice as hard as before. God, what a nasty habit.

"Give me more credit than that, Allie. I—"

The door opened and the officer asked me to come in. Sloane was standing over the body. Her back was to me, but the way her shoulders were convulsing left no doubt she was mourning the loss of her father, despite their difficult relationship, as only a daughter could.

I stepped up to Matt and kept my voice low. "You want me to give you credit? Earn it." Then I went to comfort my friend without giving him a second look.

"I'm so sorry, Sloane." I put my arms around her and let her cry. It would haunt me to the end of my days that I didn't get home in time to say good-bye to my father, but that was on me. I'd have to live with it. Sloane never got the chance to say good-bye. As I tried to comfort her, I made a vow to do everything in my power to right the injustice done to Thornwell.

And Sloane.

After a while, she calmed down from the initial shock and the tears came to an end. Matt asked if he could run a few questions past her. When she nodded, I got between them.

"I'll join you two. Sloane needs support right now and shouldn't have to be alone while we wait for her mom to get here."

Matt clenched his jaw and shook his head, but nodded and popped in another piece of gum. "How about a cup of coffee in the hospital cafeteria?"

* * * *

Sloane and I slipped into a booth in a quiet corner while Matt got the drinks. I made a mental note to sit at a table next time I was out in public. Between Sloane's parents and now this, I was experiencing way too much weirdness while sitting in booths all of a sudden.

Torn between my rage at Matt, grief for Sloane and guilt about Dad, I was at a loss for comforting words for my friend. So I did the only thing I could think of; I held her hand while Matt got settled across from us. And I didn't let it go for the entire conversation.

"Do you know how he died?" The roughness of Sloane's voice startled me. The poor thing had to be utterly spent.

"Not yet. What we do know is he was found facedown with a cut and a decent-sized bump on the back of his head, but that was it." Matt took a drink but kept his gaze on Sloane.

When I was in middle school, a kid had jumped off the bridge as part of a high school graduation stunt. He'd broken an arm and a leg. Sure, the water level was currently high, but if my memory was correct, the distance from the bridge railing to the water was typically about twenty feet. *And all he got from his fall was a bump on the head?* It didn't add up, but I kept my thoughts to myself. Sloane was upset enough.

Matt glanced at me and took a deep breath. "Sloane, I'd like to ask you about last night. I understand you were both at the service for Mr. Cobb."

Between sniffing back tears, Sloane recounted yesterday's events. She'd driven Thornwell straight home from the community center, arriving a little after eight. She'd gone into the house with him to get him a sandwich and some coffee to sober him up. She was there for a half hour before she left.

"And then where did you go?" Matt was taking notes as he asked the question.

"Home. It had been a tough enough day saying good-bye to Mr. Cobb, without my father making a spectacle of himself. And after all the progress he'd made." She blew her nose.

"What kind of progress?"

"With the booze. After Mr. Cobb got sick, Dad seemed to have an epiphany. He cut way back on his drinking and said he'd been working on a new book. He told me about a year ago, 'Sloane, when Walter's gone, I'm going to have to stand on my own two feet again. I need to relearn how to do that.'"

"So, he was drinking yesterday?"

"He'd just buried his agent and best friend," I said, with some extra heat. "You'd have wanted a drink, too, I'd bet."

Matt's cheeks turned red. "I'm not passing judgment. Just trying to get the facts. I want to find out what happened to Mr. Winchester as much as anyone. So, Sloane?"

"Yes. He'd been drinking. Way too much." She wadded up a napkin, smoothed it out and wadded it up again. She told Matt about her dad's sharp words with Suzette and how only Daniel had been able to get him to calm down.

An excruciating hour later, Sloane received a text from her mom, who was in the parking lot. While Sloane went to get her, I took the initiative and told Matt about seeing Charissa Mody, the woman who claimed to be Thornwell's girlfriend, and then, later that night, coming across him with his ex-wife. Sure, I was grasping at straws, but it was all I could come up with.

Then I had a lightbulb moment.

"Sloane promised Luke she'd text him when she got home. Check her phone or talk to Luke. That'll corroborate her story."

"Well." Matt cocked his head to the side. "It'll confirm whether or not she texted him, and if so, the time of the text. Look, Allie, you've been gone a long time. Times change. People change. Let me do my job to find out what happened."

"Whatever you say, Chief." While Matt's tepid response left me deflated, it didn't leave me defeated. I couldn't deny his logic, as much as it hurt to acknowledge I didn't know my hometown as well as I had in my younger days. It also didn't change my belief that Sloane was Matt's prime suspect.

And that he was mistaken.

All I needed to do now was figure out how to prove it, which was way easier said than done. I was a literary agent, not a police officer, after all. Heck, I didn't even have a single mystery writer among my clients.

I did have a couple of things going for me, though. First, Matt was right; I didn't know the good people of Rushing Creek like I once had. That could be a good thing. Being a step removed from the people in town, I could see them through a more-balanced perspective. On top of that was the one thing I'd emphasized in every job interview I'd had since I was old enough to work; my attention to detail was unsurpassed.

At the sound of voices behind me, I turned around. Sloane and her mom were approaching. They were walking with a slow, stiff gait that called to mind scenes from films in which one of the characters was making the final walk toward execution. My heart broke for both of them.

After the introductions were made, Matt told Sloane she was free to go, but he would catch up with her later.

Sloane nodded and gave her mom a quick hug. The two were as close as Indiana is to Alaska, thanks, in large part, to the divorce. But at least Kathryn was here.

While Sloane was giving Matt her contact information, I pulled Kathryn off to the side. "Thanks for coming down from Indy for this. I'm sure Sloane appreciates it."

"Someday, perhaps." She sniffed. "I just can't believe this happened. Then again, when it comes to Thornwell, nothing should surprise me."

"When did you see him last?" She hadn't made it to the funeral, so I was curious to hear her answer. Good Lord, I was getting paranoid already.

"Night before last. We'd been working on reconciling. I stayed in town after your dad's visitation, God rest his soul, and we had dinner." She got a faraway look in her eyes. "It was good. I had a nice time." She closed her eyes as she massaged the back of her neck. "And now he's gone."

"I'm so sorry for your loss, Mrs. Winchester." I'd been on the receiving end of that line too many times to count over the past few days. It was weird to be saying it to someone else.

"Thank you. Please be there for Sloane. This is all so sudden. I can't imagine what she's going through right now."

You don't know the half of it. I promised to do all I could for Sloane, and then Sloane and I made our way to her car.

At Sloane's apartment, I brewed coffee and toasted us bagels while she lay on the couch in the fetal position. While I waited for the pot to fill, I took a close look around the kitchen. A few plates and cups were in the sink, waiting to be transferred to the dishwasher. The trash can by the fridge was half full of plastic sports drink bottles and power bar wrappers. The fridge was stocked with items straight out of a health food store: wheat bread, sliced lean meats, assorted fresh fruit and vegetables and a dozen bottles of some power shake.

"How's the training going?" I figured asking about her trail running efforts would be a safe way to get her talking. She hadn't said a word since we left the hospital, which wasn't like her. In elementary school, a few mean kids called her Motormouth. It was unkind but accurate, nonetheless. "Pretty good, actually." She sat up when I handed her a bagel smeared with blueberry cream cheese. "It's bizarre. My times have improved over the past few weeks. Ever since I gave myself my sponsorship deadline, I've felt less tense. So much for that now, huh?"

Countless times, Sloane had told me a relaxed runner was a fast runner. It made total sense her sponsorship hunt, and the stress that had come with it, impeded her training. Then she found a way to eliminate that stress. And now this. The poor thing.

"I'm glad you're here." She took a sip of her coffee. "Don't get me wrong. I'd do anything to turn back the clock so your dad and my dad were still alive. But I know what people around here say about my family, and I don't think I'll be able to face the next few days without you."

Drunken father. Cold and distant mother. Aimless, screwed-up kid. Along with Sloane, I knew all too well the vicious things people said about the Winchester family. And I despised the callousness.

"I'm here, and I'm not going anywhere until this is figured out." I sat next to her on the couch and laced my fingers through hers, like we did when watching Nickelodeon as kids. Despite Matt's words, I couldn't envision Sloane killing her father in any way, shape or form.

"You believe me, don't you?" Sloane ran her finger across her plate, grouping the bagel crumbs into a little pile in the center. If I hadn't been sitting right next to her, I might not have heard the question. Her desperate plea for solidarity.

"Of course I do. Why would you even ask?"

"Matt asked if I called or texted anyone last night after leaving the wake. When I showed him my text to Luke, he took a picture of it and said he'd follow up with Luke." She squeezed my hand hard enough to crack a couple of knuckles. "I don't think he believes me."

"Matt Roberson's a jerk. I guarantee you he's freaking out right now because he's never had to deal with anything more serious than when Georgie Alonso started that brawl at Hoosiers a few years ago." I extricated my hand and flexed it to get blood flowing again. "He was probably trying to scare you."

She snorted. "You know what's scary? Looking at your father, knowing he was drunk during the last conversation you had with him and you'll never be able to talk to him again. Knowing I left him alone and then someone killed him."

In all my years of editing and agenting, years spent looking for the perfect words to convey a message, I'd always been able to come up with something to make a story, a chapter, a sentence better. As I sat with my brokenhearted best friend, I had nothing. How did you comfort someone filled with that much grief and guilt?

So, I kept my mouth shut. Instead, I put my arm around Sloane and pulled her close.

The rhythmic *swish, swish, swish* of the ceiling fan calmed us, and, after a little while, Sloane's breathing evened out. When I was certain she was asleep, I got her settled under a cotton throw and sneaked off to the kitchen to call Luke.

He let out a long whistle when I finished my report. "Holy buckets. When it rains, it pours. How's Sloanie?"

"She's sleeping right now. Matt Roberson was asking her some pretty pointed questions. Don't be surprised when he pays you a visit to confirm Sloane's story."

Luke promised to be ready and we made our good-byes. With peak leaf season, and the tourists it brought to the area, fewer than two weeks away, he'd be scrambling to make sure the town was spotless and ready for the upcoming Fall Festival. I found it unforgivable the mayor had hinted, in less than subtle terms, he needed Luke to delay any additional bereavement leave until after the festival. Lucky for the mayor, Luke was a workaholic who didn't mind channeling his grief into his work.

I, on the other hand, was in a position to take care of my clients and still have time on my hands until I returned to New York. After letting Mom know I was spending the day with Sloane, I busied myself in the kitchen. I wasn't a great cook, but I had mastered the art of maintaining a healthy diet while preparing a variety of meals for one.

A couple of hours later, I roused Sloane from her nap by waving tomato bisque soup close to her nose. Her favorite for as long as I could remember; she sniffed and opened her eyes.

"How much of that did you make?"

We didn't speak while Sloane plowed through two bowls of soup and a double-decker grilled cheese sandwich. She'd been through more than enough for one day, and I wanted to check on Mom. So I told her about the meals I'd prepared and gathered my things to leave.

At her door, Sloane hugged and thanked me for helping her through the morning.

"I'm glad I was able to be here for you." A current of understanding forged over almost three decades of friendship ran between us. It told me Sloane had more to say. "There's something else. Isn't there?" "Yeah." Sloane scratched her forehead, as if she was using the time to build up the confidence to say what was on her mind. "I know my dad was an arrogant jerk. I know he was unfaithful. I know he drank too much. But I also know he turned his life around and didn't drown in that creek. Someone killed him." She pounded her fist against the doorframe. "I don't trust Matt. Will you help me find whoever killed my daddy?"

My daddy. Sloane hadn't referred to Thornwell that way since we were little. There was no way I was going to do anything less than what Atticus Finch did for Tom Robinson.

"Yes, Sloane. Yes, I will. I'll find his killer."

Chapter Five

The walk home from Sloane's apartment helped clear my head for the task at hand. I'd read enough mysteries and police procedurals over the years to give me an idea of where I needed to start. The stories also reminded me I had no business meddling in a police matter. My closest brush with the law was a public intoxication charge back when I was in college. I paid a fine, did community service by spending a day picking up trash and put the embarrassing affair behind me.

A murder was a great white shark compared to the guppy my public intox charge amounted to.

No matter. I promised Sloane I'd do whatever I could to help her. It was a promise I intended to keep. It wasn't that I didn't trust Matt. Sure, on a personal level I thought he was a cheating scumbag, but on a professional level, by all accounts, he was a decent cop. He'd served the community of Rushing Creek his entire career, the last two as chief of police. What I didn't trust was the department's ability to conduct a murder investigation.

An Internet search when I got home confirmed my worries. The last murder in Rushing Creek had been committed over thirty years ago. A couple of guys had gotten into a bar fight over the song choices one had made at the jukebox. The brawl spilled into the parking lot, a gun was pulled and shots were fired. The gunman was too drunk to flee the scene and Matt's grandfather made the arrest with minimal fuss.

This was Matt's first murder investigation.

Awesome.

I scrounged around Dad's office and found a yellow legal pad he used for making editorial notes. In one column, I wrote down the names of every person I could remember seeing, talking to or being mentioned since I'd returned to Rushing Creek. Next to each name, I noted whether the person was a local or from out of town.

There were eleven out-of-towners on account of Dad's funeral. I'd have to contact Matt and ask him to make sure nobody left. And soon. While I pondered how to approach him with the request, Ursi jumped into my lap and bumped her head against my hand.

"Sorry, girl." I scratched her ears. "I'd planned on spending the day here with you and Mom. So much for that, huh?"

A knock on the office door interrupted my kitty scratching. It was Mom. Her eyes were tear-filled.

"Oh, Allie. What is going on? The world's gone insane."

We hugged each other, squishing Ursi a little, but my kitty must have sensed our grief because she started purring while we embraced. After a while, we went to the kitchen, where Mom made us a late lunch. Food was one thing definitely not in short supply at the moment.

I made a mental note to take some things to Sloane. I wasn't certain the community would be as generous to her as to Mom.

"I'm proud of you for going with Sloane this morning." She sat across from me, a steaming cup of tea in her hands. "I can't believe Thornwell's gone. Does Matt have any idea what happened?"

"He's trying to gather as much information as possible right now." I didn't have the heart to tell her Sloane appeared to be at the top of Matt's suspect list. After all, it was possible my stressed-out emotions were creating a problem that didn't exist. On the other hand...

"Let me know if there's anything I can do. I know you want to be there for Sloane, but you need to be able to grieve for your father, too."

"Thanks, Mom. Maybe you could check in with Mrs. Winchester. I don't know what her plans are."

"Probably tracking down Thornwell's will." She covered her mouth with her hand. "I'm sorry. That was a horrible thing to say."

The Winchesters' divorce had taken its own toll on my family. Dad felt he had a duty to his client. On top of that, they'd been friends since meeting in a literature class as sophomores in college. Dad had encouraged Thornwell to follow his dream of writing a book. When Thornwell finished it the summer after they graduated, he insisted Dad serve as his agent. They'd been together ever since.

Mom had initially supported Mrs. Winchester, but when the woman moved to Indianapolis and didn't take Sloane with her, Mom had gone off. For the better part of a week, she told anybody who would listen that a decent mother would never leave her daughter to remain in close proximity to such a difficult man.

Over the years, the members of the Cobb family came to terms with the divorce, and each of us did our best to support Sloane and keep Thornwell on as straight a path as possible. Evidently, Mom hadn't been as forgiving as I'd assumed.

"I saw them together the other night." I told her about my observations at the pub, along with an admission I was so shocked to see them together, and apparently happy, I'd hidden from them.

With a world-weary sigh, Mom slumped into the recliner. "I'm not surprised. Thornwell talked to both your dad and me about reconciling. We didn't think it was a good idea, at least not yet, but he chose to ignore our advice, as you saw."

"Why?" Sloane's words about her dad getting better echoed in my mind. They didn't line up with what Mom was saying. Did she know something important? Was Mrs. Winchester the killer? Good Lord, I was already seeing murder in everything.

"You have to understand, we had Thornwell and Sloane's interests above everything else. The change in him once he got sober was stunning. Between the progress on his new book and his improved relationship with Sloane, we were encouraged he'd finally changed for the better." Tears welled up in her eyes.

"I'm sorry, Mom. I shouldn't have brought it up. You have enough to deal with right now."

She brushed some cat fuzz from her sweater. "It's fine. You deserve to know. We were worried Thornwell was taking things too quickly. We suggested he focus on his writing and rebuilding things one person at a time instead of with both Kathryn and Sloane at once. Between the two of them, Kathryn probably needed his money more than he needed anything from her. Still, I never thought..."

I gave Mom a hug. Once again, words seemed pointless, so when Ursi jumped into Mom's lap, we sat in silence for a while. Despite my best efforts to not think, I couldn't help wondering if Kathryn Winchester had murdered her ex-husband. That would be a minefield to navigate. I could see it. *Hey Sloane, I know you didn't kill your dad, but your mom did.* Yeah, that would go over like the proverbial lead balloon.

Still, I'd promised her I'd find the killer. And I had every intention of keeping that promise.

Even if that meant one of her parents was dead and the other was in jail.

Mom's phone beeped. "It's the office. I better take this."

Ursi followed Mom out of the room. She knew who the boss was in her temporary quarters. With nothing but my thoughts to keep me company, I went back to my list and added a name at the bottom.

Kathryn Winchester.

A little while later, I left the house, ready to get to work helping Sloane. My first stop was the police station. I needed to talk to Matt.

He was in his office, so I breezed by a woman with short, black hair at the front desk, knocked on his door once and stepped inside. "I need a few minutes, Matt."

"Allie? What the...?" His eyes were wide as he glanced over my shoulder. "Jeanette, why is this woman in my office without an appointment?"

I turned to get a look at the woman. She closed a manual she'd been reading.

"I'm sorry, Chief. She was by me before I realized what was happening." She scratched her ear and glanced at me. "I'm sorry for your loss, Miss Cobb."

"Thank you. I don't believe we've met." I offered to shake. I would need this woman on my side if I was going to get anywhere. "I'm Allie. Sorry about that. It's just there's something I need to speak with the chief about, and after yesterday, I guess my head isn't quite where it should be."

Jeanette took my hand while putting an arm around me. "Don't apologize. I can't imagine how hard things must be for your family right now. Can I get you something to drink?"

Since I was probably going to go to hell for lying anyway, I figured why not go all in. "Some water would be very nice. Thank you."

When Jeanette was gone, I slipped into the chair.

Matt was staring at me with a half-grin. "Nice work at manipulation there. Your sister would be proud."

"Matt, please. I don't want to be enemies. I'm here because I'm worried about Sloane."

He raised an eyebrow and popped a piece of gum in his mouth. "The situation with her dad's understandably a shock. We gave her grief counseling information. Beyond that, there's not a lot I can do for her."

I needed to make my move while we were still alone. "Do you really think Sloane killed him?"

After glancing at the ceiling, Matt shook his head. "I can't talk about an active investigation. Is there another reason you came by? If not, you should go."

"I don't understand. This morning, you acted like you were ready to lock her up and throw away the key." A knock at the door stopped me.

Jeanette handed me a plastic cup of ice water and left.

"And now you won't talk about it? What's up with that?"

"Look, Allie." Matt leaned forward and placed his hands on the worn, wooden desktop. His fingernails were chewed down to the nubs. "I understand you're upset. First your dad. Now your best friend's dad. I'm sure you want to help." He got to his feet, using his height advantage to loom over me. "The best way you can help is to let me do my job. Fair enough?"

"No." I took a deep breath and crossed my arms. "I'm not going to let you railroad Sloane. I want you to make all of the out-of-towners stay here until you find Thornwell's killer. His real killer."

"That's enough. I've had enough of you breezing into my office telling me how to do my job. I'm not going to let you start bossing everyone around just because you left all of us hayseeds behind for the bright lights of the big city."

My blood began to simmer. Just because he was taller than me by a foot and outweighed me by a hundred pounds, it didn't mean I was going to let him intimidate me. I'd learned a thing or two making my own way, first in college and then in New York. One of the things I'd learned was how to spot a bully. I'd seen it before, and I saw it now.

Matt Roberson was trying to bully me.

All his life, his good looks, athletic ability, and charisma had gotten him what he wanted. He was the hometown legend who became police chief and had the princess on his arm. And when the princess started to push back because she wanted a partner in their marriage, not a boss? The legend turned into a bully.

It was time for me to push back against the bully.

"I'm not trying to boss you, or anybody, around. I'm simply asking you to show a lifetime resident of this community the benefit of the doubt. For now. I'm sure people will understand you asking them to stick around for a few days."

"People will understand." Matt laughed and pointed at the wall behind me. "Look at the calendar. The most important weekend of the year is ten days away. You know what the Fall Festival means to this town. The mayor has made it crystal clear we can't have an unsolved murder hanging over our heads when the leaf peepers arrive. I do not intend to let my boss, along with each and every business in this town, down. Have I made myself clear?"

"Absolutely." I placed my fingertips on the desk and leaned toward him. "By my calculations, you'll have no problem having our current out of town visitors stay for a few extra days. They'll be long gone by the time the festival starts. On behalf of Sloane and Thornwell, thank you for your time and cooperation."

I took the water and left his office without turning back. At the receptionist desk, I made a show of taking a few drinks and thanked Jeanette for her kindness.

"Is everything okay? I heard raised voices." She tilted her head toward Matt's office.

"Nothing to worry about." She seemed like a nice person, so there was no point in dragging her into the swamp of the Cobb versus Roberson family feud. "Chief Roberson and I have known each other since elementary school. He's got a tough job to do, and I wanted to let him know I appreciated his efforts in serving the good people of Rushing Creek."

"Really?" Jeanette tapped her finger on the desktop. "Forgive me for saying so, Ms. Cobb, but lying isn't your strong suit." As my cheeks got hot, she smiled. "It's okay. I've worked here long enough to know these aren't normal times in Rushing Creek. If there's anything I can help you with, let me know."

She handed me her business card. I blinked to keep my eyes from welling up.

"Thank you, Jeanette. I really appreciate it." I cleared my throat. "And please call me Allie."

"Will do, Allie. Why don't you give me your number? I assume you'd like a copy of the police report when it's complete?"

Jeanette's phone rang, so I scribbled my number on a Post-it Note while she took the call. As I made my exit from the police station, it felt as if one brick had been lifted from the load I was carrying. I had no clue what I was doing and no idea what I was looking for, but I had one new item in my toolkit.

I had an ally. With access to information.

Chapter Six

I left the police department feeling a foot taller than my five-one frame. Standing up to Matt had been empowering. Followed by making a friend, or at least forming an alliance with Jeanette was gratifying. I didn't feel like a detective, but I was hoping my next stop would fix that. It was time to see the scene of the crime.

The Rushing Creek Bridge was a 170-foot-long steel and concrete structure. It was wide enough for two lanes for motor traffic, along with sidewalks on either side to accommodate pedestrians going into and out of Green Hills State Park. At some point, since I'd last visited the bridge, the sidewalk railings had received a new coat of red paint. The bridge was the main access point to the park, so the town went to great lengths to make sure the structure was well maintained.

The crossing was also an important part of the town culture. High school seniors had their senior pictures taken there. For generations, stories had been told about who had lost their virginity to whom under the bridge. It was a common sight to see people using it as a fishing spot.

I leaned against the railing and peered down at the clear water beneath me, flowing at an easy pace that reminded me of a lazy Sunday afternoon. It looked to be a fifteen-foot drop from the bridge deck, which seemed like an insufficient distance if someone was going to kill himself or herself. I dictated a note into my phone to ask Mom about that while I took pictures of the scene from the railing.

Something else was odd. The railing was four feet high. If Matt thought Sloane killed Thornwell, how did he think it happened? Did they get in a fight and she pushed him over the railing? Did she kill him first, come here and then dump the body? Regardless, it must have taken some serious muscle to get him over the railing.

Sloane was taller than me at five seven, but her dad was about six feet. The size difference would have made dumping a body, dead or alive, over the rail a chore.

I shivered at the morbid thought.

Down below, the area where Thornwell's body had been found had been marked off with yellow and black police tape. I'd deal with that shortly. First, I crept along the railing, looking for scrape marks, chipped paint, something to indicate something heavy was pushed across it. Unable to find anything, I dictated a note to ask about whether or not any red paint was found on Thornwell's clothes.

After a look around to make sure I was alone, I scrambled down the bank to the edge of the creek. The scene was a head-scratcher. In the shade of the bridge and sycamore trees, with the water bubbling by, it was a world of quiet serenity—small town, Southern Indiana at its finest. Until my gaze moved to the police tape.

The police had rounded up a half dozen garden stakes to cordon off the area where Thornwell was found. I placed my hand on one of the stakes.

"If your final chapter ended here Thornwell, where did it begin?"

The myriad gurney tracks and footprints told me nothing beyond the obvious, so I snapped a few more pictures and trudged back up the slope. A box truck rumbled across the bridge. The driver gave me a wave. Without a second thought, I waved back. Another aspect of small-town life, so different from the Big Apple. As the dust from the four-wheeled monster settled, I thought about my conversation with Matt at the hospital. Whether on purpose or not, he never mentioned who found the body. I needed to find that out.

And talk to whomever it was.

The afternoon of amateur sleuthing had left me tired, dusty and thirsty, but I couldn't resist the draw from the aromatherapy shop. Originally a one-story single-family dwelling, the building had been converted into a store in the eighties. Over the years, it had been home to an art studio, a music store and, most recently, a boutique clothier.

After having sat empty for eighteen months, the building now sported a cheerful yellow coat of paint and a forest green bench by the front door. With each step I took toward the store, bits of tension in my shoulders faded away. I had high hopes I'd leave the store with something to help me battle my insomnia.

Once inside, I had to let my eyes adjust to the dim surroundings. Native American music played in the background as I detected a scent of chamomile.

"Welcome to Soaps and Scents." A woman who looked to be about Mom's age came up to me. She had long, gray hair that spilled over her shoulders and wore round, wire-rimmed glasses. A Dave Matthews Band T-shirt and green peasant skirt completed the bohemian vibe. "I just brewed some herbal tea. Would you care for some?"

"I'd love some." I studied the items on the store's wooden shelves, fascinated that there were so many different kinds of aromatherapy oils, candles and lotions. A small glass bottle containing Bergamot oil had my attention when my host returned.

"Ah, now, that's one of my best sellers." She handed me a white mug with the store's name printed on it in green. "I'm Shirley, and this is my store. What brings you here?"

After introducing myself, I brought the mug to my nose and inhaled. The warmth commingled with the floral scent to make me smile. I took a sip and could have gone to Heaven then and there. Shirley had evidently added honey to the tea, and the hint of sweetness, along with the mild flavor, was incredible. After tasting the amazing concoction, my heart told me to trust Shirley.

"I'm looking for something to help me wind down at the end of the day. That, and I grew up here in town and wanted to see your store."

Shirley ran her fingers along the miniature dream catcher that hung on a leather cord around her neck. "A common malady these days. It doesn't matter whether one is working or on vacation, it seems everyone has trouble sleeping." She sighed. "Especially in these troubled times."

I wasn't sure whether she was referring to local events or global ones, but it didn't seem to matter, once I gave it a moment's thought.

"That poor man." Shirley wrapped her arms around herself. "So tragic."

My detective radar went on high alert. Maybe there was information to be gleaned from her. "Did you know Mr. Winchester?"

"He was one of my best customers. He said he was a writer and my oils helped clear his mind, especially my lavender. I can't believe he's gone. And to be found under a bridge. How awful." She took a sip of her tea. "Did you know him?"

"He and my father worked together. His daughter and I are friends."

"I'm so sorry for your loss. Is there anything I can do?"

"No, but thank you." I scratched behind my ear, trying to appear casual. "Word's gotten around fast about Thornwell."

"I couldn't say. Jackson Michaels, the local handyman, was in the store this morning to take measurements for some new shelves and didn't seem to be himself. When I asked what was wrong, he told me he'd found the body."

"Oh, wow. I can't imagine something like that."

I knew Jackson Michaels. The man everyone called Jax was Thornwell's property manager and took care of pretty much everything on the 120-acre estate, from grounds keeping to plumbing. Shirley referring to him as a handyman had me puzzled, but that was something I could ask Sloane about when I saw her again.

"He was shaking like a leaf. And who could blame him?" Shirley took another drink of her tea. "I'm sorry. You're here to look for something to help you calm down, and I'm talking about murder. That won't help your nerves, now will it?"

"Good point."

We laughed, but I was glad nobody else was in the store. I didn't want Matt to know I was poking around in police business. He'd find out later, but I was pretty sure the longer it was until he found out, the better.

I chose two bottles of the Bergamot oil, a bowl-shaped wooden diffuser, and a tube of eucalyptus bubble bath. "I think this will do the trick for today."

A man and a woman came in as I followed Shirley to the counter. *Close call.* Instead of a cash register, Shirley had a tablet with a credit card reader attached to it. She must have noticed my wide eyes because she chuckled.

"I may look like a hippie, but that doesn't mean I don't love twenty-first-century technology." She took my card and inserted it into the chip-reading slot. "Mr. Winchester and I often talked about looking beneath the surface to truly understand people."

"A great lesson to live by." I thanked her for the items and the tea and promised to visit again soon.

Once outside, I got comfortable on the bench to take stock of my visit. Thornwell admitting to someone he had anxiety issues was quite the revelation, but it also had a thread of plausibility given his recent change in behavior. I couldn't see how it fit in to his murder, but I made a note of it, anyway.

More intriguing was how she referred to Jax Michaels. Why was he no longer working as Thornwell's property manager? I always figured that was a pretty cushy job, even if he had to put up with the man's drunken tirades from time to time. Had he finally gotten his fill of Thornwell? Or, had Thornwell gotten his fill of Jax?

Most importantly, did his apparent split from Thornwell have anything to do with the fact that he was the one who found the dead man?

My phone broke my train of thought when it pinged to let me know I had an e-mail. One of my clients was checking on how I was doing. My clients were as precious to me as my family. The thought that one of them took the time to check in on me warmed my heart. I responded that things were fine.

They weren't fine. They were totally not fine. But I was going to fix that. The house was dark when I got home, so, after feeding Ursi and cleaning her litter box, I made a beeline for the fridge. I thought I wouldn't have much of an appetite, but the second I laid eyes on the leftovers, my stomach rumbled loud enough to make Ursi give me a dirty look. By the time I took a seat at the kitchen table, I had ham, fruit salad, green bean casserole and a slice of apple pie.

The feast energized me, so I fetched my laptop and headed to Dad's office to edit a contemporary romance manuscript one of my clients had submitted over the weekend. I'd fallen in love with the synopsis and was looking forward to reading the completed work. On top of that, I hoped a story with a happy ending would lift my troubled spirits.

Dad's recliner was as comfortable as a pair of worn blue jeans as I got settled, and a blanket I'd grabbed from the hall closet made me all warm and snuggly. Ursi joined me and, after kneading my abdomen for a few minutes, curled up in a ball between my hip and the arm of the chair and fell asleep. The only thing to disturb the blessed silence was the warm air blowing through the floor vents.

I'd just made a note in the manuscript, asking the author for more background on the hero's military service, when there was a knock on the office door.

"Hey, there," Mom said. "I wanted to let you know I'm home. Have you been crying?"

I laughed as I wiped tears from my cheeks. "It's the story I'm editing. It's *sooo* good. I think I want to marry the hero."

Mom scratched Ursi's head on her way to the chair behind Dad's desk. The cat opened one eye, yawned and went right back to sleep. If I couldn't marry the story's hero, spending the rest of my life as a cat wouldn't be a bad consolation prize.

"I remember your father talking about characters in his authors' books he fell in love with or wanted to have a beer with. Unless I'm mistaken, he usually sold those books quickly. I hope that's a good sign for you, too."

Notwithstanding the incredible manuscript, I was in need of a good sign. Lance had left a short voice-mail message saying he hoped I was doing okay, but it sounded more perfunctory than anything. It was almost as if someone at work read him the riot act for being AWOL in my life right now, so he did the bare minimum to clear his conscience. Then again, we'd only been going out for a couple of months, so maybe he didn't know what the expectations on him were, if any. I'd give him the benefit of the doubt and call him in the morning. It would do me some good to talk to someone not from Rushing Creek.

At the moment, Mom was the perfect person for me to chat with, though.

"So, Mom. About Thornwell's death. I was at the bridge today, and it looked like a fifteen-foot fall from the bridge to the creek. Would that be far enough to be fatal?"

"It depends. If he hit his head or there were contributing factors, it could be. For instance, we know he was intoxicated, so that would have to be worked into the equation. It would also depend on how deep the water was where he landed. Why do you ask?"

"When I was looking around, I couldn't find anything to indicate how he was pushed over the rail."

"What makes you think he was pushed?"

The question caught me unprepared. Why did I think that? "I guess I assumed that if he was still awake when he went over, someone would have to push him to get him over the railing. If he was unconscious, again, someone would have had to roll him over the railing, or something like that. He wasn't small. I'd bet he was two hundred pounds."

Mom raised her eyebrows. "You assume he was pushed. Therefore, you're jumping to the conclusion he was on the bridge with someone else and the someone else managed to get him over the railing, where he dropped into the water."

"I'm not jumping to any conclusions." I scratched Ursi's ear in response to her nipping at my thumb for waking her. "Okay, maybe I am. But what other explanation can there be?"

"In the medical world, we try to avoid speculation and follow the science with an open mind. I imagine police work has similar guiding principles."

I snorted. "I wish our police chief had guiding principles."

"I don't care for Matt, either, but I'd like to believe he'll investigate this situation thoroughly, regardless of what he already told you."

"What if I don't trust him to do that? I can't sit back and not do anything. There has to be an answer out there."

Mom smiled. "You sound like your father. He loved to challenge people to look past the obvious when searching for an answer to a problem. So, it's my turn for a question. What are you going to do?"

"I'm going to follow the science. Or in this case, follow the clues. Wherever they may lead."

Chapter Seven

I was drinking coffee and going through work e-mails when Mom joined me in the kitchen. She was showered and dressed as if she was going to work.

"You're up early." She was waiting for her own cup to brew.

"Trying to stay caught up on work. Don't want a client to miss out on something on account of me. What's your excuse?"

"The same, actually." She made herself a bowl of granola and yogurt then joined me at the table. "I thought I'd head into the office for a few hours."

"Come on, Mom." I brushed a few crumbs of my bagel from my Bill the Cat T-shirt. "Isn't it a little early to be returning to work? You need to allow yourself time to grieve."

"You mean I need to allow myself time to mope around the house feeling lost and sorry for myself?" She shook her head. "I grieved when we received your father's diagnosis. I grieved when we had to admit he was fighting a battle he couldn't win. I grieved after your sister and I told the twins their grandpapa wasn't going to be able to be with them anymore. I may grieve again, but for now, I've grieved enough."

We sat in silence for a while, as Mom ate her breakfast and I sipped my coffee. While Dad had always been my hero, Mom had always been the rock of the family. She was the one who literally bandaged my cuts and scrapes when I was little. She was the one who stayed up late with Luke to help him with his high school anatomy so he didn't lose his eligibility to play sports. She was the one who gave Rachel the strength to stand up to Matt and demand a divorce.

"I'm sorry, Mom. I wasn't meaning to judge. I just thought…"

Ursi jumped onto my lap and bumped my hand with her head. Like Pavlov's dog, I scratched her black and orange ears.

"It's okay. Everyone seems to think I should be here, dressed in black, poring over memories. Your dad and I talked about this very subject not long ago. It's like I told you the other day. I'll miss him terribly, and some days will be better than others, but rather than be sad that he's gone, I choose to be happy we had almost forty wonderful years together. I could have done a lot worse."

"Wow. That's an amazing attitude."

"I don't know about that. Everyone needs to be able to process losing a loved one in their own way. After all, I sure haven't seen you dressed in black waiting for me to come sit by your side this week."

I laughed. "Touché. My clients need me."

"And my patients need me."

As we finished breakfast, Mom asked about my plans. When I told her I was going to talk to Jax Michaels, she warned me to be careful. Never the friendliest type, since he'd parted ways with Thornwell, he'd become surlier.

"What happened?" I mentioned my surprise when Shirley told me Jax was doing handyman work.

"All I know is some work Thornwell paid Jax to do apparently didn't get done. Your dad told me Thornwell went through the roof when he found out and fired Jax. Then he started doing the maintenance work himself. It seems he used his sobriety to become more self-reliant around the house."

"It wasn't an amicable parting then?"

"Not in the least. Like I said, be careful."

With Mom's words in mind, I hiked the two miles to Jax Michaels's place. I could have taken the rental car, but the chilly October air made for a pleasant walk. In fact, I'd barely broken a sweat when his farmhouse came into view—which was good, since I had a feeling my conversation with Jax was going to make me do just that.

I strode up the stone path to the front door. The lawn was so green and lush, it was like I was back in Ireland on vacation. The house was as tidy as the yard, with windows so spotless their reflections almost blinded me, despite the cloudy skies and mums in bright shades of red, orange and yellow.

The property conveyed a sense of tranquility, of contentment. It was quite the difference from the man I recalled crossing paths with when I hung out at Sloane's house growing up. Simply put, in those days, Jax scared me. He was ill-tempered and on more than one occasion threatened Sloane and me with his nail gun when we interrupted his work. At first, I was convinced the man hated me because he had no reservations about calling my parents to tell them when Sloane and I had skipped through his flower beds, destroying his hard work. As the years went by, I realized he didn't hate me, it simply wasn't in his nature to be friendly, especially to two rambunctious girls.

As I knocked on the door, I couldn't help but wonder if part of his surly nature came from working for the unpredictable and imperious Thornwell. On more than one occasion, I'd seen Thornwell storm through the house shouting at the top of his lungs for Jax because there were rodents in the garden or the bathroom faucet leaked. Maybe if I gave him a chance to talk freely about his former boss, I'd pick up a few clues.

I kept that thought in mind as, after getting no answer at the door, I went around the house to the backyard. Towering red and white pine trees lined the property's border, creating a feeling of seclusion. On a normal day, it would have been enchanting. Today, it made the hair on the back of my neck stand on end. I pulled my phone out of my back pocket. Two bars out of five. That was life in a rural community. Oh well, at least Mom knew where I was.

A two-car garage stood twenty feet behind the house, both painted the same cornflower shade of blue. Another hundred feet farther was an aluminum-sided pole barn. The garage doors were closed, but the barn door was open. Somebody was sawing wood. Great. Single girl, spotty cell service and an unfriendly person with power tools. God, I was in the middle of a scene from a slasher film.

Keep it together, girl. I rolled my shoulders then marched toward the pole barn—with my phone in my hand.

Jax was at a table sawing boards in half. Between the safety glasses and industrial-style headphones, he didn't seem to notice me until I was halfway inside the building and waving my hand across a shop light to get his attention.

As the saw came to a stop, he removed the glasses and slipped the headphones down around his neck. His brows were furrowed as he stepped toward me, like I was a multisyllabic word he couldn't figure out how to pronounce.

"Who the hell are you?" He brushed sawdust from his shirt with his gloved hands.

"Hi, Mr. Michaels, I'm Allie Cobb. I don't know if you remember me, but I used—"

"To cause me nothing but trouble vandalizing Winchester's place with that brat, Sloane." He stared at the hand I'd extended in an offer to shake like it was the carcass of a dead animal. "Your father's funeral is over. Shouldn't you be going back to the big city and leaving us hicks to our small-town ways?"

I took a deep breath. He was trying to goad me into running away before I could talk to him. Well I wasn't the little girl he'd intimidated years ago.

"I was chatting with Shirley Price yesterday. She mentioned you're building some new shelves for her store." I pointed toward the stack of boards. "Is that what this wood is for?"

"What's it to you? I haven't heard anything about Matt Roberson adding you to the force."

Don't take the bait. Don't take the bait. I smiled. "Nope. He hasn't. It's just that Shirley said you were the unfortunate soul who found Thornwell. That must have been a shock to the system."

He grunted. "You could say that."

"Would you mind telling me about it?"

With a grimace, he took a seat on a sawdust-covered stool. "I already told Roberson everything. Why should I tell you?"

"I'm trying to help Sloane come to terms with losing her father by making sense of what happened. She's pretty shell-shocked right now." It wasn't exactly the truth, but it wasn't an outright lie, either. I slipped a hand in my pocket and crossed my fingers.

"Guess I can understand that. Not much to tell, really. I'd been out fishing in the park and was on my way home. I hadn't used all my worms, so I decided to spend some time fishing from the bridge. When I went to the rail, something caught my eye. I looked down and saw the body floating facedown. That's when I called nine-one-one. Didn't know who it was until Roberson's officers got there and ID'd the body."

I made mental notes of potential holes in his story. Antagonizing him wouldn't get me anywhere. I needed more to go on.

"Ironic, huh? You finding the body of the man who fired you after all those years? What are the odds of that?"

He looked away. I followed his gaze as it settled on his boat parked at the other end of the barn. Even with a cover on, the low profile told me it was a bass boat. When I was little, Mom and Dad took me and the sibs out for a pontoon boat ride on Lake Monroe once or twice a summer. It was always a blast and I learned a lot about boats that way. What I would have given to be able to look under the cover of Jax's boat.

His gaze returned to me. "Pretty good around here. You should know that. It's a small town and that bridge gets plenty of traffic. Are you accusing me of something?"

"No. Like I said, I'm just trying to help Sloane through a tough time."

"I had a tough time working for that drunken jerk for years. Put up with his arrogance and foolishness. And then, when he cleaned up his act, instead of thanking me for putting up with him all those years, he accused me of mismanaging funds and fired me." He pointed his finger at me. It was shaking. "If you ask me, the man got what he deserved."

"So, you think he was murdered, then. Why do you think that?"

"I never said I thought he was murdered." He picked up a new piece of wood and placed it on the worktable.

"Then what do you think happened?" I was running out of time. I couldn't leave without more digging.

"He magically sprouted wings and went flying, but when he tried to cross the creek, his wings disappeared and he drowned." With a smirk, he put his safety glasses back on.

I wasn't ready to be dismissed, so I put my hand on the piece of wood he was preparing to cut. "So, you were fishing all night. How'd you do? Catch anything?"

"It's none of your business, young lady. It's time for you to go. Unlike some people, I have work to do." He fired up the saw.

"Fine. One final question. Who do—"

He let out a long, dramatic sigh. "Who do I think killed Winchester? I don't know, and I don't really care. I'll tell you this, though. If you're going to keep butting into people's lives, I suggest you pay Charissa Mody a visit. If Sloane didn't kill him, Charissa's crazy enough to."

With a nod, I left Jax to his work. As I traipsed home, dictating notes as I walked, it was like a cloud descended on top of me. His story fit, for the most part, but there were still holes big enough for me to crawl through. On top of that, his comment about Sloane worried me. How did he know about Matt's suspicions? Or did he say that just to throw me for a loop? If so, mission accomplished.

A chilly breeze made me shiver, so I texted Sloane and told her to meet me at the diner. I needed hot coffee and we needed to talk.

I was halfway through my first cup, black with two packets of sugar, when Sloane slipped into the seat across from me. She smiled, but her eyes were red-rimmed and accompanied by dark circles beneath them. Her brown hair, which normally had a salon-like sheen, was dull.

She poured herself a cup from a carafe on the table, added three packages of creamer and downed half of the concoction in a long gulp. "Sorry," she said with a shrug. "Haven't been able to sleep. Thanks for dragging me out of the apartment. I've been driving myself crazy not knowing what to do. I can't even plan his funeral because Matt said they can't release the body until they know for sure what happened."

"I'm so sorry." I signaled for another carafe of coffee. "I've been talking to a few people, but I'm afraid I haven't gotten very far yet."

With a shrug, Sloane reached for a menu. When the waiter arrived with the coffee, she ordered a western omelet with a side of bacon and an English muffin.

"What? This is the first I've felt like eating in two days. Besides, the more I've thought about it, the more I get the feeling Matt has an idea who the killer is. There's that, at least."

My poor, clueless friend had no idea about the current state of affairs in Rushing Creek. Of course, having been holed up in her apartment for two days, how would she know Matt's suspicions about her were getting out? I couldn't let her find out through the grapevine. I could let her eat her breakfast in blissful ignorance, though.

While she ate, I told her what I'd learned. I left out the part about Jax finding Thornwell lying facedown under the bridge. That would have been too much.

I waited until we were outside to drop my bombshell question on her. "Sloane, you said you went home after dropping your dad off. Do you have any way to verify that?"

"I told you. I texted Luke when I got home." She showed me the message on her phone.

"That's great, but bear with me. While the text is helpful, it doesn't exactly prove you were home all night. Does your building have security cameras that would show you in the parking lot or going into your apartment?"

"Come on, Allie. This isn't New York. My building doesn't have anything like that. What's the matter? Don't you believe me?"

"I believe you." I stopped and waited until she was looking at me eye to eye. "But other people, other important people, don't."

Chapter Eight

"What do you mean, other people don't?" Sloane crossed her arms. In a split second, the temperature seemed to drop fifteen degrees.

I tugged at my earlobe. It was what I did when anxious. "There's no good way to put this. Matt considers you his top suspect." When she gave me a blank stare, I took a deep breath.

"He thinks you killed your dad."

I told her about my exchange with the police chief, emphasizing with great care the fact that one of her credit card statements had been found on Thornwell.

Sloane's eyes got watery, but then she blinked the tears away and gave me a hard stare. "I didn't kill my dad."

"I know that, which is why we need to find proof of your innocence to give to Matt." I grasped her arm. "I'm on your side."

She bit her lip and started drumming her fingers against her legs, a classic sign of Sloane Winchester nervousness. We were quite the anxiety-ridden duo.

"Come on." I guided her toward her car. "We can talk at my house."

Sloane's silence on the way home was as oppressive as a summer night so humid you ended up drenched just breathing. It was a relief Ursi was the only one around when we arrived, since I needed to talk to Sloane alone, without any distractions.

Once we were seated in the living room, I took Sloane's hand. "You're my best friend. You can trust me. Tell me what you're holding back."

"I'm sorry. I wasn't straight with you before." She hung her head. "I wasn't home all night. I was so upset about Dad's setback, I couldn't sleep, so I went out for a run."

I held my tongue. This didn't sound good, but we'd deal with it. Matt would be angry she hadn't been honest with him, but he could get over it. Besides, as a trail runner, it wasn't unusual for Sloane to go for a night run. She did it once or twice a week.

"That's great. I totally understand. It was a tough day for all of us and your dad's drinking didn't help. What time did you leave the apartment?" She ran her fingers through her hair. "I don't know. Midnight, I think."

"And when did you get back?"

"Um. I'm not sure."

"Sloane, come on. This is important. I want to help you, but I can't if you won't level with me. I know you track all your workouts, so when did you get home?"

"I didn't exactly go home when I finished my run." She kept her gaze on Ursi, who was busy playing with a catnip-filled fabric mouse I brought with us from New York.

"Okay. Where did you go?" It wasn't like Sloane to keep secrets from me. She was the personification of an open book, and we'd prided ourselves on maintaining our friendship through total honesty.

"You're not going to like it."

"I'm not going to like it?" My sharp tone stopped Ursi in her tracks. "I don't think you're going to like it when Matt shows up on your doorstep with an arrest warrant. Now, out with it. Where were did you go after you left the apartment?"

"I, uh...went to a friend's house." She nodded, as if attempting to convince herself that was what she did.

"Good." A river of relief flowed through my wall of frustration with Sloane. At least we were making progress. "Who is it? We need to talk to her about providing you an alibi."

"It wasn't a *her.*"

That brought my inquisition to a screeching halt. Sloane hadn't mentioned a boyfriend recently. A part of me couldn't help feeling a bit hurt at the revelation. Nonetheless, I needed to stay focused.

"What's his name, then? Do I know him?"

"Oh yeah, you know him." She sighed. "It's Luke."

I ran through the list of all the Lukes I knew. Other than my brother and an agent I worked with, I came up blank. Given that agent Luke was based in Southern California, it was easy to mark him off the list. That left...*no way, no way in the world.*

"Sloane, honey." I rubbed my temples. My return to Rushing Creek, Indiana, was turning into a trip to *The Twilight Zone.* "Are you telling me you left your apartment around midnight to go for a run and ended up at my brother's house?"

"Not exactly." She was squirming like a six-year-old who'd been caught doodling in her father's favorite book with a red ink pen. Something with which I was all too familiar.

At that point, I wanted to strangle her. Since I was supposed to be looking for a murderer, and not becoming one, I counted to ten before opening my mouth. I needed to nail down where she was and when she was there so we could prove her innocence. Any additional details regarding my dear brother, well, that would have to wait.

"For the last time, what *exactly* did you do when you left your apartment?"

"You're not gonna—"

"Sloane Winifred Winchester—"

"Okay, okay." She despised being called by her full name. I'd only done it to her three times, each occurrence when I was mad as a hornet at her.

"I was telling you the truth when I said I couldn't sleep, so I went for a run. I'd planned on running the loop that takes me through the park along Sycamore Ridge. I thought a long run like that would leave me worn out enough to sleep."

I raised my eyebrows. While I'd never run them, I knew Sloane's routes from the countless times she'd talked about them. The Sycamore Ridge run was seven miles long with a back breaker of a climb just inside the park's north gate. I'd ridden it on a mountain bike once and vowed never again, happily returning to my kickboxing workouts.

Sloane got to her feet. "I was running by your brother's house—it's on the route, and the light in the front room was on, so the next thing I knew, I was knocking on his front door. He invited me in, and well, I kind of spent the night there. His alarm went off at six, and I came home.

"We've been seeing each other for a few months. It's not super serious, at least not yet, so we didn't want to tell you. We figured you had enough on your mind with your dad." She shrugged. "Sorry."

"I need a drink." I went to the kitchen, bypassed my usual stop at the wine rack and went straight for a bottle of rum in the liquor cabinet. It was all too much. First Dad, then Thornwell, now Sloane and Luke dating. As I added Diet Pepsi to my tumbler of ice and spiced rum, I blinked back tears that were making my vision blurry.

"Hey." Sloane put her hand on my shoulder. "You okay?"

The question made me feel worse than if I was one of the ogres who lived under the bridge. Sure, my father was dead, but I'd known his time was coming and had time to prepare for his passing. Sloane had

had none of that. Shoot, I'd been so wrapped up in my own affairs, I'd barely paid attention to the reports about Thornwell's changes for the better. I needed to get over myself and focus on things I could control, like finding the man's killer.

"Yeah." I looked at her and laughed. "Spending the night at my brother's house wasn't what I expected to hear."

"Yeah, about that, there's something, something good I need to tell you." She leaned against the counter while I made a drink for her. "A few months ago, Dad asked me to run a package over here. It was after one of your dad's chemo treatments and Luke was looking after him. We hung out for a while and when I got ready to leave, Luke asked if I'd join him for a beer at the pub. One thing led to another, and we've been out a few times."

I took a drink and swirled it around in my mouth. The carbonation and sweetness of the Diet Pepsi took the edge off the tart rum. It was an apt metaphor for Sloane and Luke. She was sweet and bubbly and kind, and he could be smooth and agreeable one moment and leave your head spinning the next.

What did it say about me, that neither one felt they could tell me? Had I really drifted that far from two of the most important people in my life? I took another drink, this one for courage.

"I'm happy for you. I'm a little hurt that you didn't confide in me, though. I mean, come on, you've had a crush on him for forever."

"I know, right?" Sloane bumped her shoulder against mine. "We talked about telling you but thought if things didn't work out..." She shrugged.

"I get it. But if the past few days have taught me anything, it's embrace the present and don't get hung up on what might happen." I clinked my glass against hers. "I think we should call your boyfriend. He's your alibi, after all."

A little while later, Luke, Sloane and Mom were seated at the dining room table while I scooped a steaming casserole onto plates. Just when I thought Mom and I were making a dent in the fridge, she came home from work with containers of sliced turkey, a pumpkin pie and a gallon of milk. It was a good thing I was getting in plenty of walking.

"So, Mom." I took my seat. "Sloane told me some good news she and Luke have. Did you know about it?"

"Of course. You know this town. Rumors fly around here faster than a car at the Indianapolis Motor Speedway. Luke tried to deny it, but he should know better than trying to lie to his mother."

Luke's casserole-laden fork stopped in midair. "I wasn't lying, Mom. I was trying to keep expectations low."

Mom raised an eyebrow, a gesture I'd never mastered and was envious to no end that I was the only member of the Cobb family who couldn't do it. "I asked if you'd been seeing anybody when I knew full well you and Sloane had gone out at least three times." Mom leaned toward Sloane. "I raised Luke to be a gentleman, but it appears I may have fallen short on a few points. For that, I apologize."

With a grin, Sloane leaned toward Mom. "He has a few shortcomings, but they're not your fault. If you give me a chance, I think I can straighten him out."

Luke shook his head as his cheeks turned bright pink. He was grinning, though.

"I think that's the first time I've seen you smile this week," I said to him as he chewed on a piece of garlic bread. "It's good to see."

He opened his mouth, glanced at Mom and shut it again as his cheeks went from pink to ruby red.

"Discretion's the better part of valor, son." Mom patted his hand and winked at me. "Having said that, it is good to see you smile. You look like your father when you do."

"Thanks. I can't believe you knew about Sloane and me and didn't say anything."

Mom shrugged and took a drink of her sparkling water. "I figured you'd tell me when the time was right. Both of our families have their struggles, I didn't want to put any pressure on you."

"In that case." Luke straightened up in his chair and cleared his throat. "Mom, Allie, before you find out from someone else, Sloane and I are dating. Feel free to shower us with good wishes and presents. Cash works, too."

It was Sloane's turn to get red in the face while Mom rolled her eyes. I threw a napkin at Luke.

The dark cloud hanging over me retreated as I raised my glass of water. "Luke, Sloane, thank you for bringing some sunshine into these dark times. I'm sure Mom will agree with me that we wish you happiness, but you better tell Rachel or she'll never forgive you."

"No worries, Allie," Sloane said. "She's known all along. She saw us at the pub that first night, and we swore her to secrecy."

I put my hand over my heart. "You wound me, Sloane. I thought I was your bestie and here I'm the last to know. I'm going to have to hang this over your head for the rest of our lives."

When dinner was over, I made Luke and Mom clean up as punishment for keeping secrets from me while Sloane and I hung out on the back patio. The clouds that moved in earlier had cleared out, leaving a star-filled sky.

I wrapped a stadium blanket tight around me to ward off the chill and let out a long, stress-releasing breath. "I'd forgotten how many stars you can see at night."

"Can't you see any in New York?"

"You can, but not this many. Too much light pollution."

Sloane and I had talked dozens of times about her visiting, but she was an admitted small-town girl, and the thought of spending time in the largest city in America intimidated her. Then again, when I gazed up, and lost myself among the countless pin pricks of light, it occurred to me that maybe I was the one who was missing out, not Sloane.

"You sound like you miss this." Sloane propped her feet on an empty chair. "I thought about leaving town a few years ago. Kind of following your lead. But, I always found an excuse that kept me from leaving. Now...looks like I'm not going anywhere for a while, at least."

My heart went out to Sloane. Sure, it hurt that Dad was gone, but I had two siblings and Mom to help carry me through my darkest valleys of grief. Who did Sloane have? Me? Her mom, maybe? Luke, perhaps? Regardless, when it came to a support system, she was sorely lacking.

"That wouldn't be so bad, would it? Staying here, I mean. Especially if things between you and Luke work out, right?"

"Sure, but there are times I wish I'd been more adventuresome, like you. Living in a place like New York must be nonstop excitement with the restaurants, theaters, museums."

"Traffic, noise, pushy people." I laughed. "It can be great, but it isn't paradise."

I gestured toward the stars. Part of the Big Dipper was obscured by a massive white pine from the neighbor's yard. Somewhere nearby, something scurried through the foliage, probably a squirrel, but maybe a coyote. I saw coyotes every now and then from the kitchen window when I was growing up and was always thrilled by the experience.

"This, Sloane, my dear, is much closer to paradise."

Chapter Nine

I woke up the next morning feeling better than I had in years. Between the aromatherapy and the good news from Sloane and Luke, I felt somewhat in control. I actually had to nudge a protesting Ursi off my leg so I could get out of bed. It was the first time since I'd returned to Rushing Creek that I woke up before my kitty.

Since it was Saturday, Mom didn't have to get up to go to work, so I sliced some fruit and toasted a bagel while the coffee machine did its magic. My first order of business was to catch up on work e-mails. My heart stopped for a minute when I opened the reply from the editor I'd been hounding. After reading it, I let out a sigh and looked at Ursi, who was winding her way through my legs.

"Good news, bad news girl. The editor likes it, so she's bumping it up to her boss for a final decision. Gonna be a few more weeks until a decision is made, though." At the report, Ursi yawned and trotted to her food bowl. There was never any doubt about what was at the top of her priority list. She could hold on until I updated my client, though.

When my inbox was caught up, I spent an hour editing another client's proposal for a three-book sci-fi series and sent it off to her with my comments. Satisfied I'd done enough work, I called Lance. After four rings, I got his voice mail. With a growl, I hit the End key. I was done playing message tag.

My annoyance with Lance wasn't going to get in the way of my plans, though. I had two people to visit, and nobody was going to get in my way.

Stop number one was a return visit to the police station. Jeanette wasn't at the front desk, which was a bummer. Instead, it was the officer who had stayed with Sloane while she identified Thornwell's body. When he looked at me, his eyebrows narrowed, so I switched my tactics. Time to try a little New York attitude.

"Good morning. I'm Allie Cobb, a friend of Sloane Winchester. I've come for a copy of the police report regarding her father's murder." When he didn't move, I pressed on. "I was in the other day and Chief Roberson said one would be available by now. I believe the report is subject to a public records request."

"Yes, Ms. Cobb. I can pull up a copy for you." The officer looked over his shoulder toward Matt's office as his fingers went to his computer keyboard.

"I have information for the chief, too. While you're getting the report, I'll have a word with him." Without another look, I stepped through the swinging gate and strode to Matt's office, trying to exude an air of bravado I didn't actually feel.

I knocked on his office door and opened it without waiting for an answer. In for a dime, in for a dollar, as Dad liked to say.

Matt was on the phone, but he shook his head when I took a seat. Through clenched teeth, he ended the call.

"Who do you think you are? You can't just waltz into my office whenever you feel like it. I have a job, a real job, to do. I can't do it if you're going to keep bothering me."

I refused to lower myself to respond to his insult. It would just drag things out and I had other places to be.

"This won't take long. I have information regarding Thornwell Winchester's murder."

"I'm listening." He flipped open a notepad and grabbed a pen.

"Sloane didn't kill her father. She has an alibi." I told him the major points of Sloan's confession, omitting the challenge I had in getting it out of her and the dinner conversation that followed. For good measure, I gave him Luke's contact information, both work and personal.

"You realize I can't just take your word for this." He put down the pen and rolled his shoulders. The dark circles under his eyes betrayed his confident tone.

I couldn't help sympathizing. His first murder investigation couldn't have come at a worse time. It didn't change the fact that Sloane was innocent, though.

And the killer was still out there.

"Of course. They're ready and willing to cooperate in any way they can." I stood. "I'll let you get back to work finding the murderer. You know how to reach me."

On my way out of the station, I stopped long enough to pick up the report and thank the officer for his help. There was no reason to antagonize the rest of Rushing Creek's finest because the man in the big chair could be such a jerk. Besides, I was far from accomplishing my mission to find the killer and would, no doubt, cross paths with the police again. I needed them with me, not against me.

Once outside, I paused to soak up some sun. Indiana weather in October was notorious in its unpredictability. One day we could have rain and temps in the fifties, the next, bright sunshine with the thermometer reaching near seventy. Today, it looked like we were in store for the latter.

I took that for a sign my next stop would be a success. I'd never met Charissa Mody, so introducing myself and then asking if she was a murderer in the same conversation was insane. Oh well, Rachel told me more than once I was insane for trying to follow in Dad's footsteps and doubly so for trying to make it in New York. I'd proven Rachel wrong then. Hopefully, I'd prove myself wrong now.

Nodding to my realist streak that I was pulling at my earlobe due to my nerves, I stopped for a little chocolate therapy. The moment I stepped through the doorway of Creekside Chocolates, my confidence doubled. The blissful aroma of milk chocolate commingled with the sweet aroma of peppermint. The place even had a coffee and hot chocolate bar.

I was in Heaven.

A youngish woman with spiky purple hair and brown skin was behind the glass display counter. She must have noticed my wide-eyed, ravenous look because she raised her eyebrows with a smile and offered me a sampler dish.

"White, milk or dark?" she asked.

"Yes," I laughed, the tension draining away from my shoulders. There was a blackboard mounted on the wall behind the counter. The selections were written in stylish print, using pastel chalk. There were truffles, solid blocks that could be cut into single serving pieces and countless other irresistible delicacies, including drinks.

"You're my kind of customer. I'm Diane." We shook and, in that instant, I wanted to be friends with Diane and it wasn't just because she smelled like powdered sugar and had a sign on the wall that read Without Chocolate, Why Bother?

I introduced myself with the usual former resident and only member of the family to leave town spiel.

"Well, I'm glad to have you back home, even if it's only for a little while. And I'm sorry about your dad. I met him one time when he came in with your mom. She's a regular customer."

Mom's love of chocolate was stuff of legends in the Cobb household. My sibs and I, who didn't see eye to eye on much, reached a pact years ago that when in trouble with Mom, the go-to gift was chocolate. That way, she couldn't play favorites when it came to bribes to get us out of the doghouse.

"Like mother, like daughter." I closed my eyes and took a deep breath. I never wanted to leave Creekside Chocolates. "How about a hot chocolate with whipped cream and peppermint sprinkles."

"Excellent choice."

My mouth watered as Diane made the drink. I hadn't had decent chocolate since I was in New York and it had been one whale of a week. I was going to revel in the indulgence and not feel an iota of guilt about it.

While she made my drink, we chatted about what brought Diane to Rushing Creek. She'd grown up in Chicago and studied business at Indiana University in Bloomington. She literally hit the lottery—winning only a small sum, she insisted—and used her winnings to study the art of chocolate making. When she became confident enough in her knowledge of chocolates, she put together a business plan and landed in Rushing Creek, having visited a few times in college and fallen in love with the town.

Diane handed me my drink and turned her attention to a quartet of customers who were hovering over the display case and chatting in breathless tones. A surge of pride in my hometown coursed through me. I couldn't deny that Rushing Creek had a spirit that had attracted artisans and entrepreneurs for years. In its own way, it wasn't that different from New York. People came, people went. Shops opened, shops closed. Underneath it all flowed a current that carried the message if you were courageous enough to try something new, this was the place to do it.

Odd that I'd never noticed that current before. Then again, maybe not so odd. Maybe my time away from home had gifted me with an ability to look at tiny Rushing Creek, Indiana, with a new appreciation.

Breathing deeply to inhale every bit of the drink's sweet aroma, I wandered toward a few tables and chairs strategically placed by the store's picture window.

The boulevard was busy with shoppers and sightseers on this fine October Saturday. Every parking spot was taken. It was busy, but not overwhelming. In another week, the boulevard would be packed with bumper-to-bumper traffic and the sidewalks would be every bit as crowded. Business was good in Rushing Creek. Times were good, too. If you didn't think about Thornwell Winchester. Which was a luxury I couldn't afford. While I sipped the divine hot chocolate, I studied the police report. It didn't contain much I didn't already know. One thing kept bugging me, like an itchy spot on my back that, no matter how hard I tried, I could never quite reach.

Why did Thornwell have one of Sloane's credit card statements?

We'd never kept secrets from each other—well, except for a certain boyfriend and brother—so I was familiar with her money challenges. But that was an issue she'd pledged to resolve without anybody's help. Especially her father's.

So, if Sloane hadn't approached Thornwell about her financial woes, did somebody do it on her behalf? I shook my head. Sloane had been scrupulous in keeping her finances out of the town's rumor mill, so that scenario seemed unlikely.

Then I had a lightbulb moment. It was one of those glorious times when I felt as if I was smarter than I actually was. Assuming the document was planted on Thornwell the night he was murdered, then the murderer had to know both Thornwell and Sloane. And the murderer would have to have access to a credit card statement and be bold enough to snatch it.

This was progress, actual, measurable progress. Sure, pretty much everybody in town who knew Thornwell knew Sloane, too. I drummed my fingers on the oak tabletop. Access was the key. To both of the Winchesters.

A surge of adrenaline flowed through my veins as I added tasks to my to-do list. Cross reference my suspect list to prioritize those who knew both Sloane and her father. Confirm the date on the credit card statement. Make sure it was an actual statement and not a copy. Ask Sloane if she hadn't received any statements.

As I drained the last of my drink, I wanted to let out a tiger-like roar. A killer was out there, and little Allie Cobb, all five feet, one inch of me, was on the hunt.

It was time to visit the infamous Charissa Mody.

Chapter Ten

When people asked me to name the can't-miss business in Rushing Creek, my answer was always the same.

Rushing Creek Winery.

Established in the early nineties, the winery was at the forefront of the Indiana wine scene. While there were dozens of fabulous wineries across the Hoosier State—most of which I'd visited—Rushing Creek was my favorite. Maybe it was the fact the winery included fifty acres of vineyards on site. Or that the tasting room was built from locally sourced Indiana hardwoods. Or the fact that my first job was at the winery.

At the end of the day, visiting Rushing Creek Winery was like visiting a second home.

I crossed the winery's full parking lot, which pleased me to no end, and took a moment to savor the gorgeous brushed steel sign situated above the tasting room's entrance. The place emanated good vibes, and the feeling of contentment at being home returned.

A gray-haired man and dark-haired woman, each laden with a case of wine, said hello as I held the door open for them. Before entering, I knocked on the wooden doorframe. My progress notwithstanding, I figured I still needed as much luck as I could get.

The tasting room was bursting with energy as employees, in the familiar royal blue Rushing Creek Winery polo shirts, assisted customers with their wine choices. The textured concrete floor was familiar under my feet as I passed one of the cedar posts that supported the cathedral ceiling. Sunlight spilled through the four-foot-high windows, giving the room a bright, festive feel. At the center of the room, visitors waited two and three deep to reach the bar for tastings. Contemporary jazz, featuring a trombone virtuoso, was playing over the speaker system. The upbeat, syncopated rhythm fit with the movements of the crowd.

I weaved toward the tasting bar, tapping my thigh to the beat of the music. I'd spent two summers after I turned twenty-one working behind the bar. Thanks to that wonderful experience, I'd amazed my East Coast colleagues with my ability to speak at length about all things wine. I'd forced them to admit, some begrudgingly, that there was, in fact, more than corn in Indiana.

With platinum-blonde hair, Charissa Mody was impossible to miss. She was on the far side of the massive, polished wooden bar, pouring a red wine for a trio of women who looked to be about my age. I couldn't hear her over the din, but I hoped she was giving them a little history of the wine, along with suggestions of foods with which to pair it.

A spot close by opened, but I kept moving until I settled a few feet behind the women Charissa was serving. She had a high-pitched voice, kind of nasally, which made me think of the character Janice Litman from *Friends*. When she laughed, she covered her mouth and didn't make a sound.

I didn't like Charissa Mody.

My chance came when a couple next to the three friends left. I stepped to the bar and pretended to study the wine list. I knew the list, and the product, better than Charissa probably did, but wanted to play the part of curious customer. At least until she recognized me.

"Welcome to Rushing Creek Winery. Would you like to try a sample of Southern Indiana's finest from the vine, or are you waiting for your husband?"

Check that. I hated Charissa Mody.

"No. I'm not waiting for anybody. Thank you, though." I forced a smile and reeled in my inner tiger. "I'll try the Cabernet Sauvignon."

Charissa gave me the standard spiel as she poured. Her work was fine technically, but it lacked passion. Then again, she didn't grow up knowing the winery's owners like I did. I sniffed the wine, took a sip, swirled it around my mouth and swallowed. Still too dry for my preference, but that was okay. Starting with the dry wines was part of the tasting routine. Besides, there was a Catawba and a Moscato down the list that would more than make up for the dry varieties.

"Are you from around here?" I asked. Figured I had to break the ice somehow.

"I'm originally from Oklahoma City, but I've lived here for almost two years now." She gave me a long stare as she poured me an oak-aged Chardonnay. "You look familiar. Do I know you?"

Since I was basically busted, I gave her my name. Maybe it would generate some sympathy.

It did.

"Oh, I'm so sorry for your loss." She placed her hand on mine. It was warm, not cold, like I'd expected. "I missed you at your father's visitation. That was quite the gathering. He was a wonderful man."

"Thank you." My level of disdain for Charissa decreased a touch. Her words would have been easy to dismiss, but her pinched brow convinced me. She really was sorry. But that was about Dad, not Thornwell.

"How did you know him?" I took my time with the Chardonnay. I needed to pace myself. At my size, it didn't take much to get me tipsy.

"I met him through my boyfriend." Her smile disappeared and she went back to the power trio beside me. Those women were sampling every wine available. Made me glad to be on foot.

When she came back, I finished the Chardonnay and asked for a Pinot Gris. I needed to speed this up.

"Who's your boyfriend?" It was a crappy, underhanded maneuver, but the wine was making me bold.

She stopped with the bottle halfway to my glass, tilted at a forty-five-degree angle. "Thorny Winchester. God rest his soul."

Thorny? Nobody called him that. "My condolences to you. How long had you been together?"

"Thirteen wonderful months." She let out a long, dramatic sigh. "The best thirteen months of my life. And now he's gone."

"You know, that's so sad." I'd had enough of playing games. "I'm friends with Thornwell's daughter, Sloane, and she's never mentioned you. And yet..."

Her eyes narrowed. "Yes. Well, Sloane and I never connected." She nodded toward my still untouched sample. "Are you going to drink that, or is it time for you to give your space to someone else?"

"I have a few more wines I'm planning on trying." Without breaking eye contact, I took a sip. A small one. She tried to stare me down. This amateur had nothing on the sharklike New York editors and attorneys I dealt with.

"It must hurt. Your boyfriend's ex-wife shows up and then he ends up dead, amid rumors of you being a gold digger." I finished my Pinot Gris and pointed at the Catawba on the list. "I'll have this next."

She chewed on her lip for a minute. It was as if nobody else existed. Like one of those old Western stare downs Dad loved but I thought were utter clichés. I knew better now.

"I can't imagine what you're talking about. I loved Thorny."

"Yeah, well, that's the problem." I leaned across the counter to get as close as possible to Charissa. "I have it on good authority Thornwell was reconciling with his ex-wife. That doesn't exactly square with what you just told me, does it?"

"I think you don't know what you're talking about. And I think you need to leave." She turned away.

"I worked here when I was in college and am on a first-name basis with the owners. Plus, I'm not driving."

She turned back and gripped the bar with her hands on either side of me as if she was trying to box me in. "What do you want from me?"

I made a point to look around the tasting room. It was like a contract negotiation, and I had her where I wanted her. It was time to make her sweat.

"This is my hometown. Your boyfriend's murder was the first in thirty years." I looked into her eyes. "Where were you the night he died?"

With a deep breath, Charissa straightened and stepped back. "None of your damn business."

"Yes, it is my business." I leaned across the bar, grabbing a fistful of her shirt in the process. "My best friend's father was murdered in cold blood. Because of that, my friend's alone."

I dug into my purse and dropped a twenty-dollar bill on the bar. "I'm going to find his killer and make sure that person is brought to justice. With or without your cooperation."

I bought a bottle of the Chardonnay and made a hasty exit before my temper got the best of me. For the most part, I was shy and quiet, the introvert of the family. But just because I was small in stature and reserved in demeanor didn't mean I was a pushover.

Not by a long shot.

Mom and Dad had taught me the importance of the Golden Rule, and I try to live by that ethic every day. But Dad also taught me how vital it was to defend my clients' interests. Right now, Sloane was my client, and I was going to do all I could to help her out.

When I reached the edge of the parking lot, I took a deep breath and stopped. My heart was racing and my neck was as sweaty as if I'd just finished an hour-long kickboxing session.

Slow down, Allie. I couldn't let my emotions rule the day. The only way for me to find Thornwell's killer was to keep a clear mind.

I made my way to a nearby sugar maple. It was still mostly green, but, in another week or two, it would be bursting with red, orange and yellow leaves. I ran my hand along the tree's grooved bark and let the nature's peacefulness center me.

I sat at the base of the tree, closed my eyes, and let the sun's rays warm my face. I had to see this investigation through. More importantly, I believed I could. If I kept my feelings in check. I believed I could do that, too.

With the day's positive vibe returning, I texted Sloane to tell her I wanted to get together for brunch tomorrow, to fill her in on my progress. I didn't mention I had questions about the credit card bill. Those questions were going to upset her, so they needed to be asked in person.

I took another few moments to sit and enjoy the October sunshine. Back in New York, it seemed like I always had someplace to go, or something to do. There weren't many times like this, when I could simply stop and sit under a tree. It was nice to be doing it now.

Sloane texted back that she'd be at my house at eleven. With that detail set, I got up, brushed some dirt from my pants and set off for home.

* * * *

Mom was in the living room, reading a magazine, when I arrived. I dropped onto the couch and took off my shoes.

"And how was your day." Her attention was still fixed on her magazine.

"Not bad. Made a mortal enemy and figured out a way to bug Matt more."

She closed her magazine and gave me a long look over her reading glasses. "Causing trouble on Sloane's behalf, I take it?"

"Yep." I handed her the bottle of wine. "A peace offering in advance. For when people start complaining about your nosy daughter from out of town."

"Rushing Creek's new Chardonnay. Love it. You must have stirred up quite the hornet's nest to have brought me this."

My cheeks got hot. "I might have almost climbed on top of the bar at the winery and strangled Charissa Mody."

Mom raised her eyebrows. "'I might have.' You have your father's art for the qualified statement. As a doctor, you know I can't condone violent behavior like that, so if you do it again, make sure I don't hear about it."

"Deal. Interested in joining me for a late lunch? I'm starving." I headed for the kitchen without waiting for her.

By the time Mom joined me, I had a ham sandwich, a double serving of green bean casserole, and a slice of apple pie on my plate. For good measure, I added some baked beans.

"What?" I asked when she raised an eyebrow. "I haven't eaten since breakfast, and I've been walking all over town. Fighting crime makes for a big appetite. It's hard work."

"Yes. Tasting wine is *so* exhausting. It's a wonder you had the energy to walk all the way home without collapsing." Since there was only one piece of apple pie left in the pan, Mom took it and started eating it without bothering to get a plate.

We ate in silence, Ursi weaving herself between my legs to get attention, despite the fact I filled her bowl before I raided the fridge. The buzz from my wine tasting was wearing off and, with that, the euphoria from the day's accomplishments.

Sure, I'd made progress but, in the grand scheme of things, had I honestly accomplished anything? By now, the *Law & Order* team would have the murderer behind bars and be preparing for trial.

Me? I had Sloane in the clear, assuming Matt believed me. If not, there was Luke. Matt wouldn't hesitate to disrespect me, but he wouldn't dare tangle with my big brother. The two had known each other too long, and knew too much about each other, for any game playing. No, I was confident Sloane wouldn't be spending any time behind bars.

"What's on your mind?"

"What?" I looked at Mom.

She was grinning. It was good to see.

"You've been swirling your fork around for ages, just like when you were little and didn't want to eat your mashed potatoes."

I glanced at my plate. Sure enough, there was a figure eight in the middle of the green bean casserole. Busted.

"Back then, I thought mashed potatoes were gross."

"And what about now? I know for a fact you adore green bean casserole. That's why there's so much in the fridge." Mom sat back and crossed her arms. "Talk to me, Allie."

I scooped some of the casserole into my mouth, just to prove some sort of childish point, and chewed while I tried to figure out how to put into words the things that were on my mind.

I told her about my conversations with Jax and Charissa and my supposition about the credit card bill.

"I have no idea what I'm doing. I don't know if I'm helping or hurting things. And, on top of everything else, now I'm threatening people."

Mom leaned forward. "Between you and me, that Mody woman could use some sense scared into her." After a moment, she smiled, evidently pleased she'd shocked me into silence.

"In all seriousness, let me ask you a question." She patted her thigh and, when Ursi jumped into her lap, started scratching my fur baby between the ears. "Why are you pursuing this? I mean, it's a police matter, after all."

"I want justice for Thornwell and for Sloane." I took a deep breath and let it out slowly. "And, I don't trust Matt."

"Fair enough." Mom got up and took the pie pan to the sink. "Thornwell had his detractors, but I'm sure nobody wanted to see him murdered. Except, whoever did it, obviously. And I understand your distrust for Matt."

"But…" I waited while she ran the garbage disposal. I hated this kind of talk with Mom. She was so deliberate, with long pauses to make me think, and sometimes sweat.

She sat back down. "Your reasons still don't explain why you. Based on the reasons you just gave me, a third of the town could be looking into this. But they aren't, and you are. Why do you think that is?"

"Well, Sloane was so upset the other day when she came to see me. I couldn't stand by and do nothing."

"Exactly." Mom gave me a wide smile like I hadn't seen from her in months. "Your best friend came to you in her darkest moment. Even after all these years apart, when Sloane needed someone, she didn't go to her mother or someone else in town. She came to you."

"So, I'm doing this because Sloane asked me?"

"Correct me if I'm wrong, but I don't remember you saying she asked you to find her father's killer."

I thought back to that awful morning. As hard as I tried, I couldn't recall her actually asking me to investigate. It was something I decided to do. To right a wrong. To try to fix things.

"You're right, Mom." I got up and gave her a hug. As she'd done so many times over the years when I felt lost, she'd guided me back to my path.

"I'm doing this to help my friend."

"That's my baby girl." She held me close as a tear, I wasn't sure if it was hers or mine, fell to my shoulder. "Keep that in mind until you find Thornwell's killer."

Chapter Eleven

After making an early night of it, I woke up at dawn on Sunday. The house was quiet, so I got my computer and slid back under the covers. With Ursi snuggled by my side, I lost myself in editing one of my client's manuscripts. It was a spy thriller set in Eastern Europe involving the sale of drugs to finance a terror plot planned against the Winter Olympics.

I got so engrossed in the story's high-stakes gamesmanship and skullduggery that I let out a little yelp when my phone went off, letting me know it was time to get ready for Sloane's visit.

"Sorry, missy." As I got up, I scratched Ursi, who had retreated to the end of the bed when the alarm went off. She nipped my finger then rubbed her fuzzy orange and black striped head against it. Evidently, I was forgiven for disturbing her.

While in the shower, I took stock of my situation, still unsettled about my mood swings following my encounter with Charissa. I could try to use the alcohol as an excuse, but there was no excuse. Clearheaded analysis and thought was what I needed. If there was any Sherlock Holmes in me, I needed to start channeling him right now.

To make Mom and Dad proud. To make sure Sloane got closure. To make sure Thornwell received justice.

I was energized and ready to keep fighting the good fight when there was a knock on the front door.

"Hey, girlfriend. Ready for some awesome Allie Cobb home-cooked delicacies?"

Sloane had a plastic grocery bag in one hand. She hugged me with the other. The dark circles were still under her eyes, which wasn't surprising, given the circumstances. Her hair was shiny and smelled like lemons, though. And she'd added a touch of makeup to give her cheeks some color. It was reassuring she wasn't falling apart.

Our embrace went longer than usual, even for two best friends, but I wasn't going to break it. If it helped Sloane, I'd keep hugging her until it got dark.

Or until our stomachs started rumbling.

What got us moving was Ursi bumping Sloane's jeans with her head. After rubbing her head for a minute against Sloane's left leg, she did the same to the right. I took the bag as Sloane laughed and picked up my kitty.

"And hello to you, Miss Ursula." Sloane wrapped her arms around Ursi and rubbed her nose against my feline's neck.

In response, Ursi licked Sloane's nose and then her cheek.

Sloane giggled like when we were nine and chatted and snuggled with Ursi all the way to the kitchen. I'll admit, for a second I was put off by my cat. While she could be affectionate when she felt like it, she'd never licked my nose or my cheek. One time she bit my nose, but it was when I was doing a lousy job of clipping her front claws, so I couldn't hold that against her.

I stopped pouting when I recalled a blog post about cat behavior shortly after I brought Ursi home. Its main point was that, despite cats' natural tendency to be standoffish, they were amazingly adept at sensing when their human was upset. The rule didn't apply one hundred percent of the time, but it was a common behavior.

So, that's what Ursi's doing. You go, girl. My heart swelled with pride at my cat's efforts to make my best friend feel better. There would be a kitty treat for Ursi tonight.

Mom breezed through the kitchen on her way to Mass while I sliced veggies to put into omelets. She gave Sloane a hug, but she wagged her finger at me and said I was going to hell for abandoning my good Catholic upbringing.

She was out the back door before I could remind her I was a registered parishioner of St. Anthony's in New York and made it to Mass monthly. Okay, more like once every other month, but I hadn't missed either of the big ones—Christmas and Easter—since the dreaded Easter egg hunt fiasco when I was ten.

The Catholic guilt complex a mother could bestow upon her child was darn near all-powerful, so I made a note in my calendar to make sure I didn't miss church next Sunday.

While I cooked, I gave Sloane a general update on my progress. I would wait until after we ate to raise my questions. Between handling two skillets, the toaster and the microwave, I was working too hard to take the chance of ruining brunch by losing my concentration. Besides, it wasn't often I got to cook for more than just myself.

Once, I'd cooked for Lance, a delicious chicken stir fry, after he told me he liked Asian. I spent an entire afternoon preparing the vegetables, chicken and fried rice. I even made egg drop soup and bought a six-pack of Kirin Ichiban beer.

Then he arrived at my door with takeout from a Cantonese restaurant he liked.

I should have known then we had communication issues. Like the fact we kept missing each other over the past week. Whatever. I was with my best friend and was going to enjoy some uninterrupted Allie and Sloane time.

When the microwave dinged to let me know the sausage patties were ready, I slipped Sloane's omelet onto a plate, spooned some breakfast potatoes next to it and filled the remaining space with two sausage patties.

"*Bon appétit*," I said, with an awful French accent.

I filled my plate every bit as much as I'd done with Sloane's. All the walking around town was leaving me hungry twenty-four, seven. But it was a good hunger, and the fact that my jeans were a touch looser around the hips than they were a week ago made me smile.

Over brunch, we got caught up, truly chatted girlfriend to girlfriend. The past few days had been such a whirlwind that we'd never had the chance to simply chat. When I thought about it, we hadn't really chatted for months. If we had, I would have known so much more about Thornwell's change. While I couldn't change the past, it made me feel good to fix things in the present.

Sloane told me who was dating who, though I insisted she refrain from talking about my brother in that way. I told her about the deals I'd landed for two of my authors. One deal was for three books with a five-figure advance.

"Wow. Way to go, though it still amazes me publishers are willing to pay authors anything before a book is finished." She stabbed a piece of sausage to go with some potatoes already on her fork. "That'll be a nice commission for you, right?"

I shrugged and got myself another cup of coffee. Discussing specifics of my clients' contracts was a no-no, but I didn't mind sharing information that was available on the Internet. Besides, it wasn't like I was going to receive a windfall tomorrow.

The contract my client signed provided she would be paid one-third of her advance upon executing the contract, a second third when the finished manuscript was accepted by the publisher as ready to go into production and the final third when the book was actually published. Because of the time involved between the stages, it wasn't unusual for months to go by between payments.

When you took into consideration my commission was fifteen percent of the advance payments, I wasn't getting rich, by any stretch of the imagination. On the other hand, I was building a solid client list, was making deals twice as often as the year before and was beginning to build a savings account. It wasn't much above a month-to-month subsistence, but nobody said being a literary agent would be lucrative.

And I loved what I did, which made it all worthwhile.

"I have a few questions I need to ask you." I took Sloane's plate to the sink when we were finished eating.

"Do I get an award for being a member of the Clean Plate Club?" She picked up Ursi and began snuggling with her again.

The feline's purr filled the room. Make that two kitty treats in store for my little girl.

"You're getting it right now." I sat back down and waited for Sloane to make eye contact. When she did, I swallowed. My throat was dry. I recounted my conversation with Matt. When I was finished, I slid the police report across the table to her.

"My guess is Matt will track down Luke to verify what I told him."

"That's fine." Sloane was studying the police report, like she was trying to memorize it for an exam. "I mean, it's true. Luke and I have nothing to hide."

"About that. Matt said they found one of your credit card bills on your dad. Do you have any idea how he could have ended up with it?"

Her eyes went wide as she shook her head.

"Were there any months recently where you didn't receive a statement?"

"No." She tensed up enough that Ursi leapt from her lap and dashed down the hall. "I've got copies at home. I keep them so I can deduct my trail running stuff at tax time."

"Good." I rose from my seat. "Let's go take a look."

"What do we need to do that for? Don't you trust me?"

"Of course I trust you. It's other people I don't trust."

Sloane's eyes narrowed to slits when I told her why I wanted to see the records for myself.

"I'll drive," she said, through gritted teeth. Her words dripped with more venom than I'd ever heard spoken by Sloane Winchester.

An hour later, we had statements for both of Sloane's credit cards going back three years spread all over her kitchen table.

With one exception.

"I can't believe this." Sloane choked back tears. "I know I got that bill because I remember making the payment."

The missing statement was from two months ago. My hope that the document they found on Thornwell had been a copy.

"As bad as this is, we knew it could be a possibility." On the drive from my house, I'd explained my suspicions. "Now we need to make a list of people who had access to both your dad's house and this place. Shall we?"

The process was agonizing and slow. When the subject returned to her father, Sloane started chewing her fingernails and complaining of maladies ranging from indigestion to a migraine. It was time to back off when Sloane pulled up WebMD on her laptop in an attempt to diagnose her condition.

It didn't take a genius to diagnose her problem. The poor thing was guilt-ridden because she hadn't done something to protect her father, anxiety-filled because the killer was still at large and sleep-deprived due to both.

When we had the list down to five suspects, I called it quits. Sloane was toast. She simply couldn't deal with the stress of her situation. Who could blame her?

In spite of growing up in a household that became more toxic as the years went by, she was an example of the credo "See the good in people." She was the one who fretted over a litter of baby bunnies we discovered one summer. Twice a day, she checked to make sure they were warm and safe. When they left their nest, Sloane cried tears of joy.

Sloane was a kind, gentle soul who was emotionally fragile due to the damage her warring parents inflicted upon her. She deserved better than to be stuck indoors on a sunny October afternoon trying to figure out who killed her father.

I had to do better.

Sloane had retreated to her bedroom, so I gave her door three light taps and opened it.

"Hey, girl," I said in a quiet tone. The curtains were drawn, shrouding the room in a dusk-like setting. Sloane lay on the bed with a washcloth covering her eyes. The sound of Native American flutes came from her phone.

When she didn't respond, I sat on the corner of her bed. My fingers traced the intricate pattern of her quilt. It was a starburst pattern that featured all eight colors of the spectrum on a white background. It was gorgeous.

She lifted the washcloth, glanced at me for a few seconds and put it back in place.

"You did great today." I rubbed her ankle through the quilt. "I can't imagine how hard this must be, but I'm going to find whoever did this. You rest easy and when you feel better, you should go for a run."

I got her a glass of ice water and slipped out of the apartment in stealth ninja mode. On the walk home, I mulled over my lists of suspects—Kathryn Winchester, Charissa Mody, Jax Michaels, Daniel Godwin and Luke Cobb.

Five people who had access to Thornwell's house and knew where Sloane lived. I didn't consider Luke a real suspect, but, since he fit the mold, I included him. Maybe he would be able to shed light on this so far unsolvable puzzle.

At home, I switched into workout clothes and headed to the basement for an appointment with the kickboxing bag. By the time I was born, all of Mom and Dad's athletic ability genes had been distributed. Growing up, I contented myself by either walking or riding my bike to stay fit. It was during my freshman year in college that I discovered kickboxing. As a tiny woman, I signed up for a class being offered in my dorm to learn self-defense skills. I got that and more. I fell in love with the fact I could get the heart rate up, improve my balance and build muscle while not having to worry about someone hitting back.

Over time, I found it was also a perfect way to reduce stress and clear my mind. The rhythmic punching of the bag, using both hands and feet, forced me to concentrate on my body movements. In doing so, all my worries about a term paper or an editing job would be worked out of me, like the sweat flowing from my pores.

For the first few months, I ended my workouts sweat-covered and exhausted, but over time, as I grew more adept with the discipline, I still finished in a puddle of perspiration, but my mind was sharp and my spirits high.

I needed to get to that place now.

The basement was typical of a house built in the fifties. The concrete floor was painted gray, but a few spots the paint had flecked away to reveal a previous coat of forest green. The cinder block walls were flat white to take maximum advantage of the natural light that shone through the safety glass windows. The overhead fluorescent lights hanging from the wooden joists cast an artificial light to make the room feel comfortable, but not so much that it took on an antiseptic, hospital corridor glare. In one corner, Luke's bench press collected dust. Mom and Dad had been after him for years to get it out of the basement. I made a note to give him a hard time about it. In another corner, my training bag awaited. The heavy-duty vinyl covering had lost its sheen over the years, a victim of neglect since I'd moved to New York and purchased a new one when I'd settled into my apartment. Still, it was comforting knowing I still had my original bag available for a workout whenever I returned home.

I put my earbuds in and cued up Linkin Park. The fast and aggressive music fueled my workout and took it to a level of intensity I hadn't reached in months. After an hour of nonstop punching and kicking, I dropped to the floor, my back against the training bag. As I wiped my face and neck with a towel, Ursi ambled up to me and licked my shin.

"Girl, that's gross. You don't need a drink that bad." I removed my gloves and squirted some water into my palm. She gave my offering a few licks then crawled into my lap and fell asleep. The life of a cat.

While Ursi napped, I took deep cleansing breaths and meditated. With the focus on my breathing and my warm snuggle-buddy, by the time the fifteen-minute session was complete, my heart rate was at a comfortable sixty-two beats per minute and the knot at the base of my neck was gone.

The workout brought me peace of mind but no answers about the investigation, so I got cleaned up and paid the bridge another visit. With an uncluttered mind and a narrower list of suspects, I was confident clues I'd missed before would reveal themselves.

* * * *

I was standing beside the creek, letting the water brush against the toes of my shoes while I studied the scene. A rustling of trees broke my concentration. Matt was making his way down the path from the road.

"Thought I might find you here." He came alongside me. His gaze swept from the bridge supports on one side of us to the pebbly water's edge at our feet, and finally upstream to where the creek bent to the right and disappeared.

"Why? Am I a suspect?" I shut my eyes. Responding to every word from Matt's mouth with venom wasn't productive. "Sorry. What's up?"

"I talked to Luke and he agreed to come to the station tomorrow and give his statement. That should clear both him and Sloane. Thought you'd like to know."

"Thank you." I swallowed and tugged at my earlobe. "I appreciate that." As we stared at the water, an uncomfortable silence developed and, with it, a black cloud of doom descended upon me.

"There's something else." He lit a cigarette. I shuddered at the rancid cloud of gray smoke he expelled from his nostrils. Rachel had told me he'd started smoking after the divorce, but I'd had a hard time believing a former athlete like Matt would take up such a nasty habit. Guess I was wrong.

"Okay. What is it?"

"The mayor had a talk with me earlier today. He told me to inform the witnesses from out of town they're free to go home."

Chapter Twelve

Like an enraged bull barreling down the boulevard after having escaped from a nearby farm, I stomped to the home of Larry Cannon, Honorable Mayor of Rushing Creek, Indiana. I'd known the man all my life and was on a first-name basis with him. Then again, when you lived in a town of fewer than four thousand, you tended to be on a first-name basis with just about everybody.

As far as small-town mayors went, Larry had a decent track record. Being the figurehead of a community that relied on something as fickle as tourism couldn't be easy, and he'd balanced the need for economic development with the equally important need for Rushing Creek to maintain its quaint, rustic atmosphere. Before becoming mayor, Larry had been a successful realtor. Dad once joked that Larry had represented either the buyer or seller of over half the homes in Rushing Creek. He was driven without being pushy, talkative without being a blabbermouth and energetic without being wearisome.

In his seven years as mayor, he'd kept the streets plowed in winter, the tourists coming the rest of the year and had grown the town with a thoughtful plan that kept people happy.

Except for Thornwell.

Because of Larry's career, Thornwell grouped the man with used car salesmen, lawyers and talk radio hosts. In short, Larry was not to be trusted, especially as mayor. While I wasn't in town to see all of it firsthand, Thornwell spent a great deal of time existing as a thorn in Larry's side.

For years, Larry had tried to get Thornwell to sell a piece of his property that bordered the state road running through town. The realtor saw the twenty acres as prime land for commercial development. He tried time and again to convince Thornwell the property, which contained undeveloped woodlands, would be a boon for business, increase the tax base and be a win-win for the community.

Thornwell saw the tract of land as a haven for wildlife and a source of inspiration for his writing. He claimed that one time when he was walking through those woods, he found a Native American arrowhead estimated to be over six thousand years old. He said he was doing the community a favor, that nature in its finest undisturbed state was infinitely better than asphalt parking lots and prefabricated buildings with no character or history.

Things between Larry and Thornwell came to a head during Larry's first term as mayor. A developer approached the town about building a hotel and was interested in Thornwell's property because of the highway access. Thornwell refused to sell, which surprised nobody, so Larry initiated eminent domain proceedings on the land.

The ensuing legal fight was vicious, full of underhanded mudslinging and made national headlines when an environmental group started demonstrating at town council meetings. The case went all the way to the Indiana Supreme Court. By this time, the developer had cut its losses and found a site to develop in a neighboring county, but for Larry and Thornwell, it was personal.

Thornwell won the case and kept his land. Larry was victorious in the court of public opinion, though, by portraying Thornwell as a drunken, out-of-touch recluse who had no regard for anybody in the community but himself. It didn't help that Thornwell's drinking was at an all-time high, dueto the fact he and Kathryn hit rock bottom around the same time.

Given Larry and Thornwell's history, and that word was getting out I was looking into Thornwell's death, I shouldn't have been surprised the man greeted me with guarded suspicion when I rang the doorbell.

"Good afternoon, Allie." His eyes darted from side to side, and he kept the screen door closed. "Can I help you with something?"

"How could you tell Matt to let the out-of-town suspects go? What if one of them is the murderer?"

He cocked his head to the side. "Whose murder are you talking about?"

So, he wanted to play games. I stepped forward until my nose was microns from the screen. I didn't feel like playing. "Thornwell Winchester. The man found under the Rushing Creek Bridge last Thursday, four days ago. The man whose killer is still at large. The man who lived in this community for almost forty years and is as responsible as anybody for this place being on the map, thanks to his book sales. Am I being specific enough?"

Larry stepped back and placed a hand on the door. "That's no way to speak to the mayor of this community, Ms. Cobb. Especially since you haven't been a member of the community for over a decade."

"You haven't answered my question."

"And I don't intend to in this setting. If you have a concern about city services, you may contact my office tomorrow morning and request a meeting. I will remind you this is a matter for the police. Despite whatever big-city delusions of grandeur you may possess, this doesn't concern you. Furthermore, please stop harassing residents of my community. With the Fall Festival next weekend, the local businesses can't afford to have you continuing this misguided quest and spreading unsubstantiated rumors about a killer being on the loose."

He slammed the door, the *whoosh* of air rocking me back on my heels.

I turned around to find Matt leaning against his cruiser, arms crossed. From the frying pan into the fire and back into the frying pan. With my chin held high, I left the porch, making a point to look at everything but the police chief.

Ten steps away from the sidewalk, I started a silent countdown. Once there, I could turn left and be on my way home. At six steps, a bead of sweat trickled down my back. At three steps, my heart began to flutter that I'd avoid further humiliation at Matt's hands.

Two steps. One step. Avoid eye contact at all cost. Turn. And home—

"Got a minute, Allie?"

My foot landed wrong and I almost lost my balance, swinging my arms like Rachel did in her cheerleading golden girl days. Once I regained my balance, I whirled on him, my cheeks burning with the heat of a thousand suns.

"Why? So you can give me a review of the show? Would you give it five stars?" I stepped toward him. "Was there enough emotional conflict for you?" I took another step and poked him in the chest. "Did it provide you with a satisfying emotional ending?"

I was nose-to-nose with him, well, more like nose-to-Adam's-apple, but I had five years' worth of holding my tongue about the way he treated my sister stoking the sudden fire within me.

"Did I mention to you earlier how Sloane's doing today? She's beginning to suffer migraines and is scared to death because someone got into her apartment and stole that credit card statement you guys found on Thornwell."

He grabbed my wrist to stop me from poking him. "Why didn't you tell me this earlier?"

I wrenched my wrist free and stepped away from him. "Maybe because you didn't ask. Or maybe because you were too busy telling me you're letting suspects walk out of town scot-free."

"Let's go for a ride." He opened the passenger door of the cruiser. It was like I was staring into the mouth of a black and white steel monster waiting to swallow me up and spit me out the tail pipe.

"No way. You can't arrest me. I haven't done anything wrong."

With a sigh, he removed his sunglasses and gave me a long, penetrating stare. After thirty seconds or so, he put his sunglasses back on.

Stare down victory. Yes!

"Some might say I could charge you with assaulting a public official, thanks to your exchange with the mayor. They might also say I could charge you with battering a peace officer for poking him in the chest." He rubbed his sternum.

"You wouldn't dare." It was false bravado, but it was all I had at the moment.

"Oh, I could, but I won't." He gestured toward the car. "I just want to talk."

I glanced up and down the street. Just when I needed someone, nobody was out decorating for the Fall Festival or planting mums or even walking their dog. If I disappeared forever, nobody would have the slightest idea what happened to little Allie Cobb.

With as much defiance as I could muster, I made a show of pulling out my phone and sending Luke a text that I was meeting Matt to talk about the case. I even recited the words as I typed to make my point.

Matt removed his Rushing Creek Police Department baseball cap, ran his fingers through his hair and put the cap back on, chuckling the entire time.

"To think people say your sister's the scary one." Without another word, he went around the cruiser and got in. When I held my ground, he leaned across the passenger seat to look at me. "You need my help, Allie, and I need yours. Let's work together. For Sloane."

At the mention of my friend, I got in. We didn't talk as he drove away from the mayor's house. The street, Cedar Lane, was one of the nicest streets in town, with mature white oaks and red maples lining the way. The homes were immaculate two-story colonial and craftsman-style structures that belonged in the middle of a chamber of commerce brochure. Kids played football on the manicured lawns, which were as green as Jax Michaels's lawn, a sign of their intent on defying the inevitable coming of winter.

When we turned onto the boulevard, the quiet became too much. "Are you trying to make me sweat, Matt?"

"I thought I'd get a couple of to-go coffees from the diner so we can talk in private."

"Don't want to risk Maybelle Schuman eavesdropping on us?"

Maybelle was a retired teacher who took on a new profession when she stepped away from the classroom. These days the widow, whose four children lived out of town, kept herself occupied as the town busybody. When you combined the fact that she taught just about everyone and therefore knew everyone, with the reality she had a lot of free time, she was a natural for the role of Rushing Creek Rumormonger.

Matt laughed. "It seems like her hearing improves as she gets older."

"I never got away with anything when I had her in the fourth grade. She sent notes home to Mom every week busting me for something or other."

"I know the feeling. I've thought about deputizing her from time to time. Could use all the help I can get." He pulled into an open parking spot in front of the diner and took my coffee order.

While he was away, I considered the situation. The conversation during the drive was our most civil in years. And as much as I wanted to, I couldn't deny the olive branch he'd extended. What did I have to lose by cooperating with him?

"One coffee two sugars for the private investigator." Matt handed me a steaming cup with the diner's logo stamped in bright red on the paperboard coffee sleeve.

I took a sip. "Well done, Chief Roberson. Where to now?"

"Thought we would drive through town and find crime to fight."

"Wow, you must be really desperate to talk to me." I took another sip and studied the cruiser's interior. The dashboard seemed like any other, but a laptop computer was mounted on a platform between us. Below the computer, in the area between the driver and passenger seats, was a console that housed presumably two radios because of the two different microphones. A dash cam was mounted between the windshield and the rearview mirror.

"Impressive ride you've got here. Can I turn the lights and siren on?" I reached for a random switch to see what he would do.

"The only civilians allowed to do that are Theresa and Tristan." He moved my hand away from the panel with a firm, yet nonthreatening touch. We cruised the boulevard, the trailer park, also known not so affectionately as the Lowlands and then Rushing Creek Memorial Park, where Matt pulled over under the shade of a Sycamore tree. Our parking spot had a clear view of the basketball courts, where a group of teen girls was playing a pickup game on one and a group of men, who looked to be about my age, was playing on the other.

Our field of vision also encompassed a playground and the bandstand. Moms pushed their little ones on the swings, while a couple of adventurous tweens were trying to scale the dome that covered the bandstand.

It was the American Midwest at its best.

I chuckled at the memory of when Sloane and I tried to climb the bandstand dome. It was an unofficial rite of passage for Rushing Creek kids to attempt to reach the top before they started high school. As far as I knew, only one kid had ever accomplished the task, and he was sitting to my left.

"You going to stop those two before they get hurt?" I pointed toward the bandstand.

"Nah. A couple of years back, I introduced an ordinance to stop the kids from trying to climb it. This was after Phillip Bowman fell and broke his leg. He was in a cast for eight weeks.

"It was only going to be a five-dollar fine, but I didn't anticipate the blowback. The residents complained I was trying to take away something that made Rushing Creek unique and that the ordinance was an example of government overreach."

"Wow. What if one of those kids falls and busts his head open?"

"I'll administer first aid while you call nine-one-one." He took a drink of his coffee and rolled down his window to prop his arm on the bottom edge of the window frame.

"You tried, though. My dad would say you deserved an A for effort."

"I envy you for the relationship you had with your dad." He took another drink and kept his focus forward, as if he wanted to avoid eye contact after delivering such a bombshell.

A car pulled up near the playground. The tweens gave up on their attempts to climb the bandstand when the driver honked the horn.

Matt pulled out a cigarette then slid it back into the pack. "Your dad did good work and made people happy. When you wanted to follow in his footsteps, everybody knew it was the right decision. We were all happy for you."

I had no idea where Matt was going with this out-of-the-blue topic of conversation. "You followed in your dad's footsteps, too. It doesn't get much more honorable than being a police officer."

"Yeah, but that's the thing. I never wanted to put on a badge and sure as hell never wanted to become chief. I did what was expected of me, though. Just like marrying your sister."

"What are you talking about?" I was totally freaked out now, half of me afraid he was going to make a move on me and the other half afraid he was going to take out his gun and off himself.

"My whole life, I've done what was expected of me, instead of what I wanted to do. The old man said I was going to be a cop just like him and his dad, so I became a cop. I loved your sister and everybody said I should marry her, so I did. I knew from the start it was a mistake. I tried, but I didn't love her enough to stay married. None of what happened was her fault."

He let out a long, jagged breath and finally looked at me. "I'm out of my depth here. I asked for permission to bring in assistance from the state police, but Larry denied it. I can handle the drunk drivers, the occasional breaking and entering, the assault and battery cases." He removed his sunglasses. "What I'm trying to say is, I want your help with this murder case. I need your help."

I was stunned.

Without knowing what to say, much less do, I got out of the car and went to a nearby trash can to dispose of my cup. So, tough guy Matt Roberson wasn't the pillar of alpha male strength he was made up to be. In fact, he seemed to be every bit as messed up as half the people I knew back in New York. There was a difference, though. As opposed to my colleagues, Matt knew he needed help and was willing to ask for it.

And I was in a position to give it.

After a few minutes, I got back in the car, still reeling from Matt's confessions but determined to hear him out. For Sloane. "Okay, Chief. How can I help?"

He took a notebook from his breast pocket. "Tell me everything you know, even if you've shared it with me before, and then tell me everything you suspect."

With a surge of optimism, I went back to the beginning and recounted what I'd learned over the last four days. When I was finished, he asked if he could make a copy of my notes. Then he told me everything he knew, which wasn't much.

"What gives, man? You have six people under you, yet you have nothing beyond a couple dozen witness statements and some surveillance video."

"I know. That's why I asked for help from the state police. Larry's got me and my team running ragged getting ready for the Fall Festival.

When I told him Sloane had an alibi, all he did was put his hands in his pockets and say it must have been suicide."

"You don't believe that, do you? Because I sure don't."

"Not by a longshot. The thing is, I can't help thinking that's what Larry wants everyone to think. He wants everyone to move on and focus on the festival."

Matt's theory was like getting a rejection e-mail on a manuscript I loved. The pain cut me to the core. Still, given Larry's behavior during my visit, it rang true. And the potential ramifications were earth-shattering, at least as far as the good people of Rushing Creek would be concerned.

"You can't possibly think Larry did it, do you?"

Matt held up three fingers. "He had motive—they hated each other. He had means—he's big enough to toss Thornwell in the creek. He had opportunity—his whereabouts the night of the murder are undetermined. What do you think?"

"I think it's time for some research into our mayor."

Chapter Thirteen

Monday morning was a reverse image of the previous day. Exhausted, both mentally and physically, from my investigation, I'd eaten a quick dinner and crashed early Sunday night. I didn't roll out of bed until Mom popped her head in my room to tell me she was leaving for work. She was dressed in her classic Janice Cobb family doctor ensemble—a knit top under a sweater with cartoon animals on it and black slacks. Her young patients loved the animals and her older ones got a laugh out of them. The sweater was so popular, over the years, she'd accumulated a dozen variations of it.

"I should be back by six. What's on your agenda?" Holding her car keys in one hand and the Wonder Woman lunch box the twins gave to her for Christmas in the other, Mom was ready to get back to work full time. People depended on her, and she wasn't going to let them down.

Intentional or not, the message wasn't lost on me.

"I'm off to the library. I thought I'd sweet talk Mrs. Napier into letting me do some unsupervised research."

"Be patient with her. Her hearing isn't what it once was." She was silent for a moment as she jiggled her keys. "And be careful. I'm worried you're going to find yourself in over your head."

"I'll be fine." I got out of bed and yawned while I stretched. "The killer's probably gone by now, anyway. No thanks to jerk-face Mayor Cannon."

"If you believe that, why are you visiting the library?"

"I'm not ready to give up. If I can't find the killer, so be it, but I won't be able to sleep until I know I've left no stone unturned."

With a nod, Mom headed downstairs.

I followed, rolling my shoulders and neck to work out the stiffness from the previous day's kickboxing session. I'd slept well again, thanks to the aromatherapy oils, but a question I hadn't put much thought into was bothering me more and more. How did Thornwell get from his house to the Rushing Creek Bridge?

With no answer jumping in front of me to present itself, I made a beeline for something that could offer me certainty and reassurance; the coffee machine. I breathed in the sharp, dark roast aroma and smiled. In my world, coffee couldn't solve every problem, just most of them.

Mom hugged me, scratched Ursi between the ears and blew us both kisses as she made her way out the door. With the house to myself, I pulled up some Kelly Clarkson on my computer. Between the singer's upbeat melodies and empowering songwriting, it was the kind of music I needed to start the week off on the right foot.

Which was good, because the first work e-mail I saw was a rejection from the editor I'd been after. *Fudge.* The rejection letter was the kind I hated. It said all the right things about the manuscript, complimented the author on her hard work but passed because it didn't quite fit. Sure, there were other publishing houses I could offer the manuscript to, but this one was my client's top choice. And I'd failed to come through for her.

In a surge of self-pity, I texted Lance. One of the things I liked about him was that he was a history buff. He'd been a good sport letting me ask him questions as I edited the book so I could make sure the historical portions of the story were accurate. I don't know. I guess I was looking for someone with whom I could share my disappointment, and he was the first candidate who came to mind.

Then I sent my client an e-mail, breaking the bad news. Giving clients bad news was the worst part of the job. I received many more rejections from publishers than acceptances, and it was my duty to give that information to my clients, even if it left them in tears or so down they wanted to quit writing.

That was the thing about publishing, a writer didn't last long if he or she didn't develop skin as thick as a rhino.

It was the same for agents. It didn't matter I hadn't written my clients' books. What mattered was I loved those books and wanted to share them with the world every bit as much as my clients did.

So, yeah, receiving a rejection from an editor was always tough, but the key was to keep going. To keep working until I found an editor who would answer me with the most glorious three-letter word in the English language.

Yes.

It was eerie how many similarities there were between my hunt for Thornwell's killer and my job. In both situations, I was looking for the right answer, the right fit, the right person, so I could connect the dots and give my client, or my friend, the good news he or she deserved.

When I was caught up on e-mails, I read queries while I ate a bowl of oatmeal with diced apples for breakfast. Queries were the unsolicited e-mails the agency received from writers hoping to attract an agent's attention. While the odds of landing a deal with an agent were against the writers who submitted their work this way, from time to time, it happened.

And when it did, it was like a bright ray of sunshine breaking through the clouds after a rainstorm. It signified hope and positivity and the good things in the world. On this morning, there were no rays of sunshine, though. By the time I finished breakfast, I'd read thirty queries and responded to each with a respectful rejection.

After taking a shower and getting dressed, my next task was to develop a research plan while I got ready to go to the library. Matt had promised to send copies of witness statements and other materials to a Dropbox account I used. Hopefully that information, combined with whatever helpful research I unearthed, would help me find the killer. And sooner, rather than later.

With his actions of yesterday, Matt was proving to be quite the enigma. Maybe the bully-type behavior was his way to cover up the fact he was insecure. I had no doubt in the world his change in attitude wasn't due to a sudden burst of affection for me or my family.

No. I'd bet my trusty *Roget's Thesaurus* the change was due to a sense of duty. Unlike Larry, Matt wasn't willing to ignore the evidence, or lack thereof. While I'd have to be content that the change was due to the latter, not the former, I closed the front door, happy to get any help at all, regardless of the reasons.

The dew on the grass sparkled like millions of tiny diamonds as I strolled down the house's front walkway. It was a brisk morning, but with clear skies the day promised to turn into a picture-postcard fall day in Indiana, the kind that included sweatshirts, hot chocolate and outdoor sports like touch football played in Memorial Park.

With a smile, I strolled to Rushing Creek Public Library. I chuckled at the thought that, even after so many years away, I could still walk to the library blindfolded and not take a single misstep. During my summers in elementary and middle school, I trekked to the library almost daily. With a backpack bursting with books over my shoulder, I traipsed into the building, waved at Mrs. Napier, slipped the books one by one into the return slot and then hunted for new reading material.

During my primary school years, Dad went with me. When we arrived, he told Mrs. Napier he needed me to guide him so he didn't get lost. They laughed and sent me on my way to the children's section to pick out the latest Junie B. Jones or Boxcar Children adventure. When I arrived at the checkout counter loaded down with my day's selections, Mrs. Napier, with her dark brown hair in a side braid, complimented me on my selections and made me promise I'd get Dad home safely.

The summer between fourth and fifth grade was when I began my solo treks to the library. I felt like an adult, sauntering up to the library's glass front door accompanied only by the books to be returned and my unquenchable desire for more.

I'd asked Mrs. Napier the same question every time I visited. What's new and interesting? She gave me the same answer every time. With a twinkle in her eye, she said that every book in her library was new and interesting to someone.

When I was in high school, the library became my second home. Since it was open until eight during the week, I spent hours studying there. It was also where I got my start as an editor. I'd met classmates there and edited their composition and literature papers.

Thanks to Dad's influence, I provided flawless editing. Over time, my reputation grew, and I began to make money at it. By the time I was a senior, teachers from both Rushing Creek and the neighboring school system referred students in need of help to me.

Mrs. Napier got tears in her eyes the day I told her I'd gotten an editor job in New York City. By then, her brown hair was streaked with gray and the side braid had given way to a layered bob.

Now, as the one-story limestone structure came into view, I was shocked that it had been three years since I'd last visited. The shock turned to shame. Mrs. Napier had been like a second mom to me, yet I hadn't visited the library in years.

It was time to make up for that transgression. I'd give Mrs. Napier a hug, apologize for neglecting to visit her and promise to start sending her any free books I could get my hands on.

As I pulled open the library door, I imagined I was Odysseus returning home after his extended detour. I stepped inside and inhaled the familiar smell of old books commingled with something I didn't expect—the aroma of fresh-cut wood.

Off to the right in a far corner where I used to study, walls were being constructed. Dismay sprinkled with a touch of righteous indignation hit me. *How dare they renovate my tutoring station.* I marched to the checkout counter. I opened my mouth then shut it. Mrs. Napier wasn't there. Instead of my beloved librarian, the station was staffed by a guy in rimless glasses I didn't recognize. He was tall. Okay, fine, compared to me everyone was tall, but he was tall in the literal sense. He had to be six-five. His short, brown hair was neatly trimmed, with a part on the side. He was kind of gangly. Not Ichabod Crane–thin, but he could put on a few pounds and it wouldn't hurt.

"Is Mrs. Napier in," I glanced at his name tag, "Brent?"

"I'm afraid she's gone for a few days on vacation. Is there anything I can help you with?" He smiled. It was a gentle smile, without the malice or snark in the ones I'd encountered all too often in New York.

It also took the edge off my anxiety about the construction.

"Yeah, um." *What was I going to ask him?* I closed my eyes for a few seconds. "What's the deal with the construction?"

"You're not from around here, are you?" He propped his elbows on the counter to draw even with me at eye level.

Challenge accepted. "As a matter of fact, I am. I grew up a few blocks from here."

"Uh-huh." He scratched his chin. "So, you're not from around here now. Because if you were, you'd know the construction has been the subject of hot debate around town for the last two months. Room's being created for a genealogy section."

He came around the counter and extended his hand. "Brent Reynolds. You wouldn't happen to be Allie Cobb, would you?"

His hand dwarfed mine as we shook. I had to close my eyes so I would stop staring at our interlocked hands. It wasn't until he released me that I found my voice.

"I would. May I ask how you know that?" I pulled on my earlobe, as nervous energy searched for a release.

"There was a picture of you and your family in the local paper last week." He took a look at the floor. "I'm sorry about your dad. Vicky was pretty broken up about his passing."

Vicky? I gave him a blank look.

My confusion must have registered with him. "Vicky. You know Mrs. Napier. She told me you spent a fair amount of time here back in the day."

"You don't know the half of it." I knocked my knuckle on the imitation wooden countertop. "Now that I think about it, I don't think I ever knew

Mrs. Napier's first name is Vicky. The things you learn about your hometown when you least expect it."

"I get it. I've been in town a few months, and it seems like I learn something new every day." He squared his shoulders. "But I'm sure you didn't come here today just to see me. How can I help you?"

"I'm here on a research project." I hoped I could use Brent's newcomer status to my advantage. Since he didn't know me, he was less likely to know I'd been nosing around in pursuit of Thornwell's killer. "Was hoping you could give me access to the news archives."

Decades ago, a wealthy library patron created an endowment dedicated to preserving Brown County's history. Because of that, the library had the means to store copies of *The Brown County Beacon*, the weekly newspaper. The storage method had changed over time, from physical copies, to microfilm and probably to CD-ROM or cloud-based by now, but what mattered most to me was that every edition of the paper would be accounted for.

I needed access to everything the *Beacon* published over the last eight years.

"Sure." He led the way to a small room with a sign by the door that said Research. The room had two carrels with corresponding computer hardware that faced the right-hand wall. A laser printer was stationed in the far corner. There was a window in the door to the office, probably for security purposes. Even in Rushing Creek, you never knew what might be going on behind closed doors, as I was finding out.

He fired up the far carrel's computer and wrote something on a Post-it Note.

"Here's the information to log in." He handed me the note. "Everything's stored digitally now, so you can access the complete archive from the comfort of your friendly library chair."

I took the seat he pulled out for me and logged in. Once I was in the system, Brent gave me a quick tour so I didn't have to learn by trial and error. The system was slick and intuitive. My hopes for finding something interesting rose.

Brent stepped out of the research room and took a look around. "It's pretty quiet today. I'd be happy to help you with your research. I can do it from my workstation up front."

"I'm sure you have got plenty to do. Mrs. Napier always said a librarian's work is never done."

"True." He offered me that cute smile again. "But I'm not a librarian. I'm a genealogist. Vicky told me my primary objective while she's gone is to make sure the place doesn't burn down. I'm allowed to check materials in and out and shelve returned materials. Everything else is off-limits."

I couldn't keep from laughing. Mrs. Napier was the sweetest woman in the world, but she guarded her library and its contents like a mother bear looked after her cubs. It wasn't hard to envision her lecturing Brent with the yellow number two pencil she always kept at hand.

"Well." I looked at my watch. It was already almost eleven. "I could use some help, but do me a favor and keep this between us."

"Deal."

I asked him to search for any articles involving Thornwell written in the last ten years. The information he found would be incorporated into a project I was working on for Sloane. While it was stretching the truth, it wasn't a lie, either.

"Thornwell had issues, so don't be surprised if you come across things that are less than complimentary. If he's mentioned in something, I need it."

"You got it." Brent closed the door behind him, the click echoing off the cinderblock walls.

While Brent looked for Thornwell, I searched for Larry. Their ongoing feud, as heated as it got, didn't seem to be a reason to kill a man. Sure, it would play a role, but my gut told me if Rushing Creek's mayor was also Rushing Creek's first murderer in thirty years, something else was involved.

If only I could find it.

* * * *

I was scanning a story about a commercial real estate deal Larry was trying to push the town council into approving when there as a knock on the door. Brent came in with a stack of paper an inch thick.

"Mr. Winchester was pretty colorful." He dropped the stack next to my pile on Larry, which was almost as high.

"That's one way to put it." I adjusted the computer screen so Brent couldn't see it. The last thing I wanted was to get him involved in this mess.

"So, look." He rubbed his hands together as if he was cold. "Vicky said I could close up shop for a lunch break. I was going to go get a sandwich. Care to join me? My treat."

Brent seemed like a nice guy, and he was helping me out. And he was cute, especially when he smiled.

My stomach brought my debate to a halt by growling. Not that there had been much of one, anyway. "Sounds great."

He held the door open as I exited the research room and then again as we left the library. This was the kind of guy I wouldn't mind getting to know better.

Chapter Fourteen

The library was on the northern end of a three-block stretch nicknamed Government Row. This was where the wheels of Rushing Creek government turned. As we headed south, we passed Union Park, basically a grassy area the size of a city block crisscrossed with gravel walking paths. Concrete and wood benches were stationed here and there along the paths. A few of the benches were occupied by people on their lunch breaks, munching on sandwiches with their eyes on their phones.

In a far corner of the park, a girl had spread out a blanket and was reading a paperback. She was a wonderful reminder that, despite the ubiquity of electronic gadgets in the world, plenty of people still loved the paper and ink of a physical book.

The Rushing Creek Municipal Building was next. Built when I was in middle school, the red brick structure was divided into three sections. The northern section housed the fire department, the southern was home to the police department, and the middle was comprised of the rest of local government, including offices for the mayor, building inspector and clerk-treasurer.

The southernmost occupant of Government Row was Creekview Hospital. By hospital standards, it was small, with an emergency room, surgery center, birthing center and forty or so beds. It served Rushing Creek and the surrounding area with compassion and effectiveness, though. I liked to think it was an example that, like me, what mattered was substance not necessarily size.

It also housed the county morgue. I shivered at the thought and focused my attention on the other side of the street.

"You okay?" Brent asked as we waited for a truck to go through an intersection so we could cross the street.

"I'm fine. I brought Sloane to the hospital so she could identify her dad. I guess I've been so busy, I haven't thought about the fact he's still there, in the morgue." I shook my head to chase away the melancholy and pointed at a little storefront with a sign above the door that read Big Al's in block red letters. "Is that where we're going?"

"It's not a problem, is it?"

"A problem?" I quickened my pace to one that would make an Olympic race walker proud. "It's only my favorite place to eat in the world."

As we entered the sandwich shop, my senses were tingling in anticipation of a thick double burger and a side of the best waffle fries in the Midwest, and maybe even a chocolate shake.

Once fully inside, the aroma of seared beef and grilled onions mingled with the explosive bubbles of deep fryers in action to leave me weak in the knees.

"Allie Cobb, as I live and breathe." Big Al Hammond, the man himself, was at the cash register, ringing out a customer. As soon as he finished, he took me in his muscular arms and I practically disappeared into his hug.

"I'm so sorry about your dad. Walter was the best." He led us to a booth in the back, where it was quieter, perhaps noticing I was with a man. "Lunch is on me." When I tried to object, he put up his hands. "It's the least I can do for an old friend's daughter who was also an incredible babysitter."

He patted my hand and returned to the cash register, stopping to say hi to a customer and have a word with the server who was coming our way with a glass of ice water in each of her hands.

"So, you're a legend here, huh?" Brent unwrapped his straw. "I've been coming here twice a week for a while now and sure don't get treated like that."

Between his smile and sparkling eyes, it was easy to take Brent's gentle ribbing. Not to mention that he hadn't so much as taken a quick glance at his phone once we left the library. Lance, on the oher hand, spent as much time staring at his phone as he did looking at anything else.

"I don't know about legend. I babysat for Al's two daughters for a few years. They were a handful, though. So, maybe small-time legend."

"To small-time legends, then." He clinked his glass against mine.

A few minutes later, the server returned to take our orders. His jaw dropped when I gave her my order. Brent seemed like a nice guy, so I didn't want to consider the option he was a sexist jerk who thought women only ate salads or grilled fish. Sure, I ate those things, but there was always a place in my heart, and belly, for Big Al's finest, especially when I was walking all over town.

"No way you can eat all that," he said when our lunches were placed before us.

"What? Think a dainty thing like me can't handle a man's meal like this?" I leaned toward him and stared. Hopefully, he would take my actions as a challenge, but mostly it was a way to inhale the burger's divine aroma.

"I'm, like, twice as big as you and that pile of fries you've got is a mile high. Not to mention the burger." He stared at his chicken salad sandwich and side of coleslaw. The longing in his eyes as his gaze shifted to my meal was comical.

"Prepare to be astounded, library boy." I bit into my burger and could have died a happy woman then and there. The double patties were crispy on the outside and so tender on the inside, I went through two napkins on the first bite alone. If Brent tried to engage me in conversation, I didn't notice. For the next few magical moments, the only things that existed were me, the burger and the fries.

I finally put down the burger when there was a mere third of it left. The pile of napkins I'd used was rivaling the mountain of fries. I needed to do something about that. As I reached for the catsup, I caught Brent trying to suppress a laugh.

"Enjoying yourself?" He took a bite of his sandwich. "I'm sorry. I don't think I've seen someone enjoy a cheeseburger as much as you were." His cheeks turned red. "I mean, I'm sure this week's been hard on you. It was nice to see you happy."

"Thank you." I shoved a waffle fry into my mouth. The need to focus on chewing kept me from getting teary-eyed.

He nodded once and went back to his sandwich. A man who could show empathy and also knew when to keep his mouth shut. Brent was making Lance look worse as each minute ticked by.

Not that I was looking for a new boyfriend. Or any boyfriend, for that matter. I was simply content to find I was comfortable in Brent's presence. At least that was what I tried to tell myself.

I spent the rest of lunch in rapt attention as Brent told me about his job. He was working on his Ph.D. in information and library science at Indiana University and, as part of that, was helping libraries throughout the state set up genealogy departments.

"The interest in knowing one's roots continues to increase." He munched on the waffle fry I gave him. "When you factor in all the genetic testing available today from places like 23andMe, I think the ability to research your past will become as important to some people as knowing your cholesterol level."

"That's pretty cool." I wasn't lying.

When Rachel opened the pub, she'd done some research in the hope the Cobb family had its roots in England or Scotland and would have a super cool coat of arms she could put on display. The research turned up a slick coat of arms featuring a knight's helmet and a red and gray shield. It also proved my family was a group of mutts, with a mixture of English, German, Italian and Hungarian in our past. Ever since then, a trip to Europe to trace my family's roots was on my bucket list.

When the fries were gone, Brent took a look at the vintage Coca-Cola clock above the grill. "I need to get back. I'd love to tell you more about the project on the way, if you don't mind."

I didn't mind at all.

As we were leaving, I noticed Jax Michaels and Daniel Godwin seated at the counter. Jax was perusing a menu while Daniel was drinking a cup of hot tea and staring at his laptop. They were probably Thornwell's longest tenured employees and here they were, hanging out together.

And they were both on my list of suspects.

Despite Daniel's name being on my list, I hadn't gotten around to talking to him. Now wasn't the time for a confrontation, but his presence in town piqued my interest.

I greeted Jax with a nod and tapped Daniel on the shoulder and said hello.

"Hey, Allie. How are you?" The man had dark circles under his eyes and had missed a few spots shaving. The obvious lack of sleep was understandable, since his boss was dead. I wondered if everyone in town was suffering from insomnia.

"Hanging in there. How about you?"

His shoulders sagged. "Struggling with Thornwell's death. I find I just can't leave town until justice is done."

"I understand." I patted his shoulder.

Between his appearance and the uneven tone of his voice, he seemed to be as traumatized as Sloane.

"I need to go, but don't lose hope. We'll find the killer."

After giving Daniel a quick embrace and Jax a long side-eyed look, Brent and I made for the exit, only to be intercepted by Big Al, who gave me another lung-squeezing hug.

"If you or your mom need anything, let me know. I mean it." He gave Brent a long look, his gaze covering my new friend from head to toe, twice. "This young lady's a personal friend of mine. If she's a friend of yours, then I am too."

They shook hands as Brent introduced himself.

"You treat her like royalty, understand me, son? Because Allie Cobb is royalty in this town. Don't let anybody tell you different."

With a laugh, he gave Brent a stout slap to the shoulder and opened the door for us. I looked at Big Al and rolled my eyes, but he just winked.

On the way back to the library, Brent was silent. I could imagine a million different scenarios going through his head. Sometimes life in a small town could get overwhelming if you weren't used to it. And Brent, who said he was from Cincinnati, most definitely wasn't used to it.

"Sorry about that." With my thumb, I pointed back toward the diner. "Small town life. You were going to tell me more about your genealogy work."

"Right." He smiled and, with that little action, things were back the way I wanted them. As we walked, he told me about his goal of making sure there was space devoted to genealogy in every library in Indiana. "My grandfather told me I'd never get any joy out of life by thinking small. He's the one who got me interested in my family's roots."

"Very cool." A sinking sensation came over me as Brent unlocked the library door and flipped the sign from Closed to Open. It was as if I was jealous I had to share him with the library again. Which was silly. I barely knew the man.

But I knew enough that I liked him. And was happy I had more research to do.

"I have books to shelve and some other things to do, so I'll let you get back to your work." He tapped a finger on the counter and glanced at the ceiling, as if he wanted to say something but was struggling with finding the right words. "You're looking for Mr. Winchester's killer. I've overheard people talking about it. They were talking about you."

It was a statement, not an accusation. Denying it would get me nowhere.

"Yeah. I'm sorry I wasn't straight with you earlier, but you were so nice to offer to help. I didn't want to drag you into it. With his killer still out there..." I shoved my hands into the pockets of my jeans and stared at my New Balance shoes. They were high quality, and oh, so comfortable. Plus, it was easier to look at them than risk making eye contact with Brent.

With his index finger, he lifted my chin until our gazes met. When they did, he smiled, which led me to do the same. "That's better. Why are you doing this instead of the police? Isn't it dangerous?"

To be honest, I'd only given minimal thought to the potential danger I was putting myself into. I was in Rushing Creek, Indiana, after all. My teeny-tiny hometown was hardly a crime-ridden slum. I wasn't worried about my safety in New York, a city with a population of over eight million people. Why should I be worried about my well-being here?

"I'm not worried about that. What I am worried about is finding justice for the Winchester family."

"Fair enough, but false bravado doesn't suit you."

"Doesn't matter." I didn't know whether to take the comment as an insult or a compliment. "What matters is Thornwell's daughter is my best friend. I promised Sloane I'd find the person who did this. No offense."

"None taken." Brent scratched his chin. "Gotta admit, I wish I had a friend who'd go as far as you're going to help Sloane."

A lump formed in my throat. I'd never considered not helping Sloane, with this, or with anything else. She was the most important person in my life, outside of my family. I'd do anything for her. Besides, it was the way I was raised. To help those in need.

And right now, Sloane needed me.

"Thank you. I need to get back to my research."

Once I was settled into my chair in the research room, I let out a long breath. The chat with Brent had unsettled me. I was doing the right thing, wasn't I?

The stack of paper by the keyboard provided the answer. Yes, I was doing the right thing.

By the time I'd read my last article on Larry, the sun had said its good-byes for the day. It had been a research marathon, and, despite Brent giving me some pain reliever, my head was pounding. It had been a productive marathon, though. The ream-thick stack of paper was proof.

I didn't find anything that amounted to a smoking gun, but there was plenty of proof of the bad blood between Larry and Thornwell. Enough for Larry to resort to murder? I couldn't rule out the possibility when the value of the land Thornwell refused to sell was factored into the question. Sometimes money did scary things to people.

Further research on that end could wait, though, because Matt had been true to his word. He sent me a text late in the afternoon that he'd instructed Jeanette to upload the relevant case information to the Dropbox account.

I used the library's computer to access the materials. There wasn't much—the police report, two dozen witness interview notes and a handful of video files. I printed the interviews and called it a day.

Three patrons were waiting to check out as I made my way toward the exit. Jax was one of them. *Ohmigod, is he stalking me?* I pushed away the attack of paranoia. I was in a public place. I knew how to protect myself. What was there to worry about? It was almost eight, and I didn't want to make a scene about Jax or make Brent stay late, so I gave the genealogist a wave.

"Heading home?" He ran a book through the scanner.

"Yeah." I showed him the stack of paper. "Thanks for all your help."

"My pleasure. If you need any more help, you know where to find me." He flashed me a smile and slipped a small stack of books into a plastic bag, while he handed a woman whose name I couldn't place her library card. "Thanks, Ms. Young. See you soon."

Grace Young. She was two years behind me in high school. I should have recognized her. In penance, I held the door for her as we exited and promised myself I'd get back to Rushing Creek more often from now on.

A cold wind knifed through my sweatshirt and raised goose bumps on my arms. In October, once the sun went down, it could get cold quick, so, after doing a quick e-mail check on my phone, I decided to take a shortcut home. Granted, it only shortened the walk by a block, but the alleyway I took, which ran between Brown County Custom Furniture and Taylor's Automotive, sheltered me from the wind.

I'd covered about half of the alley's distance when something hit my shoulder. I stopped and looked around, the hair on the back of my neck springing to attention.

"Who's there?" I asked in a shaky voice.

When no response came, I got moving. *Probably some annoying kid.* I laughed out loud to prove to the juvenile delinquent I wasn't afraid.

All of a sudden, I took a sharp blow to the middle of my back, which sent me face first into the gravel. The moment I landed, someone was on top of me. A knee dug into my spine and hands wrapped around my neck.

As the hands tightened around my throat, crushing my windpipe, spots formed in front of my eyes. The attacker's rancid breath was warm on my ear.

"Let it go, Cobb. Let it go." It was barely a whisper, yet it sent a violent shudder through me.

Then the attacker grabbed my hair and hit me on the head—once, twice, a third time—and I knew no more.

Chapter Fifteen

"Allie. Allie." Someone was shaking me and calling my name. The voice seemed far away, as if it came from the other end of a miles-long subway tunnel.

I jerked my shoulder away from the hand shaking me and a lightning bolt of pain scorched my entire body. Unable to open my eyes, I lifted my head but gave up on the effort when it started pounding as if it was a bass drum being double kicked by a rock and roll star.

Someone wiped my cheek with a cloth. No, it wasn't a cloth, because it was accompanied by snuffling and snorting and horrible animal breath. I managed to lift one eyelid enough to see I was face-to-face with a dog. A big dog. And it was licking my face. *Eww.*

For some reason, a feeble wave was all I could muster, but it was enough to get the dog to back away and let out an ear-splitting *woof* that brought tears to my eyes.

"Easy there, Sammy. Good dog." The voice was clearer and familiar, too.

"Brent?" I started to sit up but was overcome by an intense wave of vertigo. Okay, I needed to keep the head still for a while. "What happened? Where am I?"

"Take it easy." Brent's face came into view. He wasn't smiling. "Looks like someone jumped you."

With equal parts precision and gentleness, he eased me into a sitting position, with my back against something hard. A wall, maybe? My brain was a muddled mess. I ran my fingers across the rough, pebbly surface of the ground.

I shivered and sucked in a sharp breath as a wave of nausea hit me. To keep from throwing up, I lowered my head until it was between my knees and started counting. The swirling, spinning sensation had receded by the time I was in the thirties, and I was able to focus on Brent's voice.

"Yes, the alley behind the furniture store." A pause. "I don't know. She was out cold when I found her." Another pause. "She's got a nasty cut on her head, but no other injuries that I can see."

A few minutes later, the distant wail of an ambulance pierced the silence and made me wince, but at least I was with it enough to know it was coming for me.

Brent squatted in front of me as a golden retriever snuggled against my side and licked my ear. It was slimy, but the dog's body heat radiated into me, the warmth spreading like icing on a cinnamon bun right out of the oven.

"The ambulance will be here in a minute. Sammy wants to keep you warm until then." The dog ran its nose through my hair and started licking the back of my head. Ursi probably wouldn't approve. I liked Sammy.

"Ow." I jerked away and my hand went to the spot the dog had innocently come across. The sore spot was wet. When I looked at my fingers, even in the dark, I recognized blood.

My blood.

A moment later, the bright headlights of the ambulance bore down on us. I breathed a sigh of relief, even as the flashing lights atop the vehicle made me squint.

The paramedic, a blond woman dressed in a blue uniform, who introduced herself as Chelsea, gave me a thorough examination, paying particular attention to my head and neck. When I complained about the penlight she flashed into my eyes, she brushed a few strands of hair behind her ear.

"Sorry, Ms. Cobb. Can't be too careful with head trauma." With a grin, she ruffed Sammy's fur. "Looks like you've got a good protector here. What's his name?"

"It's Sammy, and he's not my dog, he's Brent's." I looked around. "Where is he?"

"With my partner." She pointed toward a police cruiser that had pulled up while I was being examined. Brent was talking to a police officer and a man in a uniform similar to Chelsea's.

In my life, I'd never needed the attention of either an ambulance or a police car. Now, in a single incident, I had both attending to me. I gave Sammy another hug.

When Chelsea was satisfied with her exam, she called to her partner and they helped me get to my feet. She eyed me like a hawk before asking if I wanted to walk to the ambulance or if I needed a gurney. With my head clearing, embarrassment at my situation began to creep in on me, so, in an attempt to retain some dignity, I held my head high and walked, as if I was on eggshells, to the back of the ambulance.

When my knees buckled a foot away from the back bumper. Chelsea and her partner, who she called Boomer, assisted me onto the gurney inside the ambulance. When I was fastened in, Boomer left us to get behind wheel while Chelsea busied herself hooking me up to an IV line.

Since my situation wasn't critical, the trip to the hospital lacked the drama of lights and sirens. Even so, the drive took all of maybe five minutes. The upside was that by the time we came to a stop, the pain reliever Chelsea had given me was kicking in.

After I was admitted to the ER, I was talking to a policeman, who identified himself as Officer Abbott, when Mom burst into the room.

"Allie, what have you gotten yourself into?" She rushed to my bedside and gave me a hug. Before I knew it, she was examining my head injury. When she finally released me, her lips were pursed. "Well?"

I was saved by a knock on the door. When it swung open, Matt filled the doorway, a thunderous look on his face.

"I'll take it from here, Tommy. The witness is in a conference room down the hall. He's expecting you."

"Ma'am." The officer tipped his cap to me and left the room without another word.

Matt took the vacated chair and let out a long sigh as he looked me over. "How are you feeling, Allie?"

"How do you think she's feeling, Chief? She was just attacked."

"Enough, Mom." The tension in the room had quintupled in the last minute, and I didn't feel like putting up with it.

"I'm better since the pain meds have kicked in. Not used to being body slammed to the ground."

"Can you tell me what happened?" Matt took out his notebook and wrote at a furious pace as I recounted, as best I could, all of my activities from when I left the house in the morning up to the attack.

Mom took a deep breath when I finished. Fortunately, the doctor came in to examine me before she could start in on Matt again. The doc poked and prodded me, maintaining a running list of questions like "Does this hurt?" and "Can you feel that?" Like Chelsea, he spent more time on my neck and head than my other body parts.

"There aren't any scratch marks or cuts on your neck, which is good. Don't be surprised if you have some bruising, but that should be the worst of it on the surface."

I thought I was home free after he applied a few stitches to my head and gave me his assessment. Then he pulled the rug out from under me.

"I don't think there's any neurological damage, but I'd still like to get some images of your head and neck, just to be on the safe side." He left to put in the order, leaving me between Mom and Matt.

I would have felt safer in the middle of a gunfight between the Hatfields and McCoys.

"Your purse, phone, things like that were intact when you were found, so you were obviously attacked to get you to stop looking into Winchester's murder." Matt flipped through his notebook. We reviewed the timeline of the events. "Brent called nine-one-one at eight thirty-five. Who else might have known your whereabouts?"

Despite the calming effect of the pain meds, it was hard to concentrate. I gave him the names of the people I knew who were in the library when I left. It was a short list.

"What about my research? I had a stack of paper with me. Did someone pick it up?" The night would be salvageable if I could get my research back.

"There was nothing at the scene when Officer Naughton arrived." Matt shook his head. "He's still there. I'll contact him and ask him to make a wide sweep of the area."

"Well, what are you waiting for?" Mom got to her feet. "It's obvious this Brent or Jax Michaels must have attacked her. Why don't you arrest them?"

Matt chewed on his lower lip for a moment. "Why do you think I should?"

"Well, I just…" Mom's cheeks turned bright red as she waved her hands in little circles, as if she was conjuring an answer to Matt's question. She didn't get flustered often, and usually recovered within a few seconds.

"As for Jax, Allie talked to him a few days ago and from what I understand, asked some rather pointed questions. If he's the murderer, it makes perfect sense he'd want to scare my daughter into silence."

Matt nodded. "And Brent?"

"We don't know anything about the man. There may be a psychopath under that harmless façade of his. He says he's the one who found her. What if that's a cover? For all we know, he may have tracked her down as soon as he closed the library and attacked her."

"Why would he do that?"

"He knew what Allie was researching and that material's gone now. Who else would know to take it?" Mom crossed her arms. "Besides, I'm not the investigator. You are. It's your job to solve crimes, not mine."

I held my breath as they glared at each other, the whooshing of air through the ventilation system the only sound.

"I appreciate your concern, Janice. Unfortunately, I don't have enough to make an arrest." Matt held up an index finger to stop Mom before she could say anything. "Yet."

The x-ray technician arrived to rescue me from the battle of former in-laws. The pain meds were making it tough to think clearly, but I found myself taking Matt's side. We didn't know enough to make an arrest.

The attacker was sending me a message, though. There was no doubt in my mind about that. He, or she, must have thought my research was important enough to want it out of the way, too.

I could always go back and reprint the material, but it still amounted to precious hours lost, and, as each day passed, I got more worried the trail would go cold. I'd deal with that tomorrow, though. Getting through tonight seemed like a tough enough challenge.

The trip to x-ray was a welcome break, but, all too soon, I was being wheeled back into my room, which was now even more crowded since Rachel and Luke had arrived while I was away.

I was shocked to find nobody was glaring, shouting or throwing insults. Instead, Matt was at a little whiteboard hung on the wall, listening to Rachel, while Luke was taking notes.

"If I would have known all it would take to get you guys to be civil to each other was me getting knocked out, I would have asked Sloane to do it to me ages ago."

Laughter filled the room, uneasy at first, but then more genuine. Without any warning, Rachel, her cheeks wet with tears, wrapped me in a hug so tight, Big Al would have been proud.

"You know," she kept her forehead against mine, "since you came home, this town's been gripped in the midst of a crime wave. Your big city lifestyle is a bad influence." She choked back a sob.

"If you'll hand me my phone, I'll call Commissioner Gordon. Maybe he can get Batman on the case."

"If it's the Christian Bale Batman, then yes with a capital Y." Rachel loved Batman and the Christian Bale portrayal of the Dark Knight was her favorite. I always thought it was his lawless streak that appealed to my big sister, who worked so hard at being perfect. I'd never had the guts to tell her that, though.

I closed my eyes and tried to relax as Matt and my family resumed their brainstorming session. Evidently, Matt decided the unexpected gathering was an ideal time to ask questions and gather facts while he was out from under the mayor's thumb.

The cooperation surrounding me was encouraging. It might not last, which broke my heart a little, but at least, for tonight, members of the Cobb and Roberson families were working together, not tearing each other apart.

Funny how the worst of times could bring out the best in people.

The doctor returned a little later with good news. There was no evidence of hard tissue damage. I had a concussion and would probably be sore for a day or two, but that was it. He advised me to take it easy, avoid computer screens and stick to darkened rooms if the light got to be too much.

As we walked through the emergency department waiting room, Brent was sitting in a chair in the corner, staring at his phone. Sammy was curled up asleep by his feet.

"Since when are dogs allowed in the hospital?" Rachel asked. Now the crisis was over, my good old snarky sister was back.

"Allie." Brent rushed toward me then pulled up a few feet away, his gaze landing on each family member then Matt, before finally settling on me. "Are you okay?"

"Yeah. It was lucky for whoever did this that they attacked from behind." I pantomimed a few punches at him. "If they would have come at me from the front, I would have dropped 'em."

While I was introducing Brent to the family, Sammy strolled up to me and took a seat at my feet, or rather, on my feet. "See, I have Sammy to protect me, don't I, boy?" I scratched his head and he rewarded me by licking my hand.

"Betcha that overgrown rat of yours never does that." Luke offered an open palm to Sammy.

"Ursi loves me in her own way." I yawned. The day had caught up with me. "I'm ready to go home. Thanks again, Brent."

I gave him a quick hug, which caught him by surprise, judging by his suddenly pink cheeks, and headed for the exit.

Mom was kind enough to hold her tongue on the drive home, but as soon as I was comfortable on the living room couch with Ursi on my lap, she put her hand on her hip and gave me a long, silent stare.

"I love you, Mom, but I'm an adult and I'm going to make my own decisions about my life. I promised Sloane I'll find the killer. As I recall, you were supportive of that decision."

Her hand dropped from her hip as she lowered her head until her chin touched her chest. It was a rare sign from Mom admitting defeat. Still, knowing her, she wasn't going down without a fight.

"That was before all of this, honey." She sat on the edge of the couch and wrapped my hand in hers. "You could have been killed. How do you think that makes me feel? Especially so soon after losing your father."

Bringing Dad into this was a low blow, but I had to give Mom props for the maneuver. It was a tough one to respond to, but I was ready.

"This isn't about you, Mom. Or Dad, either. To be honest, it's not about Sloane or Thornwell. It's about me. I've been a crappy daughter the last couple of years. I left the heavy lifting to you and Luke and Rachel. Shoot, I couldn't even make it back home in time to say good-bye to Dad one final time."

I rubbed Ursi's ear, looking for forgiveness from my cat, because I sure couldn't offer it to myself.

"This is my penance. I knew Thornwell as well as anybody outside of his family and Dad, and yet I knew almost nothing about all of the positive strides he'd taken. I need to make up for that." I rubbed Ursi's soft, striped belly. "I can't turn my back on this. Not now. Especially not when the killer's still out there."

"But Matt—"

"No 'but Matt,' Mom."

Ursi gave me a nasty look in response to my cross tone.

"I'm sorry, but I'm convinced now more than ever the mayor's going to keep getting in his way."

"I don't understand. Are you saying Larry killed Thornwell?" Mom's frustration was palpable.

I couldn't blame her. She believed in the basic goodness of people, which was no doubt why she was such a wonderful doctor. The violence and accusation-filled evening, on the heels of everything else over the last week, had to be taking a toll.

"I don't know. The material I gathered painted a compelling picture, though." I told Mom about what, specifically, I'd been doing at the library. Even though I didn't have the documents anymore, what I'd read was still fresh in my mind, bruised as it was.

When I finished, Mom ran her fingers down her blouse and began pacing the room.

"As long as I've known Larry, he's been able to get along with everybody except Thornwell. I suppose that's what made him such a successful realtor and politician." She stopped and looked me in the eyes. "He doesn't like being crossed, though. Thornwell was like a wasp Larry couldn't exterminate, who showed up to sting him over and over again, year after year."

Mom's words aligned perfectly with what I'd read. I'd have to have something rock solid before I went after the biggest fish in the Rushing Creek pond, though. That was when the lightbulb went on.

"I think I might have a way to sting our beloved mayor a few more times." I lifted Ursi's front paw and gave her a high five. "And it doesn't involve walking down alleys at night, either."

Chapter Sixteen

Allie's Crime Fighting Rule Number One—don't get knocked to the ground, especially from behind.

I woke up the morning after the assault with scrapes on my palms, a stiff back, stiff neck, sore shoulders...and that was when I stopped taking an inventory. The headache had dissipated, so that was good, but the eyes were still a touch sensitive to light. Lucky for me, clouds had moved in overnight, turning the sky into a dull shade of gray.

Not that I was going anywhere.

"Stay home and let your body heal." Mom slipped into a jacket before leaving for work. "Don't make me have your brother check on you."

"I'll be a good girl. Promise." It was true. My plan was to spend an hour on the phone with editors and then another hour e-mailing clients. Between early morning and late evening work, I'd managed to stay mostly caught up while in Rushing Creek. I needed to keep it that way. My clients deserved it.

When I was finished with my agent work, I turned my attention to the video files Jeanette had uploaded to the Dropbox site. They contained footage from surveillance cameras that had been installed around town over the last few years. Initially, the community had opposed the cameras and insisted their use be limited to the boulevard only. The attitude changed when a teenager from the next county over attempted a smash-and-grab at Brown County Jewelers. A camera mounted on a telephone pole down the street from the jewelry store recorded the entire incident. The perpetrator was caught and the stolen jewelry was recovered.

Since that time, eight more surveillance cameras had been installed. While most of them were found on the boulevard, a few were placed in strategic locations around town. I was interested in video from one of those cameras—the rear entrance to the Municipal Building. It was used by city employees so they could come and go from work without having to use the public entrance or take up parking spots in the front of the building.

It was grasping at straws, but I wanted to know when the mayor left work the night Thornwell died.

The black and white video was far from Hollywood quality and lacked audio, but it got the job done. With the Fast Forward function in use, I sped through the video as I snacked on a bowl of dried fruit.

At the 11:17 p.m. mark, Larry finally emerged from the building. The man was known for working late, especially in the weeks leading up to the Fall Festival, so his exit time didn't surprise me. What surprised me was his next move.

Instead of getting into the only vehicle in the parking lot, an enormous SUV, he walked alongside the building until he was out of the camera's field of vision. On a hunch, I switched to the file containing video from the front of the building and hit the jackpot. Okay, not exactly a jackpot, but I caught him crossing the parking lot, headed in a westerly direction.

Larry's home was northeast of the Municipal Building. Why was he going the other way? Was he going to Hoosiers for a drink? It didn't matter. What did matter was that he was out and about the night his most vocal critic died.

With the impatience of a five-year-old on Christmas morning waiting to for the green light to unwrap presents, I stared at the screen, waiting for his return. An hour went by, then two, until finally he returned to the camera's field of vision. I made a note of the time. It was 1:33 a.m.

I switched back to the other camera and watched in amazement as he went inside. Twenty minutes later, he came back out with a briefcase in hand, got into his car and drove out of the picture.

So, Mayor Larry Cannon, where were you for two and half hours the night Thornwell was killed? With only one way to find out, I took Larry up on his offer from the other day and called his office. Since I'd been attacked the night before, his assistant was more than willing to schedule a meeting. I suggested first thing in the morning and ended the call on an adrenaline high.

I was still sore from the waist up, but I was back on the hunt.

While I mulled over my next move, I popped into Dad's office. There was a stack of mail on his desk, which wasn't going anywhere unless I dealt with it. I scooped it up and settled into his recliner to go through the correspondence.

My highest priority was to see if any publishers had mailed royalty checks that needed to be deposited. The vast majority of people in the business moved funds electronically, but there were still a few small publishing houses who paid by mailing him a check.

I found three checks and made a note to deposit them into Dad's literary agency account tomorrow. I'd use the reports that accompanied the checks to identify the authors who were due royalties. I wasn't a math person by any stretch of the imagination, but I looked at processing royalty payments as proof my clients were living the dream. It was the least I could do for Dad's clients, too.

Next was a stack of letters from other agents. My heart ached as I opened the first one, as I assumed it was a notice that one of Dad's authors had formally changed agents. The letter was from Suzette Young, but it wasn't addressed to Dad.

It was addressed to Thornwell.

Confusion gave way to curiosity when I realized the letter was a copy of one Suzette had mailed to Thornwell. It was her offer to represent him as his literary agent and included language indicating Dad thought she was the ideal choice since she'd worked on two of Thornwell's books before she opened her own agency.

While I agreed with the logic, it was a moot point now. The letter gave me an idea, though. It was an opportune time to find out what, if anything, Suzette knew about Thornwell's murder. After all, she'd included her cell number in the letter.

We spent a few minutes on small talk before getting down to business. I needed information, so I asked her about the letter.

"It breaks my heart, Allie. Walter and I spent weeks trying to talk Thornwell into having me represent him, but he wouldn't budge. He said he wanted Walter to sell this secret project of his so they could publish one final book together."

And there was another comment about Thornwell's mystery book. Countless times, I'd overheard Dad talking to Thornwell about a book idea, but I never gave those conversations a second thought. What I'd give to be able to transport myself back in time so I could have been around to listen to a recent conversation between them to verify whether the stories were true or not. Without proof of a new story, it was tough to believe it existed. Still, hearing someone talk about it like it was something real was a blow to my heart.

"So, your encounter at the wake. I saw that." Despite the ugly scene that flashed before my eyes, I wanted to hear her response.

"A low point of my career. I thought I could talk sense into him, but I couldn't have been more wrong. God, that whole day was one nightmare after another." She sighed. "I'm sorry. That was thoughtless."

"Don't worry about it. Dad's in a better place." Time to make my move. "The party was still going strong when I left. How late did you stay?"

Suzette lived in Louisville, a two-hour drive from Rushing Creek. Matt didn't have a statement from her, so my guess was she was already out of town by the time Thornwell was found.

"A little after ten. I wish it would have been sooner. Daniel kept trying to bring up a manuscript he sent me. I didn't want to talk business after things went sour with Thornwell, but I couldn't refuse to listen. It would have been hypocritical. I didn't want to be that way the day we laid your father to rest."

"I saw Daniel yesterday. Said he can't leave town until Thornwell's killer is caught."

"I feel for him. When he first told me about his manuscript, I was so pleased at the thought of him finally moving out from under Thornwell's shadow."

"What did you think of his manuscript?" While there was some pain in talking about these issues, it also felt good to be talking business with another agent.

"It needs a lot of work. I saw Thornwell's influence in Daniel's writing, though." She chuckled. "Of course, there are those who are convinced Daniel ghost wrote the majority of Thornwell's books in the last decade, so who knows."

I'd heard the same rumors. When I asked Dad about them, he told me Thornwell presented them as his own, with the usual acknowledgment to Daniel for his research and fact checking efforts. If Daniel wrote them, Dad didn't know about it.

The rumors of Daniel's increasing involvement with Thornwell's books might help explain why Thornwell was keeping his new project a secret. If Dad was the only person who had seen it, nobody could claim Daniel wrote it or contributed to it in any way.

Suzette said she had to make a call, so we said our good-byes. I promised to let her know where Dad's remaining clients landed, and she promised to send me any manuscripts she thought would be a good fit for me.

She hadn't been on my suspect list before the call and definitely wasn't on it now. She had her own agency, with a robust client list, and didn't need Thornwell. My guess was she and Dad were convinced Thornwell still needed an agent, if for no other reason than to look after his backlist, the books he'd already published. It was a sizeable list, twenty-two books, and continued to generate steady income.

None of that added up to a reason for Suzette to want Thornwell dead. On the contrary, I could totally see how she would want him alive. She was a literary agent through and through, and Thornwell, flawed as he was, had been a vital voice in the world of books for thirty-five years. Suzette wouldn't want that voice silenced forever. I couldn't imagine anyone in the literary world who would. Which begged the question.

Who *did* want Thornwell's voice silenced forever?

The lack of an answer didn't get me down. The morning had been way too productive for that. And for some icing on the cake, since the doctor told me the headache might come and go for a while, I decided to take advantage of its absence and go for a walk.

I slipped my laptop in my bag, threw on my favorite Indiana University hooded sweatshirt and marched out the door with sunglasses on and Creekside Chocolates as my destination. My mouth started to water the instant the idea of one of Diane's delightfully decadent hot chocolates came to mind. I could settle in at the table by the window and prepare query materials to send to editors.

My hope was to build up enough body heat during the walk to loosen my achy shoulders and neck. It wasn't that I was opposed to taking pain medication. It had been a godsend in the hospital, but ibuprofen upset my stomach and I had a phobia that acetaminophen was going to ruin my liver.

Because of those issues, I was a naproxen sodium gal. The downside to taking it was that it hadn't had enough time to build up in my system to kill the pain, so, hopefully, good old-fashioned exercise would work out the kinks. And if that didn't work, there was always chocolate to soothe my soul.

The gray skies had cleared out, leaving puffy clouds to pass in front of the sun from time to time as I strolled down the boulevard. No alleys for me today. The merchants and store owners were busy as bees sprucing up for the upcoming tourist crush. I could track the movement of the clouds in the windows of the steakhouse, thanks to efforts of a window-washing crew.

The owner of the used bookstore, Renee Gomez, was creating a display of Thornwell's novels. I knew Renee. She was a kind woman who'd admired Dad, but adored Thornwell. I'd avoided the store, unable to find the strength to cross the threshold, knowing the tears that would burst forth when Renee inevitably hugged me. We'd chatted at the viewing and she understood. I'd come see her when I was up to it.

On a happier note, a young man and woman, in matching orange polo shirts, were hanging a Welcome, Leaf Peepers banner in front of the Greek restaurant. Even Ozzy was using a leaf blower to rid his storefront of sawdust. He stopped blowing it toward Soaps and Scents when I shouted "hi" and waved to him.

A little farther down, on the other side of the street, Maybelle Schuman was sitting on a bench in front of the Rushing Creek General Store. Basically, it was a glorified convenience store and pharmacy, but it also was home to an information booth run by the Visitor's Bureau, so Maybelle loved to hang out in front and greet folks from out of town.

My need for hot chocolate was bordering on an obsession, and I wasn't in the mood to chat, but since the retired teacher knew everybody and everything, I put my obsession on hold and went to visit her.

The most important thing to keep in mind when visiting with Maybelle was that you had to be prepared to set aside at least thirty minutes. First, we hugged, then I accepted her invitation to join her. She asked about the family and went on and on how wonderful Dad had been and how the town was better because of his contributions to it.

I smiled, thanked her and said all the right things when she asked about my family. She gave me an update on her health by complaining that Mom was being mean to her by telling her to cut down on her salt intake.

"Speaking of health, I hear you had a scare last night, young lady." She took hold of my head and twisted it so she could get a look at my stitches. After a few minutes of poking and prodding, she released me. "Could have been worse, I suppose. And you have no idea who did this?"

"No. I was hit from behind."

Maybelle was a Rushing Creek legend and was treated accordingly. Because of that, she spoke her mind, fearless of any consequences. Sometimes she could go a little too far with her opinions, like I sensed she was ready to do now.

"Allie Cobb, I thought you had more sense in that head of yours. I think it's perfectly obvious who attacked you." She pushed her glasses up her nose and gave a little *humph*.

Yeah. The same person who killed Thornwell. Instead of sharing my honest assessment, I drew inspiration from a decoration in front of a law firm down the street and went the sarcasm route. "It sure wasn't the Headless Horseman."

"Watch that sassy mouth, young lady. Just because I'm old doesn't mean I'm not deserving of respect."

"You're right. I'm sorry." If I wanted information, I needed to play her game. "You think Brent did it. Why?"

"He was working at the library and he's the one who 'found' you after you were attacked." She used her fingers to make quotation marks when she said found.

"Fair enough. Go on." How much Maybelle knew and how quickly she'd found out about it made my blood run cold. The rumor mill ran at warp speed when the topic was juicy. Like a violent attack on a woman was, evidently.

Did she know what my attacker said? I'd repeated the words to my family, Matt and Officer Abbott, who took my initial statement, but nobody else, so I was betting not. Unwilling to tip my hand, I wasn't going to tell her, either.

"I know you've been snooping around into Thornwell's death. Don't act surprised. Jax Michaels told me you paid him a visit and that you were rude to him. You need to apologize for that. Did you know that Brent Reynolds met with Thornwell a few weeks ago?"

"No. I didn't." I kept my expression neutral, but I couldn't deny it was odd that Brent had spent so much time with me the day before and never mentioned he knew Thornwell.

"Not surprising. I wouldn't want someone I'd just met finding out I got into a screaming match with the man who was murdered a few days ago. Would you?"

I tightened my grip on the bench until my fingers began to ache. As with any busybody, Maybelle thrived on gossip. If I showed anything beyond general curiosity, she'd turn into a great white shark and I'd be a helpless injured fish in its path.

"I suppose it would depend on what the cause of the shouting was. Maybe they had a disagreement over something historical. Brent's a genealogy expert, after all. You know how experts can be."

"Perhaps." If she caught the gist of my subtle jab, she didn't show it. "I have it on good authority that wasn't why your Mr. Brent got so angry. I heard he asked Thornwell for money and didn't take too kindly when he was turned down."

Maybelle painted an unflattering picture of Brent, but his program was based on grant funding. It wasn't unreasonable that he'd ask a prominent historical fiction author for financial help. But resorting to murder?

"So, you're suggesting Brent was so angry at Thornwell he killed him. Then he attacked me to scare me into giving up snooping around." Saying the words aloud made the scenario sound ludicrous, but Maybelle patted my hand and nodded like back in the day when I got a difficult math problem correct.

"Let me ask you this." She wrapped a liver-spotted hand around mine. "Keep in mind I'm asking for your own good. How well do you know this man? More to the point, do you really know anything about him?"

I swallowed as I tried to come up with a decent response, which I was unable to do. Facts were facts. I knew virtually nothing about Brent Reynolds.

Despite the man's warm smile, I added him to my growing list of suspects. God, I needed to solve this. And in a hurry.

Chapter Seventeen

It was time to extricate myself from Maybelle's clutches, but I couldn't simply say thanks for the chat and then walk away, so I asked her about her grandchildren.

She literally clapped her hands before digging into her quilted Vera Bradley purse. Instead of pulling out a wallet-sized photo album, like I expected, she withdrew a cell phone.

"Don't look so surprised. I've got a two-in-one Surface at home. You have to be tech savvy when you have family spread all across the country." She pulled up a photo of a smiling toddler in a blue dress and, before I knew it, I'd been updated on all five children, nine grandchildren and two great-grandchildren.

I was about to tell her I needed to go when a shadow crossed in front of us. It was Daniel coming out of the store.

"Daniel Godwin, you poor dear." Maybelle got to her feet and gave the man a hug. "How are you?" She patted him on the arm in a way only a grandmother could.

"I'm okay." He looked my way and his eyes went wide. "Allie, I heard a rumor about you. Is it true?"

"It's—"

"Every bit of it," Maybelle said. "In fact, Allie and I were just wrapping up. I'm off to the police station to demand Chief Roberson arrest that librarian."

"Come on, Maybelle." I joined them. "The chief has a lot on his plate right now. I'm sure he and everyone there are working as hard as possible."

Maybelle sniffed. "If that's the case, then why are you sticking your nose into things?"

"Ladies, it was lovely to see you both, but I need to run." He gave Maybelle a hug. "Off for a drive. Hoping it will clear my head." Daniel headed for a black sports coupe, his keys in one hand and a brown paper bag in the other.

The roads in Southern Indiana were full of twists, turns and climbs. Because of that, it was a haven for hard-core bicyclists, motorcyclists and auto enthusiasts. I wasn't a speed demon, but Rachel often talked about people who spent hours driving the local roads on the weekends and then ate dinner at the pub, raving about the thrilling time they had.

I gave Maybelle a hug and promised I'd tell Mom she was taking her high blood pressure meds. With my mind racing like a car at the Indy 500, I sprinted to catch up with Daniel and reached his car as he started the engine.

"Hey." I tried to catch my breath. "Do you mind if I visit you tomorrow? I'd like to talk to you about Thornwell."

He crossed his arms and it seemed as if his eyes misted up behind his glasses. "Of course. Any way I can help. I'm in room one oh seven at the inn. Give me a call before you come so I can make sure the place is tidy." He gave me his cell number as he slipped on a pair of driving gloves. Watching him drive away, I made a wish for him to enjoy his four-wheeled respite from the trials and tribulations in Rushing Creek. A respite was something we all could use.

With Maybelle headed north to the police station and Daniel headed south out of town, it was time to return to my mission.

Hot chocolate.

With school out for fall break, the chocolate shop was humming with action. Short-haired young men in blue and white Rushing Creek High School letter jackets hovered over the glass display case while they flirted with girls in formfitting skinny jeans who were ordering drinks.

Diane handed one of the girls a cup. "Mocha latte with a dash of spearmint. Which one of you gentlemen is paying for the lady's drink?"

After a moment's hesitation, a boy whose cheeks were as red as his hair handed her a few bills and followed the girl out the door.

"The rest of you young men would do well to follow his example." Diane prepared another drink. "We ladies deserve to be treated like queens, am I right?"

The remaining girls responded with an enthusiastic chorus of "Yeah" and "Preach it, girlfriend" as they gave the boys long, expectant looks.

With Diane busy, I wandered to an open table by the window. It was fast becoming my second favorite spot in Rushing Creek, after Dad's recliner. I could envision myself working from here while it snowed, while it rained and while the sun shone bright in the sky.

It was funny how I never got comfortable working in the myriad of coffee shops and diners in New York. The places were always too busy, with too much going on, for me to concentrate. Creekside Chocolates, on the other hand, exuded tranquility, even with a handful of hormone-controlled teenagers nearby.

Between the strong Wi-Fi signal, the cheerful paintings done by local artists displayed on the walls and the strategically placed lighting that provided the perfect amount of illumination for reading, this place was ideal for being productive outside the office.

I was compiling my list of editors to whom I was going to send the query materials when someone placed a hot chocolate with peppermint and whipped cream on the table.

"Hope I wasn't being presumptuous. Thanks for waiting while I took care of the kids." Diane rolled her eyes. "They're harmless, but they can be *so* slow."

She gestured at the open chair across from me. "May I?"

I closed my laptop, a habit learned from Mom's need to maintain patient confidentiality. A few colleagues called it overkill, but I considered it a small display of my commitment to my clients.

"Please do. To what do I owe the honor?" I took a sip of the hot chocolate and wiped some whipped cream from my upper lip with a laugh. "God, you are a magician with this stuff."

"I heard about last night."

I suppressed a growl. Diane was nice and I wanted to be friends, so I chose to believe she only had the best of intentions.

"Welcome to life in a small town, where your business is everybody's business, if it's juicy enough."

Diane traced a small circle with her index finger on the wood grain of the tabletop, humming a pleasant, but unfamiliar, melody as she did so.

"I'm new here, so I'm not going to insult you by pretending to know Rushing Creek like you do. What I will tell you is being an outsider has its benefits when you're willing to keep your mouth shut and your ears open."

The squeak of the front door being opened distracted her for a second. She relaxed back into her seat when a woman who looked to be about Mom's age greeted the incoming customers.

"I'm taking on some help to be ready for the weekend. Still getting used to not having to do everything myself." She dabbed at some whipped cream on her apron with a napkin. "Anyway, this is about you not me.

What I've heard today is that people are concerned about you. And they're rooting for you."

"Rooting for me? I know this town. People rooting for me is a little hard to believe." I let the urge to behave like a petulant teenager prevail. I'd learned the hard way growing up that your status in my beloved home town was largely determined by who you associated with in high school.

While being bookish had gotten me plenty of work, for which I was well paid, it didn't change the fact I wasn't athletic or pretty enough to hang out with the jocks and cheerleaders, artistically talented enough to perform in band or theater or self-destructive enough to chill with the stoners.

So, without a place to fit in, when the time came, I got out and didn't look back. No more would I live in Luke and Rachel's shadows. Nobody would ask me after I introduced myself if I was Luke or Rachel Cobb's little sister.

For the first time in my life, I was going to have my own identity. One that didn't have any comparisons to Luke's athletic achievements or Rachel's looks, as so often happened in small town Rushing Creek. As massive as New York was, it was a place where I could make my own mark and fill that place with so much light and goodness there would be no room for shadows.

Diane shook her head. "From what I can tell, you don't know this town as well as you think. You're quite the topic of conversation. The older folks say they're happy you're back and the younger ones, like that group of teenagers who were here when you walked in, they talk like you're one of the Avengers."

"That's crazy. I'm no hero. I'm the furthest thing from it."

"All I know is these people see one of their own returning home under the cloud of grief, and, the next thing they know, she's putting her life in danger to catch a killer."

I loved my family and I loved Sloane and a few other people like Mrs. Napier and Big Al. My relationship with the rest of the town was complicated at best. So, while my heart warmed at Diane's words, it was tough to put a lot of belief in them.

"It's not like that. You know that, right?"

"What I know is people are scared. I see it in the way they jerk to look over their shoulders when the door to the store opens. I see it in the way their eyes dart back and forth when they're talking in hushed tones. I see it in the way the police officers are joking less when they drop by.

"What I also know is that people have faith in you. They know you knew Mr. Winchester as well as anybody, so they take comfort in knowing you're helping the police."

I stared at my hot chocolate. A few remaining peppermint sprinkles danced on the surface of the drink. They were so tiny, and yet, seeing them defy science by refusing to be dissolved into the liquid made me proud of them.

"I'm just trying to follow through on a promise I made to my friend." I kept my focus on the sprinkles.

"Where I come from, a lot of people struggle to get by. They don't have a lot. When a friend makes a promise, that's a big deal, because, over the years, my part of Chicago has been on the receiving end of a lot of empty promises from the powers that be. We've learned the only people we can count on are friends and family. The people who won't make a promise unless they plan on fulfilling it."

"Don't take this the wrong way, Diane, because you make an amazing cup of hot chocolate." I took a drink to emphasize my point. "But I think you got into the wrong line of work. You should have been a preacher."

She laughed. It was light and friendly and symbolic of the person she was.

"My grandfather was a minister at the St. John A.M.E. Church on the south side of Chicago. I like to think I inherited a little of his gift of persuasion. My brother says I just like to hear the sound of my own voice.

"Break time's over." Diane got to her feet. "Do me a favor and think about what I said, okay? This town needs you. Now more than ever."

I nodded and looked out the window. A lump in my throat made it impossible to respond. People were coming and going along the boulevard. Fall Festival decorations were in place. It was a scene of small-town America at its best. And yet...

And yet, underneath the façade of wholesome Americana, there ran a current of worry, of unease. I didn't want to believe Diane, but once I gave it some thought, I couldn't deny she was right about the way people in town were acting.

Like she said, it was the subtle things, not unlike a manuscript I was assigned to read. On first glance, it might look like an instant bestseller, but when read with a careful, trained eye, the problems rose to the surface.

So, similar to when I needed to push a client to improve a manuscript so a publisher would want to buy it, it was time to return to the task at hand.

I texted Sloane to ask her to meet me at her father's house the following morning. I'd visited the crime scene but not the man's last known location.

Maybe, like the manuscript, I'd find something important by taking a close look around the place.

With a sigh, I drained my hot chocolate and went back to the document I'd been working on. I'd spend the next hour on it. Before I set a stop watch on my computer, I ordered another hot chocolate. I was still recovering from a head injury, after all.

When the timer pinged, I was pleased to find the query package almost ready to send to editors. Finishing it and sending it out before I called it a night would be a breeze.

I thanked Diane for the hot chocolate and, more importantly, for the pep talk. She waved it away, saying that was what friends were for and asked me for a book recommendation. Naturally, I recommended a debut novel from one of my clients. After all, I still had more than Rushing Creek to watch over.

* * * *

The back of my head was beginning to ache as I pushed open the door to the police department. Jeanette was at her desk and greeted me with wide eyes. I told her I was there to see her, not Matt.

"Oh. In that case, what can I do for you?"

I took the seat in front of her desk. "Did Maybelle pay you guys a visit earlier today?"

"I'm not supposed to comment about who may or may not have paid us a visit when official police business is involved." She nodded in a slow and deliberate fashion.

Taking my cue from Jeanette, I decided to keep my questions on the vague side.

"I've heard citizens have raised concerns that Brent Reynolds may have knowledge about my attack." She nodded again, so I kept going. "As the victim, can you tell me if Chief Roberson is acting on this information?"

Jeanette shuffled a few papers on her desk, as if she was buying time to decide how she wanted to answer. After a few seconds that felt like hours, she scratched the back of her hand. "There's a picnic table in the corner of the parking lot out back. Meet me there in ten minutes."

Caught off guard by her response, I rose on rubbery legs and took a circuitous route to the rendezvous point. All I wanted to know was whether or not Matt was taking Maybelle's claims seriously. And now Jeanette wanted to meet outside, away from security cameras and eavesdroppers. This couldn't be good.

I was catching up on my Instagram account when Jeanette took a seat across from me.

She looked around before speaking. "Sorry about the cloak-and-dagger efforts, but, to answer your question, Chief Roberson sent one of the officers to the library to have another chat with Brent. That's not why I wanted to talk out here, though."

"You're freaking me out." I shivered, and it wasn't because of the breeze rustling the leaves on the trees.

"I'm kind of freaked out by this, myself. I have a police scanner at home so I'm up to speed in case something happens after hours that I need to know about. I heard about last night. Then, when I got to the office this morning, I overheard the chief and the mayor talking. Basically, the mayor was trying to make a case that you're emotionally unbalanced and you might have made up last night's events."

I stared at Jeanette, unable to come to terms with what she'd told me.

"Let me get this straight. Larry thinks I hit myself on the head hard enough to knock myself out, while managing to get rid of the weapon used to hit me before passing out." I blinked and shook my head. "Wow. That's absurd. That's—"

"I know." Jeanette placed her palms face down on the table. Her neatly trimmed fingernails were painted a shade of blue that matched her uniform. "It's crazy. Trust me when I say Matt doesn't buy it, and neither do I. The mayor seems to have it in for you right now, so tread carefully."

"Interesting. Especially since I'm scheduled to meet with him tomorrow morning. Thanks for the heads-up."

"No problem." She glanced at her watch. "I gotta get back. Check your Dropbox tonight. If anything new comes up, I'll upload it before I leave work." She nodded and jogged back to the building, leaving me even more distressed than before.

Was the mayor truly trying to discredit me? If so, why?

As I walked back home, I pulled my hood over my head. While the sun was out, a breeze out of the north was gaining steam and making the temperature drop. I already had enough on my mind to make me shiver.

Chapter Eighteen

Despite a bizarre dream in which I grew a third arm and used it to knock myself out with an empty cup of hot chocolate, when the alarm went off the next day, I got right up instead of hitting the snooze button my customary three or four times.

My enthusiastic rise from slumber wasn't shared by Ursi, because she opened one eye, yawned and went right back to sleep.

"Go ahead, be a slug. I have places to go and people to meet. Big things are going to happen today. I can feel it."

Unimpressed with my pep talk, she rolled over and covered her eyes with a leg. That was the moment I decided if I was ever reincarnated, I wanted to come back as a house cat. A stress-free life of snoozing, eating and snoozing again had a definite appeal, especially given the events of the last week.

Who would have thought I'd experience more danger and emotional upheaval in a week back in my sleepy little hometown than in years living in The Big Apple? Not me, but, then again, if I'd learned anything since I returned home, it was to expect the unexpected.

Mom fussed over me while I ate breakfast, probing my stitches and using her evil penlight to check for lingering trauma. When I started whining, she shoved the device in her pocket.

"If you had stayed home yesterday like you promised, I wouldn't have to do this. But instead of letting yourself recover, you had to spend all day in the elements, traipsing all over town."

"Come on, Mom. It was down to the chocolate shop and back. And it wasn't like I was running around in the rain in a T-shirt and shorts."

"Good. Because you did that when you were eight and ended up in bed for a week with a case of pneumonia."

"It wasn't pneumonia. It was the flu. And the only reason I got sick was because I got it from Rachel." I gave Mom a long stare and, after a few seconds, used my finger to raise my eyebrow.

With a laugh, Mom sat. "Maybe you're right. You can't blame this latest episode on your sister, though. Speaking of which, she's coming over for dinner tonight. I expect you to be here, in one piece, so the three of us can have a nice evening together."

"Promise, Mom. I'm even going to take the car so I won't be late." I shoveled the remainder of my bagel with strawberry cream cheese into my mouth and opened my notebook. I wanted to be prepared for my visit with the Honorable Larry Cannon.

Which was good because when I arrived at his office, his assistant, a raven-haired woman wearing too much eye shadow, said he was running late and asked if I wanted to reschedule. With a smile, I declined and said I'd be happy to wait, since I knew he had a full schedule with the festival coming up. I wouldn't allow the man to throw me off balance by playing games.

The woman, who I think was a cousin of Matt's, pursed her lips and turned her attention to her computer. Each keystroke carried the force of a gunshot as I imagined her e-mailing Larry, who was undoubtedly in his office trying to outwait me.

I'd waited in offices before and could bide my time. Besides, I had an ace in the hole if he made me wait too long. When my wait reached ten minutes, I decided enough was enough and sent a text message to get things moving.

A couple of minutes later, Jeanette came in the room.

"Hi, Valerie. Is the mayor in? I have some festival-related things the chief wants him to see ASAP."

"He's tied up right now, but if you'd like to leave them with me, I'll be sure he gets them."

Jeanette grimaced, looked at the papers and shook her head. "The chief said I needed to hand them directly to the mayor. Sorry." Then she looked at the beige carpeting and shuffled her feet.

It was a Tony Award–winning performance. And Valerie bought it. She buzzed the mayor, who opened his office door right away.

"What's so important I have to take personal receipt—" He stopped dead in his tracks when his gaze landed on me. "Good morning, Ms. Cobb."

I inserted myself between Jeanette and the mayor and shook his hand. "Thank you for meeting with me. I know you're busy, so I won't take too much of your time." Without looking back, I strolled into his office and took a seat in one of the two leather visitor chairs.

With Jeanette's papers in his hand, he returned to the office and stood over me. I had no doubt his looming was an intimidation tactic.

I gave him my sweetest smile and opened my folder. "Why don't we get started. Would you like to close the door or shall I? I don't want to cause your next appointment to start late."

He shut the door, tossed Jeanette's papers on his desk and glared at me. "I'm very busy and don't have time for your games. What do you want?"

"I want to know where you were the night Thornwell Winchester was murdered."

"This is insane." He rubbed his temples. "Ms. Cobb, I know you're grieving for your father and you want to help your friend, but this has to stop."

"Please answer the question." I locked gazes with him.

A single bead of sweat appeared on his forehead. "Your mother's a doctor. I'm sure she can help you find a counselor or—"

"The question, please." I leaned back and looked at my watch. "I've got all day. Do you?"

"Fine. I was here in the office, working until two, I think. In case you haven't noticed, we have an important few days coming up."

"You were here all night? In this office?"

He gave a short nod.

When I asked him if he was sure, he nodded again.

"If you were here all night, then why did you leave the building about eleven thirty, headed east on foot and return, again on foot, from the same direction a couple of hours later?"

He steepled his fingers and stared at the rectangular ceiling tiles. A moment later, he leaned forward. "That's a serious accusation. It would be awfully embarrassing to make that in public and turn out to be wrong. I understand you think Winchester was murdered and you want to find the culprit. That doesn't mean you can go around making up wild accusations about innocent citizens."

"I have surveillance video to support my accusation, so I'm not worried about being wrong. Back to my question. Where were you?"

"Who do you think you are? You waltz into town and run roughshod over everyone, browbeating people into talking to you. Well, let me tell you something, Ms. Cobb. The next time you physically threaten a member of my community, you'll walk away in handcuffs. Do I make myself clear?"

"Crystal." I stood and smiled as his accidental confession registered with me. "You know something, Mayor? I've learned a lot over the last week and a half. I learned I was wrong about Chief Roberson. He's not the bully I thought he was. He's a decent man trying to do the best he can at his job. I was wrong about you, too. Everyone always told me Larry Cannon was charming and pleasant to be around. That's wrong, too. Because you're not pleasant to be around. You're a fraud. You're the bully."

"Are you quite finished or do I need to contact the chief and have him remove you?"

"Just one more thing. I know where you were the night Thornwell died." I tapped my chin with my index finger. "I suppose that leaves you with a moral dilemma, though. You can come clean with where you were, which will clear you of any suspicion of murder but make you face the fallout from your revelation. Or you can stay silent and run the risk of leaving the chief with no choice but to arrest you on suspicion of murder. That's your call, though. Thanks for your time, Mayor."

I left him sitting there, with his mouth open and sweat covering his brow. As I got in my car, I'll admit I wasn't one hundred percent certain where Larry had spent the time in question. I was certain who he'd spent it with, though.

Now the question was whether or not he had an accomplice to murder or an alibi. Either way, it looked like Rushing Creek's beloved mayor had a rocky road in front of him.

After letting Sloane know I'd be at Thornwell's in an hour, I sent Jeanette a text thanking her for her help and applauding her performance. She responded by telling me I could buy her a drink sometime, followed by a smiley face.

Smiley face, indeed. Hopefully I could keep the positive vibes going for the rest of the day.

My next stop was the diner for a morning snack and some additional sleuthing. I'd known Angela and Claude Miller, the diner's owners, all my life, as I'd gone to school with their kids.

In a way, it was like a morning version of Big Al's. It was open from six until three in the afternoon, offered bottomless servings of coffee and served breakfast all day. My personal favorite was the biscuits and gravy, with a side of fruit to maintain the illusion of balance in my diet.

As I took a seat at the counter, Angela brought me a glass of ice water and filled my coffee cup. She offered me her condolences about Dad and asked how Mom was doing. The diner made fabulous pies, so Mom always ordered a few for my family's Thanksgiving and Christmas dinners.

"She's back to work. I think seeing patients and knowing she's helping people is good for her."

"And how are you doing?" Angela placed her elbow on the counter. "And don't try to lie to me. I've known you too long for that." She winked. It was her classic move to let someone know she was teasing.

"I'm okay. I'll miss Dad, but he's in a better place now so that's all good. I'll feel better when Thornwell's killer is caught."

"Yeah. What a mess. If it wasn't for the Fall Festival, it would be the only thing people were talking about." She shook her head. "I'm not going to lie, the man wasn't exactly my favorite customer, but I feel awful for his daughter. I wish there was something I could do."

"Actually, there is. You can answer some questions for me."

A customer at the other end of the counter asked for a coffee refill, so Angela took my order, one egg and a side of bacon since I'd already had breakfast, and promised to be right back. I was scrolling through messages on my phone when someone took the stool next to me. I let out a long sigh and told myself to avoid making eye contact with the person.

Despite my pledge, my curiosity got the best of me, and I chanced a peek at the intruder. Luke.

"Was wondering how long it was going to take to get your eyes off that phone." He gave me a gentle elbow to my upper arm. "Did that blow to your head knock any sense into you?" My brother, ever the thoughtful sibling.

I elbowed him back. "I'm seeing your girlfriend later. If I find out you're not being nice to her, I will rain blows down upon your head with the vengeance of all of the Amazons of Themyscira." Even though he was a foot taller than me, he was no match for my verbal jousting skills.

"Fair enough, Wonder Woman." He leaned in close and looked around. "Between you and me, the guys at work have a couple of pools going. One's for Thornwell's killer, the other is who gets the collar first, you or Matt."

"Gets the collar? Really? God, you guys need to get lives and stop watching so many cop shows." I took a drink of my coffee as I resigned myself to the fact I'd regret asking my next question and, therefore, dignify the juvenile behavior. "What's your money on?"

Angela brought me my order and poured a to-go cup of coffee for Luke. He said thanks as he handed her a couple of dollars.

When she was gone, he gave me a devilish smile. "I think it's Charissa. The spurned girlfriend thing. Matt will catch her, since I'm sure she's going to be giving you a wide berth. No offense." He gave me a peck on the cheek and made for the door. "Tell Sloanie I said hi."

"Is your brother ever going to grow up?" Angela asked as I started in on my egg.

"If growing up means breaking up with Sloane, I hope not. They seem to be good for each other. I'd like to think it's helped that they've got each other these days."

Until that moment, I hadn't given any thought to the fact they had someone to lean on during these difficult times. Mom and Rachel had each other. Luke and Sloane had each other. Sure, I was trying to help Sloane, but, in a few more days, my bereavement leave would be up and I'd be on a plane back to New York.

Who did that leave for me? Lance? Yeah, no. His unresponsiveness over the last week, and really the last month, made his interest, or lack thereof, clear. I was finished with that chapter of my life. Ursi? I loved my rescue kitty with all my heart, but she was still a cat and couldn't provide me with the support another human could.

That left me alone. Isolated. With nobody to depend upon, except myself. That was okay. For now, I'd use the investigation to prop myself up. I'd been on my own for over a decade, when you included college, so I could handle this.

And when the investigation concluded? I'd start that chapter when I arrived at it.

Angela shook her head. "Luke Cobb and Sloane Winchester. That's a pair I never thought I'd see. Anyway, you said you wanted to ask me a question."

"Right." I recounted what Maybelle told me about the alleged argument between Thornwell and Brent. "Didn't happen to see it, did you?"

"Did I see it?" Angela smiled wide. "For a minute, I thought I was going to have to go to the car to get my referee's whistle." It took me a minute to remember she was a high school sports official and the girls' volleyball season was in full swing.

"What happened?" There was no dispute Thornwell was a difficult person who made the lives of those around him more challenging. Brent seemed too levelheaded to get into a horrible argument, especially in public. The equation didn't add up.

"It was shock enough to see Thornwell walk in. I think the only other times he came here without Sloane were to meet your father. Anyway, it was late enough that the early crowd had dwindled, but the lunch group hadn't arrived yet. Almost as if he picked the time to be around as few people as possible."

"That sounds like him."

"But the odd thing was he was clear-eyed and friendly when I brought him a menu. He wasn't the surly Thornwell I was used to."

"A different man." It sounded like the new and improved Thornwell from Mom's and Sloane's reports.

"Right? Anyway, the guy from the library comes in. He's wearing a suit and is sweating like he's about to go in front of his lord and maker to make his case for eternal salvation. He joins Thornwell and things seem fine when I take their orders. Everything goes south after they finish their breakfasts.

"First, they get loud. Then Thornwell slams his fist on the table and starts complaining about not wanting to be taken advantage of. Thornwell gets up to leave and Brent grabs his arm. That's when Thornwell snaps. He tries to take a swing at Brent and yells at the top of his lungs, 'Leave me in peace, you monstrous cretin.'"

I scratched my head. There was no need to ask Angela if she was certain about the quote. The words had Thornwell written all over them. "And then what?"

"By the time I got to them, Brent was on his feet but still hadn't let go. I got between them, and Thornwell stormed out. Brent tried to get around me, but I told him he wasn't leaving without paying the bill. He threw a twenty in my face and took off."

"Wow. I expected a story like that to come out of Hoosiers, not a breakfast diner." It didn't sound good, but it didn't sound like there was a motive for murder there, either. "Do you remember anything else?"

"I'll give Brent credit. He came by the next day, apologized and bought everybody a piece of pie. Haven't seen him since."

I was stumped. Not for the first time, a Maybelle Schumann story turned out to be much bigger than the real thing.

"Any idea what Brent wanted?"

She shook her head. "A few people who were here at the time thought he was asking Thornwell for money. There's a rumor his genealogy project is running low on cash. I don't know if that's true or not, so take it for what it's worth."

"I will. Thanks." I leaned over the counter and gave Angela a hug. "I appreciate the info, too."

When I reached into my purse, she took hold of my hand. "This one's on the house. I appreciate what you're doing. A lot of us in town do. Promise me you'll be careful, all right?"

"That's one thing I intend to do." I promised to visit soon to get a piece of pumpkin pie and headed out the door.

On the drive to Thornwell's house, I worked through what Angela told me. Was Brent's genealogy project being funded by grant money? Yes. He told me that. Was it possible for the program to run into money problems? Yes, the funding could have been cut or there might have been cost overruns.

Did it make sense to approach Thornwell to request additional project funding? Yes and no. I could see someone running a genealogy project asking an author of historical fiction for help. There was the mutual focus on the past and the potential for both parties to benefit from the arrangement. A wider public awareness of and access to genealogy resources could lead to increased interest in Thornwell's novels. On the other hand, the author wasn't known for his generosity. Brent might not have not been aware of that key fact. And that lack of awareness provided the perfect setup for a debacle of epic proportions.

Still, where was the motive? As I waited for a tour bus to cross an intersection, the two motives I came up with were embarrassment and desperation. Embarrassment made no sense at all. Shoot, Brent had returned the next day and apologized to Angela.

Desperation had a touch of plausibility, though. I liked Brent. He was nice and cute, in a librarian sort of way. I was comfortable around him and wanted to believe he was a good guy. But I couldn't deny the possibility that, with his life's work on life support and, having been turned down by possibly his final option, desperation might have led to murder.

With a sinking heart, I motored through the now-clear intersection. I owed it to Sloane not to let my feelings get in the way of facts. And the fact was, I couldn't rule out Brent as a suspect. When I pulled into the driveway at Thornwell's house, I sent a text to Jeanette asking for any information she could share about Brent's past.

If my new library friend had a violent streak, I needed to know.

Chapter Nineteen

I punched a four-digit code into the security keypad and studied the gate as it swung open. The ornate design featured black, wrought iron grapevines that met in the middle to form a script W in bronze. In the past, the design had barely registered on my consciousness. Today, the vines reminded me of snakes. Creepy.

The brakes of my rental squeaked as I rolled to a stop next to Sloane's car, which was parked in front of the three-car garage. Yellow police tape across the front door mocked me, a harsh reminder Thornwell's murderer was still at large. My work was far from over.

Sloane was behind the house, seated on the four-foot-high rock wall that separated the patio from the lawn. My athletic shoes made a quiet brushing sound as I made my way across the patio's flagstone surface. Her solitude broken, she looked over her shoulder and gave me a sad smile.

I boosted myself to sit next to her. The breeze whistling through the still-green sugar maples provided a soothing backdrop to our meditations. We sat in silence, Sloane content to keep her thoughts to herself and me unsure what to say, or if I should anything at all.

After a while, Sloane rubbed her arms, whether to ward off a literal or figurative chill enveloping her, I wasn't sure.

"Can you believe they put that tape on the front door?" She ran her palms up and down her thighs. "They didn't even find him here, but they've searched the house twice. I feel like they're trying to keep me away."

"Not you. Other people. Troublemakers and gossips." Thornwell's house had come up in conversation while I was at the hospital. The police had searched it as part of the investigation, but hadn't found anything of note. They'd decided to leave the tape in place as a precaution, in the hope another visit would be the result of a break in the case.

Matt didn't know we were here as I'd chosen not to ask permission. I figured if I had to, I'd go the beg-for-forgiveness route. Plus, I was doing him a favor. I could guide Sloane through the house as we looked for anything that was out of place in a way that would keep her focused and cooperative. The esteemed officers of the Rushing Creek PD simply didn't know her like I did and wouldn't be able to get the same level of engagement out of her.

At least, that was my hope.

"I suppose we should get to it." Sloane launched herself from the wall and landed on her feet with the kind of grace and surefootedness that would make an Olympic gymnast proud. "The sooner we start, the sooner we finish, right?"

"Pretty much." I pushed off from my perch, contacted the ground with my tiptoes and came to a standing position with a minimum of wasted effort.

"Nice." Sloane gave me a high five. "Good to see the kickboxing's keeping you sharp." She pulled a scrunchie from her ponytail, ran her fingers through her hair and put the scrunchie back in place. "How are we going to do this?"

Honestly, I had no idea, but I was determined to be strong for Sloane and Thornwell. And for Dad, too. The men had worked together for so long, they acted more like brothers than business associates. If not for Dad, Thornwell would have become a history teacher instead of a bestselling author. If not for Thornwell, my dad would have become a sales rep instead of a literary agent.

History teacher and sales rep, both great and honorable professions, but professions I knew in my gut would have left both men unhappy and unfulfilled. As Sloane got out her key to open the side door, I recognized the flaw in my argument. If writing made Thornwell happy, why was he such a miserable and abusive drunk? As sure as the Lego Supergirl on Sloane's keychain made me chuckle, I didn't have the answer to that question.

What I did have was hope. Hope that visiting the house might help me find a clue to lead me to Thornwell's murderer. Hope that the old psychological wounds inflicted on Sloane, which would be reopened once we crossed the threshold, would one day begin to heal. Hope that my best friend might find some answers to questions she had but could only ask of her father's ghost.

Hope that the town of Rushing Creek, my hometown, would come out of this traumatic experience of losing two of its own, better for it. Hope that the sores I was picking at would get better and the secrets I was unearthing would give way to a more honest and trusting community.

Big hopes for one person to have. Especially since that one person left Rushing Creek at eighteen with no intention of returning for anything beyond summer jobs in college and family matters. As the saying went, times changed and people did, too. Obviously, I wasn't exempt.

"Allie? Hey." Sloane snapped her fingers a few inches away from my eyes. "Still with me?"

"Yeah. Sorry about that. How are we going to do this? One step at a time, my friend." I put my arm around Sloane as she unlocked the door and pushed it open. A musty smell greeted us, no doubt a symptom of the house being closed up for a week.

I dug a pen out of my purse and used it to flip on the light switch. It revealed a kitchen in need of some tidying. A few crusty plates and utensils were in the sink, still waiting to be put in the dishwasher. A ceramic coffee cup had been left on the near end of a granite-topped island. A stack of unopened mail was at the other end.

Using a flashlight I got from the utility drawer in Mom's kitchen, I gave the coffee cup a close inspection, including a sniff. "No lingering coffee smell, but it looks like there's some discoloration at the bottom."

"Probably green tea." Sloane pointed to a box of tea bags by the microwave. "It's one of the things he changed after your dad got sick. I guess he thought since your dad started drinking it, he should try it."

I nodded and stifled a comment about how unfortunate it was that the health benefits of green tea didn't help either of them. *Keep it positive, Allie. Focus on why you're here.*

A peek in the refrigerator eased my mind. There was no milk or anything else expired, but I made a note to ask Matt if I could clear out the contents before anything went bad.

"Before we go any farther, did you come in when you dropped Thornwell off?" I didn't want to spend any more time in the house than necessary and was hoping Sloane could help figure out what rooms, if any, we could bypass.

"Yeah. We came in and I followed him to his office. We talked for a while. He knew I was mad at him, but it was different this time." She leaned against the island and sniffed.

"How so?" I'd gone over Matt's notes of his interview with her the night before. According to the notes, it had been a quick in and out on Sloane's part, so her comment surprised me.

"I couldn't tell you how many times over the years I've gotten a call from your sister at the pub or someone at Hoosiers with the same story. Your dad's too drunk to drive. Will you come get him? Being the dutiful daughter, I always did, and when we'd get back here, he'd say the most awful things about how I was disloyal and an embarrassment and only stuck around town because I was after his money."

She wiped her cheek with the heel of her palm and stared out the window that overlooked the sink.

"He'd been quiet all the way home and didn't say a word until he plopped down onto his couch. Then he looked at me with tears in his eyes and said he was sorry. I told him not to worry about it and went to go, but he grabbed my hand and asked me to sit with him."

As Sloane talked, she continued to peer out the window, as if it was easier to tell me what happened if she didn't have to look at me.

"And then, and then," she sniffed, "he begged me to forgive him. He said your dad's death was too tough to bear, so he made the mistake of trying to console himself by having too much to drink instead of talking about how he felt. As we sat there, as drunk as he was, he knew he'd made a mistake and promised to make it up to me." She lowered her head and her shoulders began to tremble.

"I'm so sorry, Sloane." I put my arm around her and held her, wishing simple physical contact would take away her pain.

"He said for the first time in years, he was looking forward to the future. This project he claimed he had going on with your dad had him excited. He and Mom were making progress, and he wanted to spend the next thirty years being the best father he could be. He was going to spend every day trying to make up for being such a crappy father the last thirty years."

"He said crappy?" It was an attempt at humor, which worked, since Sloane laughed.

"I believe the word he used was abhorrent." She mimicked her father's low-pitched voice and bobbed her head side to side, which got me laughing.

"That's the Thornwell Winchester I knew. Never used a nickel word when a ten-dollar word would do." I gave Sloane a quick squeeze. "I'm sorry you guys won't have that time together."

"Me, too." She went to the stack of mail and flipped through it. "At least I got to see and feel what it was like to have a real father, like your dad, even if it was only for the last year. He was becoming a good man again, Allie. He didn't deserve to die. And after struggling with the monster for as long as I remember, I didn't deserve to have him taken from me just when we were moving in the right direction."

I couldn't agree more with Sloane on that point.

To continue our search, we walked to the front room. It was actually a formal dining room. The Winchesters had used it when Sloane and I were younger to entertain guests during the holidays and when Thornwell published a new book. As we got older, the room was used less often until it was abandoned after Kathryn moved out.

"Dad never came in here, but I thought we could start here and work our way back to the kitchen then head upstairs if you want to. There's not much to see up there, though."

I made a lap around the rectangular oak table in the middle of the room. The surface was dull from accumulated dust. The eight matching chairs had the same dull gray sheen to them. Evidently, the new Thornwell hadn't yet discovered the joys of dusting.

A china cabinet made of the same oak as the table and chairs was a lonely sentry at the far end of the room. The top half of the cabinet displayed a familiar set of Wedgwood china. Each plate featured a sterling silver band around the edge. A script W, in a similar style as the W in the gate, was centered on each plate. All of the pieces were in place. I had a feeling they hadn't been out of the cabinet in a decade.

I used the pen to open the cabinet underneath the display case. It was almost empty. There was a sterling silver set of dining utensils for eight, along with matching linen placemats and napkins, but nothing else. The storage area smelled vaguely of candles, but none were to be found.

"Nothing helpful here." I stood and, in response to a soft rumbling noise, went to the front window. A car was coming up the drive. "Shoot, we've got company."

Sloane joined me at the window. "That's Mom." She did a face palm. "Sorry, forgot to tell you. She offered to help us look through stuff since they'd been seeing each other again."

As crazy as the past week had been, the most insane thing outside of murder was the thought of Thornwell and Kathryn Winchester reconciling. Yet, I couldn't deny what I saw at the pub. And now she was coming to help us.

Sometimes the world was a really strange place.

We met Kathryn in the kitchen. She gave Sloane a hug and surprised me by giving me one as well. Like Sloane, her hair was a dark brown, though I suspected the coloring was more a product from a bottle than the result of kind genetics. As she took my hands in hers to give me a long look, I noticed the ring finger on her left hand was bare. If nothing else, she wasn't attempting some grieving widow gambit to gain sympathy.

"I'm sorry we continue to meet under such difficult circumstances. When Sloane told me the two of you were going to go through his things, I wanted to help, so here I am. What can I do?"

With Kathryn providing assistance, we made quick work of the living room, bathroom, utility room and guest bedroom. All that was left on the first floor was Thornwell's study. While I'd told Sloane and Kathryn I wanted to save that room for last because I thought we'd spend the most time there, the fact was I was scared of the room.

Thornwell's study had been his refuge, a sanctuary Sloane and I were forbidden from entering. It was where he'd brought the past to life through his novels. Some of his books, especially early in his career, had been brilliant, on par with James Michener and Larry McMurtry. His later work sold well but didn't receive the critical acclaim his previous novels did.

Some blamed the alcohol for the perceived slip in quality in Thornwell's books. Dad said he was a victim of his early success. It would have been impossible for him to maintain the brilliance of his early career. Others said Thornwell got lazy. He had the money. He had the fame. He didn't need to continue to work, but he did it for the paycheck.

As I put my hand around the ornate brass doorknob to the study, it was my hope answers would be found within.

Chapter Twenty

I took a deep breath and, for the first time in my life, stepped into the bestselling author's study. While the rest of the first floor was sparsely appointed, the study was cozy, with a warm, lived-in feel. A lush, royal blue area rug with an intricate military pattern covered most of the room's hardwood floor. The couch Sloane'd mentioned was placed against the wall to my right. Coordinating end table and lamp ensembles bookended the couch.

A double window was in the center of the wall opposite from me. Dark wooden bookcases, overflowing with tomes of all sizes, flanked the window. Thornwell's work area was to my left. In keeping with the theme, the desk was made of the same materials as the bookcases and even included a classic style banker's lamp, complete with green glass shade.

Artwork hanging from the sand-colored walls evoked scenes from Thornwell's books. One painting depicted a Native American village complete with the rounded wigwams of the Miami, one of the tribes who called Indiana home. Another was a rendering of a young Abe Lincoln, who lived in Indiana from the age of seven to twenty-one.

Among the dozen framed photos on the wall behind the desk was a black-and-white shot of Rushing Creek, no doubt taken from the bridge. The photo was as haunting as it was beautiful, and I had to look away.

Was Thornwell already dead by the time his body washed up on shore? Did he feel anything as his lungs filled with water? Why did he have to die? Why?

I shook away the haunting questions with a silent admonition to keep my emotions in check and went back to studying the room. The laptop computer on the desk and the laser jet printer on a stand adjacent to it were jarring in their refusal to conform to the room's classic ambiance. A small stack of paper was still in the printer's feeder tray.

"Do either of you mind?" I pointed at the printer.

When they said no, I looked at the pages. While I didn't recognize the story, in an instant I could tell the work was Thornwell's.

And it was good.

I offered the material to Kathryn. "Any idea if this was part of his secret project?"

"No." She passed it to Sloane, who shook her head. "It really is heartbreaking. He'd come so far. It had been such a joy to see the man I once knew and fell in love with."

Kathryn sat on the couch. "It was July fourth weekend of last year when, out of the blue, he called me. He said he'd quit drinking and now that he was clearheaded, he wanted to apologize for being such a reprobate during our marriage and in the years since."

As she talked, I slipped between the desk and the chair. The laptop was open, but the screen was dark. No surprise there. I tapped the space bar twice and got no response, so it wasn't merely asleep.

I looked from the laptop screen to the couch to find Sloane had joined her mother. There was no handholding, but at least they were sitting next to each other. It was a shocking sight from a pair that in recent years had barely been able to speak to each other without getting into a shouting match.

Could Thornwell's death be the catalyst for a reconciliation? Maybe someday down the road. The strong emotions swirling around the room would calm down once we finished our work here and went our separate ways, so who knew. On top of that, I didn't trust Kathryn. I hadn't gotten my hands on a will, so I reminded myself to be wary around the woman until that issue was resolved.

Still, it was uplifting to see mother and daughter seated in such close proximity.

"So, Kathryn," I took a peek at the contents of the desk drawer, "do you think Thornwell was really working on something new?"

"No doubt about it. Whether or not this," she waved the papers at me, "was part of it, I have no idea. As things got better between us, he opened up about a lot of things, but all he would say about his new project was he was as excited about it as he was frightened of what people would think of it."

Interesting. In the past, when people described Thornwell Winchester, they used words like arrogant and pompous. They never used words like humble or modest. And yet, I'd gotten the same story time and time again. The man had changed for the better. It was beyond doubt.

He'd been working on reconciling with his ex-wife. He'd taken steps to repair his damaged relationship with his daughter. He was writing, but without help from anybody, even Daniel. It was like Thornwell had become a real-life version of Ebenezer Scrooge.

As for the drunken episode the day of Dad's funeral? I was ready to chalk it up to grief at losing his best friend and business partner.

Which begged the question, why would someone want to kill him now?

"Is anything missing?" I went to the bookshelves. What appeared to be a haphazard mess at first look became an intriguing method of organization on closer examination. Books were grouped by subject matter and then alphabetical order by author's last name.

Sloane joined me as we searched for signs that something might be out of place.

After a while, she threw up her hands in surrender. "If there is, I can't tell. Mom?"

Kathryn was going through a two-drawer filing cabinet in a corner. She straightened up and scanned the room, chewing on the tip of her thumb as she did so. After a while, she let her hands fall to her side. "I wish I knew. He was so organized. He always knew where everything was."

"Do you know if he had a will?" I hated myself for asking, but I needed to know. The man was rumored to be worth a fortune, and people often talked about how money was a prime reason for murder.

"He did." Kathryn's jaw was clenched. "During the divorce he told me he was writing me out of it and was leaving everything to Sloane."

"I didn't ask for that, Mom." Sloane's voice cracked. "I'd gladly give it all away if that meant you and Dad were getting along again."

"Do you think I wanted a divorce? I put up with your father's abuse as long as I could. Longer than I should have. I always hoped someday the sweet, thoughtful man I fell in love with would find his way back to the surface. I never thought it would happen. But it did. And now look at us. Going through his things like vultures picking at a dead carcass."

Silence hung over us like a dark cloud until Sloane, with tears in her eyes, hugged Kathryn. Where my friend's relationship with her father had been dysfunctional at best, her relationship with her mother over the last dozen years had been poisonous, with claims of abandonment, betrayal and manipulation thrown back and forth.

Now, here was Sloane, extending an olive branch.

"No, Mom. We're here to help Allie find justice for Dad. You're totally right that he put us through hell for years, but you know better than anyone how much he'd turned his life around. I wish I could have had more time with him sober because the times we had together in recent months were good, and getting better."

"He loved you, Sloane. He was so proud of your running. He didn't understand it, but he admired how hard you worked and how you tried to forge your own way instead of coming to him for help."

Sloane leaned against the desk. "Dad was proud of me? I never knew."

"He said he wanted to fix things with us both. It was his hope that if he and I could reconcile, it might be easier to do the same with you."

Kathryn wrapped her arms around herself, the unease at which she found herself in such a vulnerable position was obvious. It seemed like a good time to allow my best friend and her mother some time alone.

"I'm going to head upstairs to have a look around. The two of you know this room better than me. I'll check back with you in a bit," I said.

As I made my way up the carpeted stairs, I heard them talking but couldn't make out what they were saying. It was just as well. If they were going to solve their issues for the long-term, they would have to work together. It wasn't something I could force.

It was something I could encourage, though. Today seemed like a first step. Sure, it was as tentative as a baby learning to walk, but if that was what it took, I'd do all I could to stand close by, ready to catch them if they fell.

At the top of the stairs, I took a break to gather my thoughts. I needed to get my focus back on the reason I was here. The first door I opened was to Sloane's old bedroom. I don't know what I expected to find, maybe her old twin bed and chest of drawers, but the room being empty wasn't it. Except for a few dust bunnies in a corner, the walk-in closet was just as devoid of furnishings.

The scene was off kilter and brought back into focus Thornwell's will. The situation there was every bit as unsettling. If Thornwell was going to leave his entire fortune to his daughter, with whom he was trying to reconnect, why would he erase all evidence of her living here? I'd have to ask Sloane what the deal was.

On the other hand, there was definitely financial motivation on Kathryn's part to reunite with her ex-husband. If her story was true, then so be it.

But what if she was using Thornwell's olive branch as a way to go straight to his bank account? They'd seemed pretty lovey-dovey when I observed them the other night. Was it possible she'd been playing the man and had gotten the will changed sometime over the last year? Who would know?

As I closed the door on Sloane's empty room, I set myself a reminder on my phone to look into the will issue.

The next room was Sloane's old bathroom. Again, it was devoid of any evidence of recent use. Even the toilet paper holder was empty. With growing curiosity, I removed the lid to the toilet tank. It was empty. When I opened the sink's cold water faucet, nothing came out.

He'd shut off the water, but why? Had he really become so secluded over time that he thought nobody would ever use the bathroom up here? Or was it simply a matter that maintenance was easier with the water turned off?

The rest of the upstairs rooms told the same story. Even the master bedroom was empty. As I went back down the stairs, the emptiness, the erasure of so many memories bothered me. And hurt a little, too. I'd spent too many sleepovers in Sloane's room to count, but there was no evidence of any of that history. What did it say about Thornwell?

Then a thought popped into my head. Mom said Thornwell fired Jax Michaels for billing for work that was never done. Was the emptiness related to Jax's termination in some way? Jax was a handyman with access to countless tools. It wasn't hard to imagine a wrench or some other heavy tool being used to kill one person and knock another person unconscious.

I stopped midway down the stairs as another question hit home. What did my upset feelings say about me? I couldn't deny it was another symptom of the tug my hometown was having on me. The old ties I thought I'd broken forever were reforming, but in a different way. When I left Rushing Creek, it felt as if I was throwing off iron shackles that had weighed me down. Now, it was as if I was being handed a life preserver and, with it, being asked to return home to be there to help those in need.

My hometown needed me.

Was it true? Or was it a figment of my imagination, a product of days spent under heavy emotional stress? I decided I was being overly dramatic, so I'd simply ask what was up with the second floor.

Sloane and Kathryn weren't in the study when I got back downstairs. "Hey, Sloane? I've got a—"

"Allie, come here, quick!"

Sloane's excited shout had me down the hall and in the kitchen in record time. Before I could say anything, she made a little leap into the air.

"We found something. It's gotta be important."

Chapter Twenty-One

I scanned the kitchen, making a three-hundred-sixty-degree turn in the process. Nothing appeared different from a few hours ago when Sloane and I started our inspection.

"What? I don't see anything."

"That's because we didn't know where to look." Sloane grabbed my hand and pointed at a wall-mounted mail rack and key holder by the door.

As she pulled me toward it, Kathryn was taking pictures of the fixture with her phone.

"Okay, Mom, tell Allie what you noticed." Excitement radiated off Sloane with the intensity of ten suns.

I still didn't see anything out of the ordinary, but, based on Sloane's reaction, whatever it was, it was big.

Kathryn stepped up to the rack and ran her finger below the four hooks hanging from the lower section. Three of the four hooks had keys hanging from them. The one on the far right was empty.

"Let me give you some background. Like I said earlier, as long as I've known Thornwell," she paused for a few seconds, "I knew Thornwell, he was always organized. Even when the drinking was at its worst, he always knew where his wallet was, his keys were and where he stored his computer passwords. He liked to joke that every author he knew had a touch of obsessive compulsive behavior. This key rack was exhibit A that it applied to him, too.

"This first hook is where he kept his car keys." Kathryn pointed to the one on the far left.

A simple, circular key chain that held a car key and two house keys hung from it. "It was easiest for him to grab his keys from this hook going out the door and easiest to replace them coming back inside."

It made sense. Back in New York, I didn't have a car, but I still had keys to my building, apartment and office. I always left them in a little ceramic bowl on a stand by the front door.

She gestured to the next hook, from which four keys were dangling. "These are spares for the house and the garage. One extra set was never enough. He always wanted two, especially when Sloane got old enough to need a key."

Sloane rubbed her forehead. "I remember one time I lost my house key. Dad was livid. Had a locksmith out the next day to rekey the place."

Kathryn took Sloane's hand in hers and gave it a gentle squeeze. The number of traumatic experiences they shared was beyond my comprehension. For today, at least, they seemed to be able to draw on those awful times for strength. I hoped today's positive moments would last and grow.

"This third hook should be empty." Instead a single house key hung from it. "This is where I used to hang my keys. I think you can imagine why he wanted to keep the hook empty after I left."

"Any idea what that key goes to?" A million possibilities ran through my mind in a flash. I crossed my fingers, hoping this was the break I'd been looking for.

"Oh yeah," Sloane said. "My apartment."

I turned to her, forcing myself to keep my jaw from dropping to the floor. "Does this mean what I think it means?"

"Dad's had a key to my apartment for years. I think it made him feel better. That he could help if I ever lost my key. It always hung from the last hook, not where it is now."

My mind broke into a full-out gallop as I tried to envision the list of suspects Sloane and I made a few days ago. Thornwell's killer had to be on that list. I didn't just know it. I felt it in my bones.

"Have either of you touched the key?" When they both said no, I got out my phone. "Matt needs to know about this."

While I left a voice mail message, Sloane told Kathryn about the credit card statement. The older woman had to lean against the island at the news. I felt for her. To find out the same person who murdered your ex-husband had also broken into your daughter's home had to be overwhelming.

"Let me get this straight," Kathryn said when I disconnected from the call. "The two of you think someone took that key, snuck into Sloane's apartment, swiped one of her credit card statements and planted the statement on Thornwell the night he died. Seems like a stretch, doesn't it?"

Okay, when someone said it out loud, it did sound crazy, but it was the best theory I had and I wasn't going to give up on it.

"I won't argue with you on that," I said. "But I also think it helps us narrow our suspects. If I'm right, whoever killed Thornwell planned it. This wasn't a crime of passion."

Sloane let out a quick laugh. "Sorry, but I never thought I'd ever hear you use the term crime of passion in real life. I guess the stress is getting to me."

My ringtone went off. It was Matt. "Why are you in Winchester's house? That's still a crime scene."

"Then you should have taped off more than just the front door. Are you on your way?"

"Getting in my car now. Nobody leaves until I get there." He ended the call as the engine roared to life in the background. Matt's interest was gratifying and justified my choice to check things out without asking.

While we waited, I asked Kathryn if she knew why the upstairs was so barren.

"Last winter, some shingles got blown off the roof in a storm. Jax was supposed to replace them. The roof started leaking and caused a lot of damage up there. When Thornwell found out the shingles hadn't been replaced properly, he fired Jax. He had everything moved to temporary storage for the repair work. He'd planned to have everything moved back, but…" She took a seat on one of the island stools. "I wish there was something more I could do to help."

"What you just told me is a huge help. There is one more thing you can help with." I asked her if she could help me access Thornwell's computer. I was inching closer to the answer and was unable to keep still and simply wait for the police.

I'd just reached the computer's main screen when Matt walked into the study. "Don't touch that. You could be tampering with evidence."

I closed my eyes and counted to ten. When I opened them, he was looming over me while Sloane and Kathryn were trying to make themselves look busy by studying the books on the bookshelves.

"Ladies, we'll be back in a minute. I want to give Chief Roberson a quick update on some things." I led Matt to the kitchen and pointed at the key rack. "There it is. What do you think?"

After taking a couple of pictures and jotting down some notes, he looked at me.

"This wasn't an accidental death by drowning. The key thing doesn't give me much to go on, though."

He used a pair of tweezers from his multi-tool to take hold of the key and drop it in a small plastic bag.

"Don't hold your breath. My guess is the only prints we're likely to find on it are the deceased and Sloane's." He pointed toward the study. "Now, about that computer. I'm going to have to impound it."

"Why didn't you do that before?" When he didn't answer, I tried a different tack. "I'm already in. Give me fifteen minutes to do a quick search. I'm trying to find out if he really was working on something new. If so, that might be important. Don't you think?"

He took in a long breath and held it while he scratched his chin. "I'll give you ten minutes. I have a few questions for Sloane and her mom. I'll talk to them while you're at the computer. Then I'm taking it. My forensics expert will know if you do anything beyond searching."

"Fair enough." I got to work while Matt asked his questions in the hall.

There were e-mails, but none to or from my dad, which was strange, given they were working on a new project. There were a number of Word documents, but nothing big enough to be even a partial manuscript. Even Scrivener, a program used by many authors to write their manuscripts, was empty.

If Thornwell had written a new novel, he'd made an effort to hide it. Well, more than one person had told me he was nervous about it, so, in a weird way, I could understand him wanting to keep it from prying eyes. But that begged a question. If Thornwell's new novel existed, where was it?

"Time's up." Matt entered the room. He kept a hand on the corner of the screen while I shut down. It was as if he didn't trust me.

Then it hit me. The reason the authoritarian Chief Roberson was back was because he didn't want anybody to know about his misgivings with the job. Our conversation had been in confidence, and I needed to keep it that way. Given the wide latitude he was giving me, I couldn't complain.

"All yours, Chief." I rose from the chair. I needed to get going, anyway. Having dinner with the family meant I needed to get cleaned up.

I gave Sloane and Kathryn hugs and promised Sloane I'd call her in the morning.

On the drive home, I went through my list of suspects. After the revelation with the key, I needed to reevaluate my theory about the killer having left town. If I was right about the planning needed to use the spare key, it seemed like a local was much more likely to be the murderer than someone from out of town. Then again, Kathryn was from out of town, had motive, that is until I got a look at the will, and had access to Thornwell's house and the key.

As I turned into the driveway, I scratched the back of my neck. I was closer, but the answer was still out of reach. It was as if I was in a field draped in fog at dawn. Everything was a pallid shade of white. While I could sense movements in the shadows and catch glimpses of darker colors and whispers of voices, any progress toward my goal amounted to guesswork until the sun came up.

I had to maintain faith the sun would rise and burn away the mist to reveal more clues to guide me toward my goal. The identification and capture of Thornwell's murderer.

* * * *

The house was dark when I unlocked the front door, so, after tending to Ursi, I headed upstairs to get a shower. And to think.

Over the years, some of my best rumination sessions had occurred in the shower, so I turned the hot water up way higher than normal, got in and let the heat and humidity turn the bathroom into a mini sauna. I closed my eyes and let the water streams become a masseuse's skilled fingers, striking the stress pressure points in my back, shoulders and neck with pinpoint accuracy.

My mind began to drift and images of Dad floated to the surface. They were happy images. Me at seven chasing him around the backyard in the snow. Him reading the e-mail to the family when my first short story was accepted for publication. The two of us at Book Expo America, a national book conference, holding our authors' books in each of our hands.

As I washed my hair, my thoughts shifted to the problem at hand. The scarcity of information about the new novel on Thornwell's computer bothered me. Did he have another computer stashed somewhere? Had he loaded everything to a cloud-based site? Did it even matter?

After the shower, as I slipped into a pair of jeans and an ivory cable-knit sweater, I decided to take another crack at the mystery folder on Dad's computer. If Thornwell had a secret book in the works, the only person I could see him sharing it with was his agent, my father.

The book and the murder had to be connected in some way. If not, I feared the foundation of my theory about the act being premeditated would be washed away like a sand castle on the beach. I couldn't let that happen.

A little while later, Mom and Rachel came into the house. My sister was lamenting her struggles as a single parent of twins. Mom was listening and offering the required motherly sympathy.

"Hi, guys." I waved at them and returned to my attempts at accessing the troublesome folder.

Mom came in and gave me a kiss on the cheek. "I'm off to make dinner. Why don't you and your sister spend some time visiting? You've barely seen her since you've been home. That's a cute sweater, by the way."

"How goes the agency wind-down," Rachel asked as Mom left the room.

"Slow, but I'm making progress." I was stretching the truth so far it was about to snap. Other than depositing the royalty checks, I'd made little headway in closing the agency. Nobody had complained though, so I wasn't worried about it.

"You've had a week. Shouldn't you be finished by now?" Rachel came around the desk to see what was on the screen. It was a classic intimidation tactic. She knew people looking over my shoulder made me as nervous as a long-tailed cat in a room full of rocking chairs.

"I've had other things on my mind."

"Yeah, like sticking your nose into police business." Her cutting tone made me feel like I was ten and I'd done something to drive Rachel up the wall for the umpteenth time.

I wasn't ten anymore, and I didn't feel like putting up with her snark anymore.

"I made a promise to Sloane and to Dad. Matt's in over his head. If not me, who, Rachel." Then a thought occurred to me. "Instead of criticizing me, you could help me. Right now."

I told her about the folder and why I thought it was so important I get a look inside of it. "Crack the password protection for me. That's all I ask. I double-checked the notecard Dad left his passwords on, and it's not there. I know you can do this. Please?"

She put her hands on her hips. "Oh, I get it. You think since I was married to a cop, I know all about cyber security? I wasn't sitting around all day reading police manuals and asking Matt about his day when he got home. I had my own career."

"Exactly." I got up to face her woman-to-woman. "Your brain works different than mine. You're a business owner. You know mathematical formulas the way I know the difference between a dangling modifier and a split infinitive. Vocabulary and sentence structure can't help me now. I need someone who can think in computational sequences. That's you."

We stared at each other, her shoe tapping on the floor the only sound in the room.

After what seemed like a week, she raised an eyebrow. "You really think I can do this?"

"I know you can."

"Why is this so important to you?"

"Because every second that goes by is another second a murderer is free to go about as he or she chooses. Because Thornwell had turned his life around, was trying to do right by his family and didn't deserve to be killed."

Rachel took a deep breath. "And you're sure the answer to Thornwell's killer is in that file?"

No, I'm not sure. But I'm sure it will tell me where to take my next step. "I'm positive."

"If nothing else, it'll give me something to hang over Matt's head." She slipped into the chair and cracked her knuckles. "Here goes nothing."

Ten minutes later, she gave me a high five. "Ta-da. I am a genius and you owe me big-time."

"You're my favorite big sister ever. Now, time for me to do my job." My heart pounded against my ribcage as if it was a kickboxing bag as I looked at the folder's contents. It was Smaug's pile of gold without the dragon around. There were dozens of e-mails between Dad and Thornwell and a dozen Word files, each of which included the word "manuscript" in the file name.

"It's true. Thornwell was working on a novel. From the dates on these files, they'd been going back and forth about it for almost two years." I leaned forward as I opened an e-mail.

At the same time, Rachel tugged on my sweater collar. "What's up with this rash around your neck?"

"Probably hives. Been a little stressed this week."

"I don't know." As I turned my head to look at her, she leaned in. "This looks a lot more blistery than hives. More like how you used to react when you got poison ivy."

Appreciative of Rachel's concern, but annoyed by the interruption, I ran my fingertips across the back of my neck then across the front, under my chin. The rash made a complete circle, but it didn't have anything to do with my sweater. Or hives.

It was right where the mugger's hands had been when I was being choked.

"Holy Mother of Edits." I leapt to my feet and ran my fingers along the rash as I used my phone's black screen as an impromptu mirror. I turned to Rachel.

"I know where Thornwell was murdered."

Chapter Twenty-Two

"I gotta go." I hugged Rachel and dashed for the front door. "Don't tell Mom."

As I sprinted to the car, I called Matt again. It was a good thing I'd put him on speed dial. I keyed the engine at the same time I got his voice mail.

"Matt, I know where Thornwell was murdered. It wasn't at the bridge. It was at the community center. Call me."

Traffic had slowed to a crawl on the boulevard. I cursed the influx of tourists who who'd arrived early. The ninety seconds I had to wait at the Main Street intersection was more anxiety inducing than waiting to hear from an editor about a manuscript I'd submitted.

When the light changed, I gunned it through the intersection, drawing an angry shout from Ozzy, who was working on a wood carving in front of his shop. Back in New York, I would have given him the one-finger salute. In my hometown, decorum ruled the day, even in my agitated state, so I gave him a friendly wave.

Once free from downtown traffic, I jammed the gas pedal to the floor and slowed only enough to keep the car on all four wheels as I turned right and blew past the winery. With a rush of adrenaline straight out of a *Fast and Furious* movie, the car fishtailed and the tires squealed as I sped into the community center parking lot and jammed the brakes to come to a stop.

I was out of the car the nanosecond the engine shut off, my heart hammering away a thousand beats a minute. The emotional part of me wanted to sprint to the edge of the deck, but the logical part made me take a trip around the building to confirm there were no security cameras.

When I verified there were none, I waited until I was calm enough to walk across the deck at an unhurried pace. As I came up against the deck's railing, I took out my phone. No response from Matt.

For a moment, I considered texting Sloane, but when I'd said good-bye earlier, Sloane and Kathryn told me they were going out for dinner. It had been eons since they'd done that, so I decided against interrupting their time together.

From my vantage point on the deck, I began my inspection of the slope between the rail and the creek at the point farthest from the community center building. A few clouds were beginning to form, but I couldn't let the diminished light rush me.

Somewhere between the start of the railing behind the community center building and the end of the railing where I stood, Thornwell had been pushed or dragged, I wasn't sure which, into the creek. Now, to find the proof.

With my trusty flashlight, for both protection and additional light, I began a systematic inspection of the foliage Luke hadn't removed. I chose to stay on the deck so I didn't trample on the evidence I was looking for by accident. It was tedious work, because there wasn't much greenery and the beam from the flashlight wasn't wide, but still, luck was with me. There'd been no rain since I'd returned to Rushing Creek. Hopefully that meant evidence of the plants and dirt being disturbed hadn't been washed away.

Throughout my life, I'd always been called detail oriented. Finding things that were out of place or needed correction, from a misspelling in a manuscript to a painting on a wall hanging sitting off kilter, was in my nature. Growing up, I treated it like a game. It was fun and I got good at it.

What I was doing now wasn't fun. One life had been lost. My own had been threatened. I couldn't take the chance the murderer would lash out again.

After some initial trial and error, I fell into a routine. I took a step to the right, scanned the ground directly in front of me up and down then left to right. When finished, I repeated the motions. It was slow going. In some sections, the distance from the deck to the water was as little as five feet. In others, it was closer to fifteen.

I was about halfway completed when my phone went off. I was so focused on my task that I yelped and dropped it. Mom. This wasn't going to be good.

"Sorry about leaving before dinner—"

"Don't give me sorry. Where are you and what are doing? If you don't tell me right now, I'm calling the police."

My ear rang from her shouts.

That last time she yelled at me like this was right after I moved to New York and didn't return her call for a day and a half. She'd been close to tears from fright. It didn't take a genius to figure out how she was feeling now.

"I'm fine, Mom." I told her where I was and what I was doing. "I'll check in with you later, but I need to finish this before it gets darker. Don't worry. Besides, I've already got a call into Matt. I need to go in case he calls back. Bye. Love you."

I ended the conversation before she could respond and got back to work.

And then I hit the jackpot.

I'd almost made it to the portion of the deck that narrowed and ran between the community center building and the creek when I found what I was looking for. I panned over the area three times before to make sure my eyes weren't playing tricks on me. The pool of light revealed a trail from the ground at the foot of the deck to the creek. Some greenery Luke had failed to remove showed signs of being bent, and the exposed dirt appeared flattened.

Given all of Luke's recent work, the differences from the rest of the area I'd studied were subtle. I had grave doubts anyone would notice unless they were looking for them. The deal was sealed by the deck railing in front of me. Upon close examination, I noticed scrapes on the railing's painted surface. Like something had been dragged across it.

I took a couple of pictures and texted Matt a request to get someone here ASAP to rope off the area then climbed down from the deck to get a closer look at the foliage.

My flashlight wasn't powerful enough to reveal traces of blood or clothing, but it exposed plenty of poison ivy. Someone who had dragged a body toward the creek wouldn't have been able to avoid coming in contact with it.

I stayed back a couple of feet from the path, as I thought of it, and took more pictures. When I reached the creek, I looked around. There were no structures within eyesight, other than the community center building. The road was too far away for a motorist to notice anything going on down here too.

In the middle of the night, nobody would have seen a thing.

The realization of what I'd found finally hit me, and the hair on the back of my neck stood at attention. I scrambled along the creek's edge until I could make a clear sprint to my car. Once I was safe inside the glass and steel refuge, I locked the doors and focused on deep, cleansing breaths while I waited for reinforcements to arrive.

As I calmed down, I closed my eyes and visualized pieces of a puzzle. The community center. Poison ivy. Hands around my neck. Thornwell's book. The credit card bill. The misplaced key. Where was the piece that finished the puzzle?

Next, I conjured images of my suspects. They could all fit the shape of the final puzzle piece, but only one of them was the perfect fit. Who?

"Come on, Allie. Think." I pounded on the steering wheel. "Who stood to gain the most from killing Thornwell?"

My thoughts were interrupted by the headlights of a police cruiser that came to a stop next to me. Jeanette emerged. She was in the same navy blue uniform the other officers wore, but this evening a shiny silver badge was affixed to her shirt.

I got out of my car. "I didn't know you were an officer."

"Finished my reserve officer training Monday. Just in time for the festival. I'm not certified to carry a gun yet, but I can do about everything else. How do I look?" She spread her arms wide and smiled.

"Congrats. You look great." It was reassuring to see an ally, but I was confused. "No offense, but what are you doing here?"

"The mayor's got Matt tied up in a festival planning meeting. He sent me your text and told me to send someone but to keep it low key, if you know what I mean."

Did I ever. With the mayor still under the cloud of suspicion, I had no desire to tip him off.

"Given the circumstances, I decided to come. I know this case as well as anyone in the department. Show me what you found."

I led Jeanette to the scene of the crime, there was no doubt about it now, and used the flashlight to point out the scrape marks, along with the disturbed foliage and dirt.

She scrunched up her nose as she studied the scene. After walking back and forth along the railing a couple of times using her police-issued, high-powered flashlight, she let out a long breath as she crossed her arms.

"This is interesting, but I don't see where it gets us closer to the killer. If this is the murder scene—"

"It is. I'd bet my life on it."

"Slow down. We don't know how Thornwell got from his house to here. For all we know, some kids may have done this." When I objected, she put up her hands. "Tell you what. I'll get someone down here to help me take a closer look. What have we got to lose, right?"

A gray cloud of despair started to descend upon me. At my moment of victory, I was suddenly plummeting toward defeat, like Wile E. Coyote in the classic Road Runner cartoons.

Jeanette withdrew a notebook from her back pocket. As she did so, all of a sudden, a parachute appeared and stopped my fall as I turned one question on its head and asked two more.

What if, instead of Thornwell's murderer being the person with the most to gain, it was the person with the least to lose? And what if that person lured Thornwell here with the intent of murdering him? And what if, instead of thinking about hands, I thought about gloves?

I circled the cars as I worked my way through the new questions. By turning the puzzle pieces around, I finally recognized the missing piece. Euphoria enveloped me as the fog finally lifted and I could see the whole scene, as clear as a Southern Indiana sky on a Sunday afternoon.

"Ohmigod, ohmigod, ohmigod. Jeanette, I've got it."

She slotted a handheld radio into a holder on her belt. "Tommy's on the way. What do you have?"

I closed my eyes and counted to ten. As I envisioned the puzzle, one piece, a small one, was still missing. I needed that piece to tell me which of my final two suspects was the killer. Without that piece, I couldn't bring myself to share my thoughts. It was a crushing decision, but I had more work to do.

"I've got an idea, but it needs more research. I'll be in touch." I opened my car door. "Promise me you'll let me know if you find anything down there, okay?"

"Count on it." She came up to me and gave my shoulder a reassuring squeeze. "I believe in you, Allie. We'll find the killer."

She stared at me for a long time, as if she sensed I was holding something back and was hoping the silence would make it impossible for me to keep quiet.

"What?" So, she was right. Sue me.

"For a minute there, I thought you were going to tell me you knew who the killer was." She shook her head. "Guess I let my emotions get the best of me."

"Totally understandable." I got in the car before I said something incriminating. "Talk to you soon."

With a wave, I drove out of the community center's parking lot. My next destination? The Rushing Creek Inn.

To find the final piece of the puzzle.

Chapter Twenty-Three

I motored along the boulevard at ten miles per hour. At the inn, tourists were scurrying back and forth across the parking lot, pulling suitcases on wheels and carrying bags of groceries. The folks checking in tonight were the Fall Festival diehards. The event didn't kick off until Friday afternoon, but these people knew that by arriving now, they could spend tomorrow in the state park and wouldn't have to deal with bumper-to-bumper traffic and full trash cans.

With the increased traffic, my slow pace made it seem as if I was another tourist looking for a parking space. Which was just as well, because I wanted to appear as nondescript as possible. I wanted the element of surprise on my side.

I turned into the parking lot and took the first spot available, which happened to be next to a familiar black sports coupe. Like Ursi after a mouse that got into my apartment, I was on the hunt, and my prey was in range. I chose to ignore the fact that the stakes before me were infinitely higher.

In an act of desperation, I called Matt a final time. And got his voice mail again.

"It's Allie. I'm at the Rushing Creek Inn. I know who killed Thornwell. Get here as fast as you can. I don't think I'm in any danger, but if he resists, I'll need your help. Get here soon, please. I don't trust anyone else on this."

I waited a minute, two minutes for a response. When none came, I squared my shoulders and walked inside. No turning back now. It was all on me. The puzzle piece had to be here, because if it wasn't, then I was in trouble.

I tried to act normal as I made my way through the lobby. According to Matt, the inn's surveillance footage indicated no guests used the lobby to come or go between one and six. An additional camera that covered the parking lot didn't provide anything helpful.

The inn had two side entrances that were locked between eleven and six and were only accessible by using a key card. The logs I reviewed, *thank you Matt*, didn't indicate any use by my prey the night of the murder.

Then again, if memory served, every other room on the first floor had a sliding glass door that opened onto a tiny patio. They would offer a simple and effective way for a murderer to avoid the prying eyes of security cameras while leaving to commit the heinous act and returning undetected.

With my palms sweaty from nerves, I marched down the hall. On the outside, I needed to exude strength and purpose, even if on the inside I felt like an anxiety-ridden teenager. At room 107, I took a deep breath and gave the wooden door three quick knocks.

After a moment of rustling around, the door opened. "I don't recall ordering—" Daniel's brows rose in almost comical fashion when he realized it wasn't room service.

"Hi, Daniel. Sorry for the surprise visit." I wasn't sorry, but I didn't want to be antagonistic from the get-go. "May I come in?"

"I thought you were going to call." He glanced over his shoulder and kept the door mostly closed. He'd unlatched the security chain, though.

In New York, it took me no time to learn you always kept the chain latched to keep people from barging into your apartment. Daniel had left himself with nothing to keep me from barging in on him at that very moment.

Big mistake.

"This really isn't a good time." He pushed his glasses up on his nose. "I'm very busy."

"Oh, come on. We've both lost someone important in our lives. It's not healthy to keep your feelings bottled up. Let's talk about it." I placed my hand on the door and put some weight behind it. It was a move he wasn't expecting, and the door gave way, allowing me to slip in before he could react.

Once inside, I scanned the room. Two open suitcases lay on the king-sized bed. The bathroom light was on and an overnight pack was in view. The curtains were drawn, blocking the view of the patio.

Behind me, the door closed with a click. "I told you this was a bad time, Allie. You shouldn't have come without calling first."

"From the looks of things, I'm glad I came when I did." I turned to face him. "Am I missing something, or are you packing?"

"Very perceptive of you. Thornwell always said you were much smarter than that dullard daughter of his." He brushed past me and flipped the suitcases closed. "I'd love to chat, but I'm checking out."

The insult directed at Sloane wasn't going to throw me off track. If anything, it intensified my resolve. "You told me the other day you couldn't bear to leave town until Thornwell's killer was caught. What changed?"

"What changed is I've waited long enough for that dolt of a police chief to arrest the librarian, Reynolds. He's obviously not going to do it during this millennium, so it's time for me to return home and get back to work."

"I see." I went to the curtain. After giving him a pointed look, I pulled it back. The glider mechanism moved with barely a whisper to reveal the sliding door. The final piece of the puzzle. I opened it.

"Very nice. Far away enough from the condos over there for someone to come in and out of their room without calling attention to themselves. Especially after dark."

Daniel rolled his eyes as he crossed his arms. "I suppose so. And your point is?"

I took a step toward him. "You know what's funny? Chief Roberson, to whom you referred to as a dolt, made certain information about Thornwell's murder available to me."

He shifted his weight from one foot to the other but kept his facial expression neutral. The man sure knew how to operate under pressure.

"A lot of people who attended Dad's funeral were staying here at the inn. I believe there were nine, including yourself. But the recordings from the security cameras showed all of the guests were in their rooms by midnight. You know, the night your boss was killed."

"Proves my point, don't you think? Obviously, none of us who were staying here could have possibly murdered Thornwell." He took a step toward the door.

"Now that's where things get dicey." I ran my fingers across the mesh surface of the screen door. "You see, with this door, someone could have come and gone without detection. A much better route for a killer to take than the hallway and lobby I'd think."

Covering my hand with the sleeve of my sweater to avoid leaving fingerprints, I opened the screen door, took a moment to look into the darkness, and slid it closed. With a flourish, I engaged the lock.

"Oh, my God." Daniel let out a long laugh. "You're implying I killed him. I understand your thirst for justice, Allie, but come on. You're embarrassing yourself. I think it's time for you to go before you make a complete fool of yourself."

"That's where you're wrong. I'm not implying you killed Thornwell. I know you killed him."

"Fine. I'll indulge you in your little fantasy. Maybe it will help find the real killer." He placed one of the suitcases on the floor and took a seat on the bed. "How could I have possibly done it?"

"You worked for the man for years. Over time, as his drinking increased, he became more and more dependent on you. He gave you access to his house, his computer, pretty much everything. Thornwell was providing you with a comfortable living."

"You're not telling me anything that isn't common knowledge. And more to the point, why would I kill the very person who was the source of my, as you inelegantly put it, comfortable living?"

"Perfect segue." I needed to keep the verbal dance going. The longer Daniel was here, the more time Matt had to arrive. "All that changed when my dad got sick. For whatever reason, it motivated Thornwell to change. He quit drinking, made efforts to reconcile with his ex-wife and daughter and, most relevant to our conversation here, he started writing. Without you."

Daniel shrugged. "Not bad. It would make a decent thriller. Maybe you can write it and get Suzette to find a publisher. Unfortunately, the rumor about his writing is baseless. As you said, I had access to his computer. He wasn't working on anything I didn't know about."

I peeked at the patio door and then at the door to the hallway. We were nearing the climax of the conversation and I had no idea if he would make a break for it or which way he would go. My money was on the patio door as he would encounter fewer people that way, so I moved in that direction.

"Wrong. Not only was he writing, he'd finished a manuscript. He and my dad were in the final stages of preparing to send it to publishers. He'd decided to let you go. You couldn't handle the fact he didn't need you anymore, which meant your income stream was coming to an end."

He rose from the bed, his cheeks turning flame red as he adjusted his glasses. "Lies. You're a poor liar, Allie. Thornwell needed me. He was nothing without me."

"You reached your breaking point when Suzette said no to your manuscript. With no book contract on the horizon, you took Sloane's apartment key from Thornwell's key rack, stole a credit card statement and returned the key while we were at the funeral. There were so many people there, nobody noticed that you arrived late. Then at the wake, you offered Thornwell a drink, which led to another, then another."

"This is slander. I'm getting the manager." He stepped toward the hallway door, but I intercepted him and pushed him onto the bed.

"I'm not finished." My voice rose in concert with my anger at the man. "Sometime after the wake was over, you snuck out of here, went to his house and lured him back to the community center."

I stood over him. The fear in his eyes emboldened me. "You hit him on the head, dumped him over the rail and dragged him to the creek. Was he dead already or did you make sure he drowned before you pushed him downstream?"

"You're wrong." He shook his head and scrambled off the bed, pulling the comforter with him, as if it would protect him from my accusations. "You don't know anything. You can't prove anything."

"Sure I can, you monster. When you dragged Thornwell to the creek, you got poison ivy all over you."

"That's a lie." He showed me his right hand then the left. "See? Nothing."

"That's because you were wearing those stupid driving gloves. The same ones you wore when you choked me." I pointed to the ring of poison ivy around my neck. "I'll bet if you pull up your sleeves, we'll see a rash on your arms. That's why you were in the general store the day you, Maybelle and I talked. You went there to get cortisone cream. That's what was in the bag you were holding."

I reached into my pocket for my phone. The sweat on Daniel's forehead told me all I needed to know. When I pressed the nine button on my keypad, he lunged at me. My phone fell to the floor as he used his greater size and weight to push me backward, pressing the edge of the comforter against my throat.

With pinwheeling arms, I stumbled and knocked a lamp off the table. It crashed to the floor, the compact fluorescent bulb exploding on contact. With another thrust, he had me against a wall, his hands tightening around my throat once more.

"I should have finished you when I had the chance. I won't make the same mistake twice." His voice was little more than a dog's growl.

Gasping for oxygen, my kickboxing training took over. Without a thought, I kneed him in the groin with all the force I could muster. He let out a howl and lost his grip on my throat.

I sucked in air and pressed my advantage by hitting him with a one, two, three combination to his chest. With space now between us, I kicked him in the gut. He fell to his knees, a dazed look in his eyes.

"Allie, please. You don't understand."

"Oh, I understand all too well, Daniel. You're a modern version of Gríma Wormtongue from *Lord of the Rings*, slithering your way into all aspects of Thornwell's life. When he was able to stand up on his own two feet, you couldn't handle the thought of having to make it on your own."

In the distance, a dog barked. Daniel tried to take advantage when I looked toward the sound by going for my legs. I was quicker, though. A roundhouse kick brought my foot against the side of his head and, like a sack of potatoes, he dropped to the floor.

With my adrenaline still flowing at top speed, I ripped a pillowcase in two and used it to bind his hands and feet. As I was securing the knot around his ankles, a dog burst through the screen and jumped on top of Daniel, a low growl making his intentions clear. It was Sammy to the rescue again.

A moment later, Brent stumbled through the ripped screen. His jaw hit the floor as he surveyed the scene.

"Allie, what in the world is going on?"

I sat back on my heels and ran my fingers through my hair. With Daniel subdued and under Sammy's watchful eyes, the adrenaline ran out and, all of a sudden, I was more tired than I'd ever been in my life. I fought back tears as I tried to make the words come.

"Call the police. Tell them we've got Thornwell's killer." Noise from the hall caught my attention. "Check the door. Maybe they're here already."

Then a wave of vertigo engulfed me and I passed out.

Chapter Twenty-Four

The nasty smell of ammonia brought me back from unconsciousness. I shook my head and tried to push the offensive scent away. After blinking a couple of times, the world came into focus.

"We have to stop meeting like this, Ms. Cobb." Chelsea, the paramedic from the alley, smiled and dropped the smelling salt into a plastic container at her side.

Behind her, the room was bursting with activity. Jeanette, with a notepad, was talking to Brent. Matt had Daniel in handcuffs and was leading him out the door. A middle-aged woman in a Rushing Creek Inn dress shirt had a cell phone to her ear. No doubt the manager talking to her boss.

Sammy nudged my arm out of the way and settled his head in my lap.

"Hey, buddy, you've got good timing." I ruffed his fur and hugged him.

In return, he flapped his ears and licked my cheek.

I laughed, which brought all conversation in the room to an instantaneous halt.

Brent came over and got down in front of me. His dorky smile was a salve to my hurting body and soul. "How are you?"

My neck hurt, my shoulders ached and my knuckles were sore. I wanted to go home and snuggle with Ursi for the rest of my life. But I'd accomplished my goal and kept my promise to Sloane.

And to Dad.

"I'll be okay. Thanks for your help, again." I winced as a jolt of pain shot through my shoulder.

"More like a day late and a dollar short, again." He frowned. "Sorry we didn't get here sooner."

"So, are you stalking her? Chelsea asked.

"No. I live in one of the condos across the way. Sammy heard something and when I opened the door to see what it was, he hightailed it over here."

"No worries. You can buy me dinner sometime to make up for it." I rattled off my cell number. Brent laughed, but Chelsea's lips were pursed. Of course, she didn't know Big Al had gently threatened Brent about treating me like a princess.

"Can I go home? I'm tired." I ruffled Sammy's coat again. "No offense, buddy."

Chelsea helped me to my feet. "I need to take a look at you, but we can do that in the ambulance. I understand the chief wants to talk to you, too."

I let Chelsea guide me to the door. At the threshold, I stopped and took a look at the ravaged room. It looked like a tornado had been through it. A shiver ran through me when I recalled what really happened. *I almost died in this room.* I said a quick prayer of thanks that Daniel's attempt to choke me to death failed.

I tried not to think about how close he came to succeeding.

"God, what a mess." I turned and headed down the hallway, with Chelsea at my side.

"Literally," she said.

Intentional or not, her comment made me laugh. It hurt my throat but lifted my spirits, so I called it even.

A few wide-eyed bystanders were hanging out in the inn's lobby. The efforts they were making to act as if they weren't watching me was comical. Then again, when tourists came to Rushing Creek's Fall Festival, they expected their excitement to come from the pumpkin pie-eating contest and Headless Horseman retellings. Finding themselves in the middle of the capture of a murderer probably wasn't on their radar.

Despite the discomfort at being the center of such unwanted attention, I kept my chin up and made eye contact with everyone who looked at me. *That's right people. Little Allie Cobb caught the bad guy.*

Then a little voice in my head gave me a not-so-gentle reminder it wasn't about me. It was about Thornwell, Sloane and Kathryn. My bumps and bruises and scratches were mere superficial injuries. They were inconveniences, to be honest, that would be healed in a week, if not sooner.

The wounds to Sloane and Kathryn might never heal. Despite my satisfaction at catching Thornwell's killer, it broke my heart when I thought of how far the man had come in fixing his life, only to have it cut short when the future was looking so bright.

My ruminations came to an abrupt halt when I stepped outside. Red, white and blue flashing lights and headache-inducing radio chatter overwhelmed me. I stood, immobilized by the assault on my senses.

With a gentle touch, Chelsea guided me to the back of the ambulance. She got me seated, wrapped a blanket around me and handed me a bottle of water. While it hurt to swallow, the clean, clear water tasted fantastic.

The exam was brief and the results, about the best I could hope for. I'd be sore for a few days, but there was no serious damage. My relief at the good news ended when Matt joined us, prompting Chelsea to step away.

"Your mom's been notified. She's on the way. I told her you're fine, but she didn't believe me."

"Sounds like Mom. Sloane, too?" When he nodded, I thanked him and took a drink. My throat was a sheet of rough sandpaper. The more fluids to soothe it, the better.

"Sorry I didn't respond to your messages. If I didn't know better, I would have thought Larry was trying to make sure I couldn't help you. When the nine-one-one call came in, he didn't have a choice."

I waved his apology away. The number of rules and protocols Matt had broken to help me figure out the puzzle had to be in the double digits. But, despite our difficult shared histories, he'd worked with me. For the good of the community.

"Sorry I put you in such a tough spot. Worked out okay, right?"

"Godwin's not stupid. He's clammed up for now. But, yeah, I think it will."

"Make sure you find his driving gloves. They're probably in his car. Have them checked for urushiol. It's the oil in poison ivy." I pointed to the rash on my neck. "It's how I got this. Check the bathroom in his room, too. You should find a tube of cortisone cream there."

He raised an eyebrow then turned away and spoke into a microphone attached to his shirt. "You going to tell me how you figured this out?" When I lowered my head, he sat next to me and offered me a stick of gum. "I know you're exhausted, but the sooner you fill me in, the sooner I can get with the county prosecutor and put this guy away for a long time."

I couldn't argue with that, so I popped the gum in my mouth and told him everything. I even admitted that until I saw the sliding door, I wasn't sure if the murderer was Daniel or Jax. By the time I was finished, I'd drained two water bottles and Mom had pulled into the parking lot.

She hurried over to me, without bothering to close her door, and took me in a tight embrace. She kissed me on the head and then started sobbing.

"It's okay, Mom. I'm okay. It's over." I held her against me as her tears fell. Mom and I loved each other, but I'd always been Daddy's little girl because of the interests he and I shared. Mom had been gracious and never put any type of guilt trip on me over it.

Now, here we were, just the two of us. I didn't know if it was a sign of things to come, but it felt good. It felt right.

After a minute or so, the tears came to an end and she gave me a long, disapproving look, complete with furrowed brows and pursed lips. "I don't know what to say right now. I'm furious with you for putting yourself in danger. I'm thankful you're okay. I," she pulled her coat tighter against her to ward off the nighttime chill, "can't believe you caught a murderer. I'm so proud of you." She hugged me again.

"I had a lot of help." With a nod toward Matt, I amended my statement. "We had a lot of help."

"Along that line, if you don't mind, Mrs. Cobb, I have a couple more questions I need to ask Allie. Can you give me five minutes?" Matt's tone was conciliatory and Mom responded with a smile.

It was good seeing them being kind to each other. Maybe it was the start of my family's acceptance of the divorce and the healing I hoped would follow. After all, on a night when little Allie Cobb took down a murderer, nothing was impossible.

When we were alone again, Matt consulted his notes. "There's part of the timeline I'm not clear about. Tell me again how Godwin lured Thornwell to the community center."

"Yeah, that part's a little confusing." I straightened up and blew out a long breath to clear my mind.

"Like I said, during the funeral, Daniel took the key to Sloane's apartment, stole the credit card statement and returned the key. I figure he did that in about a half hour, giving him plenty of time to sneak into the funeral late without anybody noticing. Fast forward to the wake. He got Thornwell drunk and when Thornwell and Suzette were arguing, managed to swipe Thornwell's wallet."

"And you saw this happen?"

"Sloane and I both saw him put his arm around Thornwell. I didn't give it any thought at the time, but when Kathryn mentioned Thornwell always knew where things like his keys and wallet were, it filled in the picture."

"I'm still not seeing the connection." Matt's brow was furrowed. He was trying to poke holes in my story. It didn't bother me. I did the same thing with manuscripts all the time.

"When the wake ended, everybody went home. Daniel knew Thornwell was already home, so he snuck out of his room through the patio door and paid Thornwell a little visit. I'm sure he pretended to be concerned for Thornwell, and, sometime during the conversation, brought up the wallet. When Thornwell freaked out, Daniel offered to drive him to the community center and help him find it."

Matt's eyes lit up and he smiled. "And when they were at the center, Daniel hit him on the head, stuffed the bill in his pocket, dumped him over the rail, and dragged him to the creek."

"With the gloves on. Don't forget that. I'd bet he tried to get Thornwell to reconsider cutting ties with him and when he refused…" I shrugged.

"We found a house key under the side door floor mat when we searched the house. Makes that a lot more relevant now." He rubbed the bridge of his nose. "People are going to breathe a lot easier around here with this resolved. The mayor's going to be relieved, that's for sure."

"I'm not so sure about that. He has a few secrets that are less secret now."

"Really? Anything I should know about?"

"He was with Charissa Mody the night of the murder. I'll tell you more later." I nodded toward Sloane, who was approaching. I stood and gave my best friend the tightest hug I could muster.

"I knew you could do it." She squeezed me and lifted me up. "Allie Cobb, the Kickboxing Crusader." There were no tears from Sloane. Instead, we laughed as she made a half circle before returning me to terra firma.

That was Sloane Winchester in a nutshell. Ever the optimist, she meant what she said. It was true she thought I would catch her father's murderer. She never lost faith in me. For a moment, I wondered how much that faith had sustained me over the past seven nightmarish days.

I let the thought go. There would be time for reflection in the future. As I sat back down with a wince, all I could think of was the one thought, the only thought, that mattered.

It was over.

I'd used up the last of my resources, both physical and emotional, for the day. I wanted my kitty and my bed.

"Hey, Chief Roberson?" A few yards away, Matt was talking to a young woman with a notebook. The reporter for the local paper, most likely.

He put up his index finger to let me know he'd be with me shortly.

"Chief Roberson?" Sloane snorted. "Since when did you start calling your ex-brother-in-law that?"

"He helped me a lot the past few days when he didn't have to. I figure the least I can do is call him by his title when we're in public."

"I suppose." Sloane sounded unconvinced and gave him a sideways glance as he approached us.

"Hey, Sloane." He extended his hand. "Crazy scene, huh? All the credit goes to Allie, here."

She took his hand. "She told me you helped, so thanks to you both. From my mom and me. I'm glad this is over."

"Speaking of which," I said. "I'm wiped out. May I go home now?"

After Matt consulted his notebook, he agreed to let me go with an agreement that he'd stop by the house tomorrow afternoon for follow-up questions.

Mom and Sloane both offered to drive me and were both disappointed when I didn't take them up on their offers. I tried to tell myself they wanted to be the chauffeur to the local hero, but I knew better. They were simply two people who cared deeply for me and wanted to make sure I got home safely.

For that, I would always be grateful.

Chapter Twenty-Five

I didn't wake up the next day until after one in the afternoon. Ursi was curled up in a ball, wedged between my arm and my chest. My eyes clouded with tears as I scratched the orange and black ears of the little creature who brought me so much joy.

It was reassuring to know she was the only one who was depending on me now. Well, that and my clients.

My clients.

I had hardworking, talented writers who depended on me to represent their interests. I'd done an okay job of that over the last week, but now it was time to get back to work.

I was in Dad's office catching up on e-mails when my phone's ring tone went off. It was my boss, Natalie.

"How's the Kickboxing Crusader? I knew you were tough, but I didn't know you were this tough. Your fighting crime while on bereavement leave story made it all the way to New York."

Oh, God. I'd avoided checking the news since I'd had enough of dealing with the world for a while. It seemed my hopes for a quiet day to recover might be over. I did a quick Internet search of my name and breathed a sigh of relief. A report had been posted on the local paper's website, so the folks back in New York City had probably gotten it after someone shared it online.

"It's a long story. I'll tell you about it when I'm back in the office, but, for now, you can let everyone know I'm fine and can't wait to see them Monday." We chatted for a little bit about the status of my client list. It was a routine conversation, covering things like monthly reports for those authors waiting for editors to decide whether or not to make an offer, and royalty reports, which were due to go out by the end of the month.

As I finished the call, Ursi jumped in my lap. I scratched her back and realized I didn't know when Thornwell's funeral was, and there was no way on Earth I was missing that.

There were no texts or e-mails from Sloane about funeral arrangements, and it would be over-the-top rude to ask her about it, so I made peace with the idea of returning to New York City when I did. If I had to leave Natalie a message that I wouldn't be able to make it to work until Thornwell's funeral was over, so be it. Sloane was family.

And family needed to come first.

It was a lesson I'd learned the hard way during my return to Rushing Creek. I would never get over not telling Dad good-bye in person, but going forward, I vowed that, no matter what, when my family needed me, I would be there.

With that in mind, once I finished my e-mails, I returned to Dad's computer. Now that I could access the files he'd kept confidential, I needed to know how far along he and Thornwell had gotten on the novel. After all, when an author submitted a manuscript to an agent, there were still hours of work to be done perfecting the story.

So, how well-tuned was Thornwell Winchester's final novel?

It didn't take me long to get an answer. In fact, my pulse quickened when I realized the manuscript I'd been reading the other night was Thornwell's.

It was finished.

According to an e-mail, Dad was going to give a final read to check for typos before sending it to Thornwell's editor to see if she was interested.

My father had finished proofreading seven chapters. The book was so close to being ready; I couldn't give up on it now. So I got a red pen, settled into the recliner and got to work. I was fully absorbed in the story, which, thanks to one of Thornwell's old superstitions, didn't have a title yet, when there was a knock at the front door.

"Come on in," I told Matt when I opened the door. I'd been hoping he'd text or call to tell me we didn't need to talk. Oh well, if it would keep Daniel behind bars, then I had all day.

"How are you?" He took off his baseball cap and popped in a piece of gum. It was probably the first time he'd stepped inside the Cobb household since before the divorce. Again, how things changed so quickly.

"Feeling better." I told him about Thornwell's book as I led him into Dad's office. "I need to talk to Sloane about what she wants to do with it. It's an incredible story. God, when the man was clearheaded, he was a genius."

"That's great." Matt took a seat on the arm of the recliner. "I've got good news. I took what you told me and used it to lean on Godwin this morning. Even with an attorney present, it didn't take long to wear him down. He confessed an hour into the interview. You pretty much nailed it. When Thornwell wouldn't reconsider dumping him, he lost it. Whacked him with a log from the fire pit's woodpile. Tossed the log into the creek after Thornwell started downstream."

"Wow. I don't know what to say." I truly didn't. A lot of my conclusions had been based on what I knew about Dad and Thornwell. To have confirmation I'd been right was gratifying, but a little scary, too. In an attempt to lighten the mood, I joked about having a criminal's mind.

"I wouldn't worry about that." Matt smiled and got to his feet. "You're smart and pay attention to details. You listen to people. You're methodical and precise. Those are traits an investigator needs. That's why you're so good at your agent job, too."

My cheeks got warm. "Thanks, but I don't know how great of an agent I am."

"All I know is Rachel brags about what you do every chance she gets." He put on his hat as he went to the door. "Thanks for all your help, Allie. It's great having you home again."

As I returned to Thornwell's manuscript, my heart swelled with pride. To think that Rachel was actually proud of me. For two decades, I'd thought Rachel considered me her annoying little sister and not much else. I couldn't be happier at being so wrong. If I said anything to her, she'd deny it, but that was okay. It was the knowledge that mattered.

A little while later there was another knock at the front door. With a growl in frustration at being interrupted again, I scanned the room. I didn't see anything Matt had left behind.

I yanked open the door and was about to ask what he wanted when I realized it wasn't Matt.

It was Brent. With a little bouquet of flowers.

"Hi. I just got off work and thought I'd stop by to see how you're doing." He offered me the flowers. "These are for you."

"Thank you." The mixture of Orange Gerbera Daisies and waxflower was a cheerful nod to the season. "Would you like to come in?"

His Adam's apple bobbed up and down as he nodded. The nervousness was cute. Instead of Dad's office, I took Brent to the living room since this was a social call rather than a business one. Mom would be proud of me. She worried I was too busy with work to find a nice guy to date.

Not that this was a date, by any means. Still, Mom would be proud.

"I was going to call, but I wasn't sure you'd remember you gave me your number last night."

Oh, yeah. Now that he mentioned it, I did recall broadcasting my cell number to everyone in the hotel room. Oh well. I didn't mind that Brent had it. It actually made me happy he remembered it in all of the mayhem.

"I do remember. You came to my rescue, after all." I gestured toward the couch.

"How are you feeling," he asked when he was seated.

"I'm okay. The police told me Daniel confessed." There was no easy way to ask the question that was on my mind, so I just went for it. "How come you didn't tell me about your fight with Thornwell?"

"Yeah, about that." He grimaced and rubbed his hands together. "Not my finest moment. I guess I was afraid to bring it up. I'm an outsider here and didn't want to bring any unwanted attention my way."

"So, instead, you let me find out from the town gossip." I stopped, my hard tone not helpful. "Sorry. I'm still tired. I hope you won't take offense that I had you on my suspect list for a while."

"On it?" He laughed. It was a friendly laugh, without any malice or anger. "I'm happy I wasn't at the top of it."

Ursi strolled in and wound her way through Brent's legs. Then she jumped on the couch and settled down next to him, with one paw resting on his thigh.

"It appears Ursi approves of you, so I guess I'll forgive the oversight. Will you get in trouble with Sammy for hanging out with a cat?"

"Given who the owner is, I think he'll be okay with it. He likes you."

We chatted for a bit about the library before he got up to leave.

"Will I see you around the festival this weekend? I'm helping with the Legend of Sleepy Hollow reenactment. Starring as Ichabod Crane. Typecasting at its finest." He gave me a long, exaggerated bow, complete with the sweeping arm movement.

My heart skipped a beat. The literature nerd in me couldn't help it. "I'll try to track you down. Got a lot on my plate before I head back to New York."

I lingered in the doorway as Brent sauntered down the front walk. He waved before he got into his car, a silver SUV. With a tightening in my stomach I never got from looking at Lance, I waved back. When

I finally closed the door, Ursi was staring at me. I picked her up and scratched under her chin.

"I agree, girl. He's a nice guy." She nipped at my index finger. "Okay, he's nicer than the guys in New York." She meowed and rubbed her head against my index finger. Message received.

With time running out before I had to return to New York, I kept a low profile and focused on getting Dad's agency affairs in order. Sloane and I got together for a drink at the pub on Friday evening, which was when she told me about the memorial service arrangements. Per his wishes, Thornwell was being cremated. There was going to be a private service in his backyard on Sunday afternoon for family and a few business associates.

"Your family's my family, so you're all welcome." Sloane wrapped her finger around a paper napkin. "Mom and I were wondering if you'd say a few words about Dad at the service since you knew him as both a writer and as your dad's friend."

"Of course I will." I took Sloane's hand. "Thank you for the honor. I have some news for you. Thornwell's book is finished." I told her about finding it in Dad's encrypted folder and spending the last day and a half finishing the final edits.

"Wow." She smiled then looked away. "I wanted to believe him, to believe in him."

"Your faith wasn't misplaced. The book, it's fantastic. It's set during the period of Tecumseh's battles with William Henry Harrison. I went through a box of tissues when I read it."

Sloane's smile grew wider. Pride radiated from her as she sipped a sparkling water. "That's awesome. Will you be the agent for the book? I know both of our dads would love that."

I stared at Sloane, dumbfounded. I wanted somebody to represent the book, as well as his backlist, but it never occurred to me I should be the one. There was no doubt the book was a bestseller on its merits alone. When the publicity surrounding the tragic circumstances around his death were factored in, I could envision an extended run on top of multiple bestseller lists.

Thornwell's and Sloane's interests needed to be protected. Was I the person to do that? I wasn't prepared to answer that question.

"How about you let things settle down before making any decisions? I've still got some work to do to finish closing Dad's agency, so we can talk later, sometime next week. How about that?"

Sloane's eyes lit up. "That's it, Allie. Instead of closing the agency, take it over."

"Now, hold on." I put my hands up. "That's a big step."

"Then think about it. We can talk later, sometime next week." She winked.

And she'd given me a lot to think about. I'd spent months trying to prepare myself, both mentally and emotionally, for the day I would close the books on The Cobb Literary Agency. I'd never given any thought to taking the reins from Dad.

I put the idea out of my head, it was too big and too intimidating, and spent Saturday morning getting ready to return to New York. Mom coaxed me out of the house to watch the annual costume parade by telling me the twins were participating and they'd be heartbroken if Aunt Allie didn't come see them.

The ploy worked. I had a blast watching all of the kids parade down the boulevard dressed as everything from fairy tale princesses to astronauts. The twins went as matching M&Ms and squealed with delight when I stepped from the crowd to take their picture.

The fun continued as Luke, Rachel and the twins joined us at the library for the Sleepy Hollow performance. Brent turned in a credible performance as Ichabod Crane, without flubbing a single line. The twins asked him for his autograph when he came over to say hi after the presentation. While he signed, he asked the kids their names and told them to spend some time reading every night. Talk about a man after my heart.

Luke had to get to the community center for his shift driving the hayride tractor, so the family piled into the bed of his truck for the ride there. The police had done an amazing job completing work on the crime scene on Friday, so the hayrides were allowed to proceed as scheduled. Matt's crew was due a major tip of the hat for their efforts.

I was tired, so I bowed out. The day had been perfect. Even having to endure Jax Michaels's cold shoulder while he and I waited in line for caramel apples didn't put a damper on things. It was my last evening in Rushing Creek, and I wanted to revel in the solitude on my walk home. Without taking any shortcuts.

As I snuggled under the covers with Ursi, my cheek muscles ached from laughing and smiling all evening. Sure, some of my coworkers in New York thought the Fall Festival sounded hokey, but the festivities reminded me it was about one of the most important things on Earth. It was about community.

It was about family.

While New York City had a lot to offer, it couldn't replace my family. A thought stayed with me as I drifted off to sleep.

I didn't want it to.

Chapter Twenty-Six

I managed to make it through Thornwell's memorial service without breaking down in tears, but the floodgates opened when Sloane hugged me at its conclusion.

Unable to figure out what I wanted to say, or what I should say, I gave up on prepared comments and talked about how Thornwell and Dad had remained close friends and business partners for forty years, despite driving each other crazy from time to time. I mentioned the authors who made it to the service, how Thornwell appreciated their skill, which I knew for a fact he did, even if he lacked the self-confidence to say it to them. Lastly, I spoke about the dramatic change he'd made in his life and how heartbreaking it was that it had been cut short just as he was getting his family back together and finishing a new book.

"That was beautiful, Allie. Thank you," Sloane said as we put our arms around each other.

We were soon joined by Kathryn and my family in what turned into a massive group hug. When it broke up, I turned to find Malcolm Blackstone standing nearby. He was the last of Dad's clients who hadn't moved on from the agency. After trading a few stories about Thornwell, he took me by the elbow and guided me away from the group.

"I was visiting with Sloane earlier," he said. "She told me about Thornwell's manuscript and that you're going to represent it and keep the agency open. That's wonderful news."

"I, uh…" I didn't want to talk business, but I didn't want to perpetuate any rumors, either.

"I understand you may not be at liberty to comment until a contract's signed. I respect that. Which is why I want to stay with The Cobb Agency and have you represent me. I'm almost finished with my latest project. I'll e-mail you this week with details."

He looked over my shoulder. "There's your mother. I need to say hi, but I promise to keep our secret between us." He gave my mother a hug as they shared something that made them both laugh.

I, on the other hand, was too stunned and on too tight of a schedule to make any decisions right then and there. Could I make a go of it with only two clients, even if one of them was Thornwell? The question stayed at the front of my mind as I drove to the airport.

On the flight to New York, I studied my client list while I rubbed the screen of Ursi's kitty carrier with my foot. Her purring floated up from beneath the seat in front of me and calmed me as I pared down the list of those who I could legally and ethically take with me if I left Natalie's agency. Technically, they were all represented by the agency, and if she wanted to play hardball to keep all of my clients, she had better than even odds of winning. With only two clients in my back pocket, and without the desire to burn any bridges if I decided to leave, I was in a weak bargaining position.

A knot had formed in my stomach by the time I walked into the office Monday morning. It was quiet. The steady hum of the HVAC system blowing warm air and the barely perceptible buzz of the overhead lighting were the only things to keep me company. I normally liked being an early bird. In the hour or so before anybody else arrived, I could get some caffeine in my system, catch up on my e-mails and, if I was lucky, do some contract review.

For some reason, today was different. I couldn't get settled. My office chair wasn't as comfortable as Dad's recliner. Even with a few wall hangings that featured shots of the New York skyline adding some color, my office felt as impersonal as a doctor's office. There was no cat to cuddle on my lap while I waited for the computer to boot, either.

On top of everything else, my office didn't have a window. After working in Dad's sun-soaked office, my office lighting was as artificial as the dusty, silk flowers on the corner of my desk.

Around midmorning, Natalie checked in with me. "It's great to see you. We've planned a little welcome back lunch in the conference room in your honor. Everyone in the office has been invited."

I forced a smile. "You don't have to do that. I mean, I've got a lot of catching up to do. I was planning on working through lunch, actually."

"You can afford an hour. Don't make me order you to go to your own party." She crossed her arms and sat on the edge of my desk. She was a good person and meant well, so I couldn't say no.

"What time?"

"That's the spirit." She squeezed my shoulder. "Noon. Don't be late. You know how people around here can get when they have to wait to eat."

We shared a laugh and then she brought me up to speed on what I'd missed while I'd been out of the office. When she was finished, I updated her on what I'd accomplished since our phone conversation.

Though she tried to hide it, as she left my office, it was clear she was less than thrilled with my report. Sure, I hadn't made a representation offer to any potential new clients and hadn't received any publication offers from editors, but I'd gotten a lot of other things accomplished. I'd also been busy mourning the loss of my father and then solving a murder. That had to be worth something, didn't it?

I tried to channel my inner-Sloane and keep an optimistic attitude as I pulled open the conference room door at five after twelve. My hopes were dashed as folks had already started eating. Lance was nowhere to be seen, either, even though there were two of his colleagues from the contracts department at the buffet. What a coward.

"I feel nauseous," I said to Natalie as I put my hand over my stomach. "Excuse me." A moment later I was in the restroom, accompanied only by my thoughts and the cold water running in the sink. I wasn't ill, at least not physically. Something was wrong, though.

In an attempt to clear my head, I switched into my walking shoes and headed outside. It was a pleasant fall afternoon in the city. A few puffy clouds floated across the bright blue sky. The breeze made me happy I had a light jacket. I got a hotdog and bottled water from a corner vendor and tried to sort out my troubled emotions.

It made sense I'd be out of sorts given it had been fewer than two weeks since Dad died. And it hadn't even been twenty-four hours since I gave the eulogy at Thornwell's service. I'd had no time to decompress and not a single person, other than Natalie, had made the effort to ask how I was feeling. I guessed they figured I was back, so that must mean I was okay. Besides, they had their own work to do.

As I chewed on my last bite of the hotdog covered in ketchup and relish, I came to terms with the fact I wasn't in small-town Indiana anymore. People were busy, and I needed to get busy, too.

With renewed drive, I motored to the office and dove back into work. Before I knew it, the clock on my computer read seven. I peeked out my door to see most of the floor already dark. With a sinking spirit, I shut down my computer and left.

The subway ride to my apartment didn't help my mood. In just a week and a half, I'd gotten used to walking anywhere and everywhere, with personal space to spare. Stuck in the crowded, mobile tin can, I had to keep my eyes on my phone to ward off an impending bout of claustrophobia. As soon as I reached my stop, I sprinted up the stairs. Back in the open, it still took until I was almost to my building before my heart rate returned to normal.

As I fed Ursi and cleaned out her litter box, I decided I was simply wiped out from the craziness of the past few days. My go-to meal when tired and stressed was cashew chicken, so I got some carryout from the Asian restaurant down the street and ate it while I watched a few episodes of my ultimate guilty pleasure, the Nickelodeon classic, *Rugrats*.

A full belly, combined with an hour watching Tommy, Angelica and their friends get into and out of trouble, improved my mood a hundredfold. There was one more self-care item to accomplish before I called it a night—a long, hot bubble bath.

An hour later, I ignored my compulsion to check my computer and phone, scooped up Ursi and got in bed.

"Tomorrow will be better, girl. Just you wait and see." As I scratched my kitty's back, she licked my cheek. I didn't know how, but yes, tomorrow was going to be better.

I woke up refreshed after dreamless sleep. With renewed determination to return to normal, I put in my earbuds so I could jam to some Pink on my way to work.

The plan was working flawlessly when I scored a seat in the subway car instead of having to stand. With the tunes keeping the blood flowing, I checked my phone. There were two messages from the night before. One was a text message from Sloane. The other was a voice mail message from a number I didn't recognize.

Sloane was checking to make sure I'd made it home safely. She also wanted to talk about Thornwell's book when I had a chance. Lastly, she thanked me again for being there when she needed me the most.

I had to blink a few times to keep my vision clear as I responded that I was fine and promised to call her to talk about the book when I got home from work on Wednesday. As I hit send, the pull I'd felt during my stay in Rushing Creek returned.

I tried to ignore the familiar pull as I accessed my voice mail. Figuring the call was from one of my authors who had a new cell number, I dug a pen and notebook out of my purse, ready to take down the message.

It was a good thing I was sitting when the recording started, because the voice surprised me. It wasn't one of my authors, but another familiar voice, a kind voice that brought the pull right back to the surface.

"Hey, Allie. It's Brent. Just wanted to call to say it was great meeting you, even if it was under some wild circumstances. Hope you're doing well back in the big city. Folks back here miss you already. Sammy and I do, too. Hope to talk to you soon. Take care."

I removed my earbuds as I stared at my phone. The one-two combination of Sloane and Brent checking in on me left me so stunned that I missed my stop. By the time I came to my senses, the subway was almost to Sixty-Third Street. When the doors opened at the next stop, I got off. Instead of work, I had a new destination in mind—Central Park.

The moment I stepped onto the park's soft green turf, a tightening that had formed in my chest loosened, making it easier to breathe. The overcast skies couldn't constrain my relief as I walked toward a tulip poplar. I laughed as I ran my hand along the furrowed, gray bark of the state tree of Indiana. The message was clear.

Under the shade of the tree, I called Natalie to let her know I wouldn't be making it to the office and was resigning from the agency. Next, I got ahold of Lance and told him we were done. Whatever we had, it was over. He didn't put up much of a fight, which was proof I was making the right decision.

Then I sent Sloane and Brent a text about a surprise I had for them.

Twelve hours later, I was seated in a corner booth at the pub. I was so excited, I had to put my hands in my jacket pockets to keep from drumming on the wooden tabletop, annoying the folks in the booth next to me.

Sloane and Brent came in together, per my instructions, and made their way to the bar. They chatted with Steve for a minute. He raised his eyebrows as he pointed in my direction.

Sloane spotted me first and practically jumped over a couple of tables on her way to tackle me as I stood to greet her.

"It's great to see you, but what's up with the mysterious text?" she asked.

Having taken a more conventional route from the bar, Brent joined us. "Hey, Allie. Surprised to see you in town so soon."

"Yeah, about that." I gestured to Steve as we got seated in the booth. "I had a lot of time to think the past couple of days."

Steve placed three champagne flutes on the table and poured from a bottle of the finest champagne the pub carried. When he was finished, I took a glass and nodded for the others to do the same.

"I learned a lot during these past two weeks. What I learned most was that Rushing Creek has changed and I've changed, too. When I left twelve years ago, I thought I needed the lights of the big city. I've learned I don't need that anymore. What I need is family and friends, like you two."

I lifted my glass. "I've decided to come home, to Rushing Creek, and carry on my dad's legacy by continuing The Cobb Literary Agency. What do you think?"

"That it's about time." Sloane, who was seated beside me, put her arm around me as we clinked glasses.

"Too cool," Brent said. "You're going to stick to books, right? No more crime fighting Kickboxing Crusader?"

"I don't know. It does have a certain ring to it." I laughed at their matching open mouths. "Nah, I think there's enough adventure ahead of me as little Allie Cobb, literary agent."

To a round of cheers, we clinked glasses and drank. I'd have to make a final trip to New York to pack my things and ship them here, but now that I was home, the pull loosened and gave way to a warm feeling that started in my heart and filled every part of me.

Without a doubt, I was where I belonged and I couldn't wait for this new adventure in my hometown to begin. Whatever the future had in store for me, I was ready to face it head-on. There was only one thing to say to the world.

Bring it!

Acknowledgments

Huge thanks to my agent, Dawn, for her continuing guidance, support and encouragement. A big thank you to my editor, John, for his faith in me. A high five to my trusted reader, Amy, for her invaluable advice. Last, but not least, a big hug to my family for their continued belief in me as this crazy writing adventure continues.

Meet the Author

J.C. Kenney lives in Indianapolis and dreams of one day retiring to a place where the water is warm and the beaches are soft.

Printed in the United States
by Baker & Taylor Publisher Services